Books by April

Audiobooks and Upcoming Releases:

For links to my audiobooks and upcoming releases, visit my website: www.aprilwilsonauthor.com

Search and Rescue

McIntyre Security
Search and Rescue Series

Book 1

by

April Wilson

Cover by Steamy Designs
Photography by Wander Aguiar
Model: Chris Hayman
Proofread by Amanda Cuff (Word of Advice)

Published by
April E. Barnswell
Wilson Publishing LLC
P.O. Box 292913
Dayton, OH 45429
www.aprilwilsonauthor.com

ISBN: 9798496289801

Character List

The McIntyres

- Hannah McIntyre, one of seven adult children in the McIntyre family
- Shane McIntyre, Hannah's eldest brother, CEO of McIntyre Security
- Jake McIntyre, Hannah's third eldest brother

Other Characters

- Killian Devereaux (former Army Ranger, works for McIntyre Security)
- Owen Ramsey (former Army Ranger, a loner who lives off-grid in the mountains of Tennessee)
- Maggie Emerson (Hannah's friend, owns the grocery store in Bryce, Colorado)
- Brendan and Riley Emerson (Maggie's teenage sons)
- Dominic Zaretti (married to Sophie McIntyre, works for McIntyre Security)
- Ruth (she owns Ruth's Tavern in Bryce, Colorado)
- Micah (former Marine, Ruth's brother, he owns an auto repair shop in Bryce and a helicopter tourism business)

1

Hannah McIntyre

The alarm on my phone wakes me promptly at six-thirty. "No," I groan as I reach over to tap the snooze button. I don't usually have an urge to throw my phone across the room, but this morning I'm tempted. I just got home the day before from a three-day trip to Chicago to celebrate the birth of my brother Shane's new baby—a darling little girl named Ava.

Yawning, I stretch my limbs and debate shutting off the alarm and sleeping half the morning away. Just this once. I think Scout—my one-year-old Belgian Malinois—agrees because he doesn't seem inclined to jump out of bed either. He flops against me as he stretches his long limbs.

I scratch behind his ears. "What do you say, buddy? Should we play hooky this morning?"

Suddenly, Scout's pointed ears perk up, and he jumps off the bed and races out of the bedroom to investigate whatever sound he heard—probably a squirrel foraging around outside our cabin as it stores food for the upcoming winter. Then he starts barking at the door, wanting to go outside to pee and chase squirrels.

So much for sleeping in.

I haul myself out of bed and head to the bathroom to empty my bladder. As I'm washing my hands, I frown at my reflection. My hair looks wild and definitely needs some serious taming before I'm ready to head to work.

Scout barks again, reminding me that he needs to go out.

"I'm coming, buddy. Hold your horses."

Usually I'm an early riser, but not today. I'm still reeling from the emotional whiplash caused by my weekend trip back home. I saw my family, of course, which is great. I have an awesome family, and I love spending time with them. But I also saw *him*. And seeing him always throws me for a loop.

Killian Devereaux gets to me in a way no man ever has. And it's not just his looks—although those are stellar. It's all of him—his personality, his presence, his swoonworthy Cajun accent. He's confident and direct and highly competent, and I find all those things very sexy.

Killian was the one who picked me up from the airport and

drove me to my brother's estate. I wouldn't be surprised if Shane sent him on purpose. Killian hasn't been shy about making his interest known. He's asked me out a number of times, and each time I politely declined.

Starting up anything with him is pointless. We live a thousand miles away from each other, and as I've told him a million times, I'm not moving back to Chicago. My life is here in Colorado—in the mountains.

Mentally shaking myself, I force thoughts of Killian out of my head. That way lies madness. And longing. And wishful thinking.

And ultimately heartache.

Scout lets out a demanding bark from the living room, reminding me that he's waiting.

The cabin air is chilly this morning as the fire in the wood-stove went out hours ago, and I was too lazy to get up in the night to replenish it. It's September, and overnight temperatures at this altitude can drop pretty low.

I make a quick stop in my bedroom to change from my flannel PJs into a pair of gray sweatpants, a black tank top, a University of Denver hoodie, socks and running shoes, and open the door for Scout to lead the way outside.

It's still dark out, as the heavy tree canopy overhead blocks much of the early morning sun. While Scout runs down the steps to the ground and saunters off to do his business, I take a moment to enjoy the quiet serenity of my wilderness home.

Living on the side of a mountain is such a contrast to living in the city. I was born and raised in Rogers Park, Chicago, in a crowded blue-collar urban neighborhood. When I was a kid, my family of nine lived in a three-bedroom, two-story brick townhouse. We were crammed in like sardines, we three girls sharing one bedroom, my four brothers in another, and my parents in the third bedroom. As a family, we were close— we still are—and we had a blast together. It wasn't until I went away to college—to the University of Denver on a full scholarship—that I discovered the vast wilderness that awaited me. I've never looked back since.

My home—a small one-bedroom cabin deep in the woods— is my happy place now. It's a balm to my soul. This is what I was born for—to live a life outdoors. To breathe fresh air and smell the scent of pine. To hike and camp and live under a quiet night sky that's so dark I can actually see the stars.

As part of our daily routine, Scout and I start each morning off with a two-mile run along a paved single-lane road that snakes up from Bryce, Colorado into the mountains I call home. Scout needs the exercise as much as I do, probably even more so. It's a necessity for a young and rambunctious Belgian Malinois. These dogs require a lot of structure and training, and in return you get a loyal companion and fearless guard dog.

Scout runs at my side with a focus that never fails to amaze me. No matter what little creature scurries across the road in front of us, he never veers off course. He's practically attached to my side, watching me intently as if waiting for a cue.

I suppose I shouldn't be surprised. I studied the breed in

depth before committing to getting one, and I knew the level of training he'd need. I was more than willing to put in the work because I knew he'd make an excellent companion and one hell of a first responder one day. My goal is to train him to do search and rescue work.

Right now, he's a handful, and he requires constant redirection to channel his energy into something productive, rather than destructive. He needs *work* to do, and I give it to him.

After the run, I bring him back to my property and put him through an agility course I made myself. Up, down, across, under, around, through... I put him through his paces. He can jump fences and scale a ladder, and he has almost mastered the balance beam. No matter how I challenge him, he excels, and he clearly loves it.

When the agility course work is complete, Scout's reward is to play his favorite game—hide-and-seek. I lead him into the barn, where I instruct him to sit, and he stays there while I run out into the woods surrounding my cabin to hide. I blow a short whistle to let him know the game is on. Then I sit back in my hiding place and wait for him to find me.

In the beginning, it took him half an hour or longer of scouring the woods around my cabin to locate me. These days, it's usually more like five minutes.

"Good boy!" I tell him when he finds me. I check the timer on my phone. "Seven minutes. Not bad, pal." I wrap my arms around his neck and bury my nose in his thick fur. "That's my good boy. Ready for breakfast?"

He takes off running for the cabin, with me right behind him. While I eat my bowl of instant maple and brown sugar oatmeal, he scarfs down his breakfast.

Exhausted from his morning exercise, Scout crashes on the rug in front of the stone hearth, while I go grab a quick shower. After dragging a comb through my hair and pulling it back into a ponytail, I dress in my usual attire—khaki cargo pants, a white tank top, a long-sleeved forest green sweatshirt, warm socks, and well-worn hiking boots.

Today I'm dressing warmer than usual because, according to my weather app, there's a snowstorm coming. I make a mental note to leave work early this afternoon so I'll have time to come home and bring in more firewood for the woodstove before it gets dark.

The last thing I do before walking out the door is slip my handgun into my ankle holster and a knife into my belt sheath. You can't be too careful this deep in the woods. It isn't unheard of to run into bears or mountain lions. A little extra protection never hurt anyone. I also carry a can of bear spray in my backpack, just in case.

Scout follows me to the door. "Be a good boy," I tell him as I scratch behind his dark ears. He sits at attention and stares up at me. "You are such a handsome boy," I say. And he is, with his thick auburn fur, dark narrow face, and dark ears. He's often mistaken for a German Shepherd.

When I sling my backpack over my shoulder, he barks eagerly, practically bouncing on his feet. "Sorry, pal. Not this time. But I'll come home for lunch, if I can, and we'll have some more fun." I hate leaving him alone for more than a few hours because he can get destructive when he's bored. He still has enough puppy in him to get into trouble at times. I just hope his basket of chew toys will suffice until I return. Then I'll put him through the agility course again, and we'll play catch with a tennis ball and hide-and-seek with his toys—his other favorite pastimes.

After locking the door behind me, I jog down the wooden steps and head for my black Jeep Wrangler, which is currently splattered with mud thanks to a recent off-road trip. I make a mental note to wash it this weekend.

It's only a quick ten-minute drive down curving mountain roads to the center of Bryce, Colorado, where I make my customary morning pit stop at Emerson's Grocery Store to grab coffee and a donut. I park right in front of the store.

"Hey, lady," I say as I push through the front door and step into the store, which smells of freshly-brewed coffee, baked goods, and lemon-scented cleaner.

It's the closest grocery store for miles around, and while it's not huge, Maggie does manage to carry just about anything we need. She gets fresh-baked goods to sell from the diner next door, and she buys fresh cuts of meat from the butcher down the street. She's even got a rack of paperbacks and magazines, school supplies, and even DVDs and VHS tapes for rent. Yeah, Maggie Emerson still rents out VHS tapes. Bryce is the kind of town that the modern world left behind long ago—and we kinda like it that way.

According to Maggie, the store hasn't changed much in the past seventy years, since her grandfather bought it. The floors are still well-worn oak boards that creak underfoot, and the sales counter is the original old oak display case. The cash register is one of those old-fashioned kind, the mechanical ones that don't make a single beep.

Bryce, Colorado—population eight hundred and twelve—is barely a blip on the Colorado map. It's located north of Estes Park—the popular Rocky Mountain Park tourist destination—far enough away to miss all the heavy sightseeing traffic, which suits us just fine. We mostly get diehard hikers and backpackers up here, and lots of rock climbers. Still, it's pretty tranquil in our little spot of heaven. You're just as likely to come across a cougar or a bear on a trail as another human being.

If you blink, you'll miss our little stretch of downtown. It consists of four blocks of businesses. Outside of that, you'll find random cabins scattered all over the mountainsides and in the valleys.

Maggie waves at me from behind the sales counter, where she's unpacking a shipment of candy bars. "Mornin', Hannah," she says as she tucks a wayward strand of wavy light-brown hair behind her ear.

Maggie was the first person I met the day I moved to Bryce after I graduated from University of Denver and accepted my first professional job here in town at the local wildlife rehabilitation center. We hit it off right away, and we've become best of friends. She and I have a lot in common—we're both independent and strong-willed, though Maggie calls it hardheaded. I'm okay with that.

At forty, Maggie is a dozen years older than me and a divorced mother of two teenage boys who are probably responsible for the onset of a few gray hairs.

The coffee counter is calling my name, and I pour myself a large cup. I dump in plenty of sugar and my favorite caramel-flavored creamer before I give it a good stir and pop the lid on. Before I move a single step, I take a sip and groan in pleasure. Just what I needed.

As I head to the sales counter, the door connecting the grocery store to the diner opens, and Maggie's two sons—Riley and Brendan—walk through. Both boys are tall for their age, like their father, Maggie's asshat of an ex-husband, whom I've only met one time. They both have the same brown hair as their mother and her blue eyes.

Riley's carrying a heaping plate of glazed donuts. "Get 'em while they're hot," he says. "They just came out of the fryer."

"Give me those," Maggie says, laughing as her sons snag two each. "Or there won't be any left for my customers."

She offers me the plate, and I take one. The donut is still warm, just as Riley said, and the sugary glaze is gooey to the touch. I take a bite of my guilty pleasure, and the tender donut practically melts in my mouth. "Mm."

Maggie sets the plate with the remaining donuts on a silver cake stand and covers it with a glass dome. "I'll bet you these won't last the hour," she says. Then she turns to her sons and points to the door. "You two, get to school. You're going to be late if you don't leave soon."

The boys grab their backpacks, sling them over their shoulders, and head out the front door, Riley dangling a set of keys from his fingers.

"And drive carefully!" she yells after them.

"Bye, Mom!" Brendan calls back just as the door closes behind them.

Maggie shakes her head at me. "Teenage boys. They'll be the death of me. Or, I'll go broke just trying to feed them."

As I polish off the last of my donut, Maggie gives me the eye. "I don't know how you manage to stay so fit when you eat so many carbs." She props her hands on her own curvaceous hips. "Obviously, I don't have your talent in that department."

"Fast metabolism, I guess." I suck the sugar off my thumb and index finger, and then I pull a wet wipe from the dispenser on the sales counter and wash my hands.

"How about joining me and the boys for dinner tonight?" Maggie asks. "I've got a pot roast and potatoes in the slow cooker."

As I take another sip of my coffee, I nod gratefully. I'm a single gal who doesn't like to cook. "Gladly. You know I would never turn down a home-cooked meal."

Maggie's cooking reminds me of my mom's cooking.

When my phone rings, I check the screen. It's Ray Calhoun, my boss at the wildlife rehab center. "Hi, Ray. What's up?"

"Where are you?" he asks, sounding more curious than anything.

"I'm at Maggie's shop, getting ready to head to the center. Why?"

He blows out a relieved breath. "Have you got your hiking gear on you?"

"Of course." I always keep my hiking gear in my Jeep.

"Perfect. I'm glad I caught you before you got too far out of town. I've received a couple of reports while you were out of town about some suspicious activity up on Eagle Ridge. We might have a poacher issue. Would you mind making a stop there on your way in? Hike up that trail and see if you can spot Betty. Let's make sure she's all right."

"Sure. Not a problem." Honestly, I'd much rather be hiking today than working indoors at the center. It'll help me get my head on straight after spending three days back home. "I'll head up there now."

"Keep me posted and call me with an update as soon as you can."

"Will do."

"Who was that?" Maggie asks as I end the call and tuck my phone into my jacket pocket.

"Ray asked me to hike up to Eagle Ridge and check on Betty. Apparently, someone's been scoping out her nest." Bald eagle poaching is a growing problem in these parts. Their feathers go for big money on the black market. It's illegal to even possess bald eagle feathers, and the penalties include fines and even jail time.

"They're probably just avid bird watchers. Do you think it's safe to hike up that far today? They're predicting some pretty serious snowfall this evening."

"I'll be down off that ridge long before the snow hits. It's a two-hour hike up, I check on Betty, and then a two-hour hike down. I'll be off the trail by midafternoon, and I'll be home in plenty of time to have dinner with you tonight. What time do you want me?"

"How about six? The boys should be home from football practice by then. I'll see if I can get my brother to close up the shop for me this evening. He owes me a few favors."

"It's a date." I salute her as I walk backward toward the front door. "Six o'clock. I'll bring the beer."

"And bring Scout!" Maggie calls. "The boys haven't stopped talking about him."

"Will do."

Maggie's sons watched Scout for me while I was in Chicago earlier in the week.

Once back on the road, I head north on the only paved road that runs through Bryce, heading toward the trailhead where I will park my Jeep. When I reach the spot about ten minutes later, I text Ray to let him know I've arrived and am getting ready to hike up to the nest.

Ray: Be careful, Hannah. Keep a close eye on the weather. A storm is coming in.

Hannah: Don't worry, dad. I will.

I chuckle as I pocket my phone. Ray thinks it's his job to watch out for me.

After hopping out of my Jeep, I walk around to the back, open the hatch, and grab my pack. Everything I could possibly need for an afternoon hike is in there: water bottle, protein bars, flashlight, thermal blanket, bear spray, and a satellite phone with a full charge. And of course I'm armed with a handgun, knife, and extra ammo. I don't want to be caught empty-handed in case I run into any vicious animals—human or otherwise.

$\backsim$ 2

Hannah McIntyre

Eagle Ridge Trail is not for the faint of heart. It's a rugged climb, popular with hardcore hikers. Part of the trail is steep, and part of it is rocky. It takes a good two hours to make it two miles up the mountain. And that's on a good day. If you throw in bad weather, all bets are off.

I glance up at the sky, which is already overcast. And it looks even more ominous to the west. Maybe a smart person would call off the hike until the weather clears, but I'm more worried about Betty's welfare than getting snowed on. If push comes to shove, I can hightail it off that mountain in record time and get back to my Jeep before too much snow has accumulated.

The snow isn't even expected until evening, and I'll be down off that mountain long before then.

There's only one other vehicle in the gravel parking lot besides mine—an all-wheel-drive black SUV with darkly-tinted windows and Larimer County license plates. I pass it as I head for the trail marker, where I stop momentarily to gaze at the info sheets pinned to the message board, but there's nothing new. No trail alerts. No recent bear or mountain lion sightings to worry about. So I proceed along the trail, ready for a good workout. It's too bad I don't have Scout with me. He loves a good hike. If I'd known I was taking this detour, I would have brought him with me.

The first quarter mile is deceptively easy, but soon enough the incline increases. Rock outcroppings and tangles of tree roots make the going more difficult. By the half mile mark, I'm breathing pretty hard and getting a good aerobic workout. A couple of relatively easy outcroppings of rock slow me down as I have to carefully pick my handholds and footholds to make my way up.

Two hours later, at the top of Eagle Ridge, I reach the spot where hikers like to camp out in hopes of spotting Betty on the far side of the ridge. Down below is a valley with a river running through it—Betty's main source of food. This time of year, she's alone up here, but when mating season arrives, her longtime mate will return, and they'll raise eaglets.

After pulling out a pair of binoculars, I scan the valley below and the air space above the ridge on the other side, hoping to spot Betty. After a few minutes, I get lucky and spot her perched high up on a bare tree branch, calmly surveying her territory. My shoulders loosen in relief when I see that she's fine. She's a popular lady in these parts.

A rustling sound to my right alerts me to the fact that I'm not the only hiker up here. I turn to spot a man dressed in all black, a black knit cap covering most of his ash-blond hair, and a pair of fancy binoculars hanging around his neck. He's a good-looking guy, probably in his mid-thirties, with hazel eyes and two gold hoops piercing his right eyebrow. He's got large black plugs in his earlobes. I don't recognize him, though. What sends my pulse racing is the high-powered rifle slung over his shoulder. That rifle's not designed for defense; it's a sniper's weapon. There's no use for it up here on a public trail. Not unless you're interested in shooting something at a far distance.

The guy makes eye contact with me but says nothing.

I glance back across the ridge at Betty, who takes flight.

"See anything interesting?" I ask him, hoping to draw him out and get an idea of what he's doing up here.

He shrugs. "Not really."

I nod toward his binoculars. "Are you a birdwatcher?"

This guy doesn't look like a birdwatcher, or even a hiker for that matter. His attire resembles tactical gear more than hiking clothes. I notice the dark aviator shades that hang from his neckline. They're certainly not necessary here under the dense canopy of trees. His boots are military grade, and he has a utility belt secured around his hips. Something about him sets my teeth on edge. This isn't a birdwatcher or a naturalist. This guy has an agenda.

I glance around, looking to see what else he has brought with him, and find a duffle bag made of camouflaged material sitting on the ground not far from where we're standing. He's been up here a while.

I glance up at the rapidly darkening sky. "Looks like snow," I observe casually, trying to draw him out. Maybe I'm being paranoid and reading too much into this. I'm inclined to see poachers everywhere I go these days.

Still, he says nothing, which only raises my concerns.

"You look familiar," I tell him. It's not true, but I'm still trying to suss him out. "Do you live around here? Maybe I've seen you in town before, at Ruth's Tavern or the grocery store."

"You sure ask a lot of questions," he says, finally turning to face me. "No, I'm not from around here."

There it is—an outright lie. The SUV—the only vehicle besides mine in the parking lot—has Larimer County plates, which means it's local. And it's not a rental. The SUV must be his.

His gaze sweeps me from head to toe as he tries to size me up, and I feel a chill creep down my spine.

Suddenly, he points to a spot on the other side of the valley. "There she is."

Out of reflex, I look to where he's pointing, but I see nothing. The next thing I know, I hear a second set of boots crunching the leaves on the ground behind me. Before I can turn to look, something hard is pressed against the back of my skull. "Don't move."

He's not alone.

The guy beside me, the blond with the piercings, turns to look at the person standing behind me. "She asks too many questions."

"Indeed she does," comes the reply. "I'd put my money on law enforcement."

"That's too bad," says the blond as he frisks me. He removes the knife sheathed on my belt first, and then he confiscates the handgun in my ankle holster. He tucks my gun into the waistband of his black jeans and tosses my knife over the edge of the cliff we're standing at.

I can hear the sound of my own blood rushing through my skull. "I'm not law enforcement." I try to keep my voice steady. "I'm just a hiker."

"Sorry, sweetheart," says the man behind me. "I don't believe you."

I glance behind me at the man towering over me. Black hair, dark eyes, and a jagged scar that stretches from his right cheekbone down to his upper lip.

He'll be easy to identify in a police lineup.

And then—

Crack!

Pain explodes in my skull, and everything goes black.

$\mathcal{e}$ 3

Hannah McIntyre

When I come to, I'm seated on the cold hard ground, propped against a tree. Dampness seeps through my cargo pants, chilling me to the bone. My arms are stretched behind me, my wrists secured with something hard and unforgiving—a zip tie, I suspect. I feel warm blood trickling down my right temple, where Scarface must have struck me with the butt of his gun.

It's my own damn fault for letting them get the drop on me. I was so focused on the guy beside me that I didn't hear the second man coming up from behind. I want to kick myself for being an idiot. I should never have engaged them at all. As soon as I spotted the first guy, I should have high-tailed it out of there and reported him to the sheriff.

My head throbs like a bitch, the pain so excruciating I'm afraid I might lose the meager contents of my stomach.

When I scan the area, I find the first guy—the blond—digging through my pack. He pulls out my satellite phone and slams it into a nearby tree trunk, shattering the plastic case. He tosses what's left of it into the woods. The second guy— Scarface, the one who knocked me out—paces in front of me. He's holding a Glock. I watch him pop out the magazine to count the rounds, then slam it back in before tucking it into the waistband of his pants.

Breathe.

Just breathe.

When I try to move my head, a burst of pain explodes in my skull, setting off more fireworks behind my eyes.

"We need to move," Scarface says to his buddy. "Now."

The blond nods as he adjusts his knit cap. "We have to deal with her first. She's seen our faces."

"Let's handle it here," his companion says.

The first guy shakes his head. "It's too public. Someone could come along."

They step farther away from me to confer in low voices, but I don't need to hear what they're saying to know they're discussing what the hell they're going to do with me. At this point, I have no doubt they're poachers. At the very least, they're up to no good and are afraid that I can identify them.

Poaching has been on the rise in the Rockies for some time now. Illegally sourced bald eagle feathers are a big part of it. I have no doubt these guys came up here looking for Betty. Her feathers would be worth a fortune.

Finally, they walk back my way, pointing their rifles directly at me. Their faces are still uncovered, which doesn't bode well for me. Two Caucasian men, both mid-thirties, average height and weight. One with an obvious scar on his face, the other with numerous piercings. I can identify them both, and they know it. And yet they don't seem overly concerned about that fact.

My stomach drops like a rock.

Scarface seems to be the one in charge. He steps forward, just a foot from me, and gazes down at me. The other guy holds back, tense and on high alert. We're on a public trail, and it wouldn't be out of the question for hikers to come up this way, especially birders hoping to spot Betty.

"This is unfortunate," Scarface says as he gently nudges my boot with his. "You should have minded your own business, sweetheart."

I grimace. "Don't patronize me, asshole."

He shrugs. "I don't think you're in a position to be telling me what to do."

"Just shoot her and be done with it," the other guy snaps. "We can toss her body over the cliff. It'll take ages for anyone to find her, if they ever do." He gazes up at an increasingly dark sky. "Come on, man. We need to get out of here. The storm's gonna hit soon, and I don't want to get stranded up here."

He's right about that. The storm is rolling in much faster than expected. The forecast is for at least two feet of snow overnight and a drop in temperature of fifty degrees. That's not unheard of this time of year. Mountain weather is unpredictable. Temperatures can swing wildly from one hour to the next.

"Just do it, man," the blond says as he gathers up his duffle bag and my pack.

Scarface glances around as if surveying the options. "I told you, not here. It's too public. We'll have to take her somewhere more remote."

I can't believe how casually they're discussing my fate, as if they have no empathy for another living being and no fear of getting caught.

The blond nods toward me as he says, "Fine. Cut her loose, and let's hike back to the vehicle."

As he unsheathes a wicked hunting knife, Scarface walks behind me and cuts the zip tie, freeing my wrists, which have grown cold and numb. As I try moving my arms, pain from lack of circulation shoots through me. My wrists are rubbed raw.

"I'm not carrying her pack," the first guy says as he slips it onto my back. "She can carry it herself."

Scarface starts walking back down the trail. "Let's go."

I stumble over the uneven terrain, my mind racing as I consider my options. One thing I'm sure of—there's no way in hell I'm walking off this trail with these guys. I know the score.

Never get in their vehicle. Once you do, you're done for.

My only option is to make a run for it.

The snow has started falling already, quite heavily, and that turns out to be a blessing in disguise for me. The sky has grown overcast thanks to a heavy, dark covering of clouds, and with the arrival of heavy snowfall, visibility quickly deteriorates. After half an hour of walking, we can hardly see ten feet in front of us. Scarface, who's in the lead, is already out of sight.

If I can make a run for it, I might be able to avoid detection long enough to find help.

I glance back at the guy behind me, who's carrying his rifle slung over his shoulder. At least it's not pointed at me. That will buy me a couple of precious seconds. I didn't study kickboxing with my youngest brother, Liam, for ten years for nothing.

Feigning a stumble, I get into position. Then I throw a heel hook kick into the loser behind me, knocking him off balance as the sole of my boot clips his jaw hard enough to break it. I hear a very satisfying *thunk* just before he goes down hard. And then I run like hell at a perpendicular angle to the trail, hoping to lose them in the densely packed woods that border the trail.

The loser behind me yells to his friend, but his voice is partially muffled by the wind whipping through the trees. I glance back and see he's still struggling to get to his feet.

I can barely make out what they're saying.

"What the fuck happened?" yells Scarface. "Where'd she go?"

"She kicked me, the damn bitch! I told you, we should have taken care of her up on that ridge."

"Which *way* did she go?" Scarface asks.

"That way, into the woods."

I run as hard and fast as I can as their voices quickly trail off to nothing. Visibility is growing increasingly worse as the snow comes down hard. Shit, I'm not dressed for this kind of weather, but now's not the time to worry about that. Branches whip at my body, tearing my jacket sleeves and scratching my face.

I can hear them crashing through the brush as they chase me, yelling to each other. They're gaining ground, and they're not even trying to be stealthy about it.

A gunshot cracks loudly in the cold air, making my ears ring. That was way too close, so I veer to the right—away from the sound of shouting—and keep running.

But still, they're gaining on me. It's hard to run through the thick underbrush. I feel like I'm slogging through quicksand. My backpack keeps catching on tree branches and shrubs, slowing me down even more, but I don't dare ditch it as there are supplies in there that I might need.

Another shot rings out, and the round strikes the bark of a tree not a foot from me, sending a piece of wood ricocheting into my right cheek. I feel the sting as the shard cuts into my face, followed by the warmth of blood streaming down my cheek.

Just as a third shot rings out, fire scorches my upper right arm. I glance down to see a jagged tear in my jacket sleeve and blood welling up from a gash. That bastard shot me! It's only a graze, but still it burns like hell. I bite my tongue hard, tasting blood, in an effort not to cry out. I don't want them to know they've scored a hit, and I certainly don't want to reveal my position. If they catch me now, they'll kill me on the spot.

My arm burns like it's on fire, and pain radiates up to my shoulder and neck. The pain is excruciating, but I keep running. I change direction, turning ninety degrees, and hope to lose them in the trees. I run as hard as I can, even though my sides are cramping and my lungs are burning. I can't risk slowing down. I move in a random pattern, changing direction frequently in an effort to lose them.

Another shot rings out, the sound echoing through the trees. "Over there!" one of them yells. "I see her."

My heart thunders as I push myself, my boots slipping on the accumulating snow, which is now starting to reach through the heavy tree canopy above to the ground. I glance down at the splatters of blood staining the newly fallen snow, leaving an easy trail for them to follow.

That's just fucking great!

I continue to run, half-blinded by the falling snow. Without warning, the ground beneath me gives way, and I drop like a stone, sliding and scraping down a wall of dirt, rocks, and roots. It's an uncontrolled free fall, and my limbs and head strike hard surfaces repeatedly as I fall into a deep ravine. Visibility is so bad that I can't even see the ground below.

Without warning, I come to a jarring stop, and screaming pain shoots up my left leg. My foot is wedged between thick roots of a tree, and as I collapse forward, my palms slamming into rocks and dirt, my ankle is wrenched brutally. Gasping at the burning pain, I manage to free my boot and smother a scream as I hit the ground face hard.

I don't have time to worry about injuries because they're up there at the edge of the ravine, both of them. I can hear them griping at each other. I roll to my back and try to get up, but my left ankle folds under me, and I hit the ground again with an involuntary scream. Shots ring out as the two men fire blindly into the ravine, hoping to score a hit. All I can do now is crawl beneath the shelter of a large tree rooted into the wall of the ravine, hoping to find protection from their bullets.

As hot tears stream down my icy cheeks, I squeeze my eyes shut and try to block out the pain and the cold. Already the temperature has dropped at least fifteen degrees. And it will get much colder before night sets in.

Shaking, I remain frozen to the spot and listen to them yelling as they blame each other for my escape.

A few minutes later, their argument is drowned out by the deafening sound of shots starting up again. They fire haphazardly into the ravine, in spite of the risk of drawing attention to themselves.

I crawl a few feet away, dragging my useless foot behind me, until I find better shelter beneath an overhang created by a gnarly tangle of tree roots. I plaster myself against the ravine wall, pressing into the cold, damp earth to make myself as small a target as possible.

I lose all track of time as they move back and forth along the top edge of the ravine as they search for me. Occasionally, one of them fires into the ravine, the shot a loud crack in the frigid air. With bad weather rolling in, there won't be any hikers up here to spoil their hunt.

I need to lie low and out of sight long enough for them to get tired of looking and head back down the trail. Once they're gone, I'll see about climbing out of this ravine, or maybe hiking down to the trailhead. But with the way my left ankle is throbbing painfully, the chances of me getting myself out of this anytime soon aren't good.

As the cold seeps into my thin jacket, my mind wanders. Two thoughts are clear. One, I'm not going to make it to Maggie's for dinner tonight. And two, I hope she realizes I'm missing and takes care of Scout for me. Surely she will. When I don't show up for dinner, she'll call me, and when I don't answer my phone—there's no way I can get a signal in this ravine—she'll come looking for me. And she's not going to find me. Not tonight. Not in this weather.

* * *

I have no idea how long I've been hiding. Darkness falls, and the temperature continues to drop, along with inch after inch of fresh snow. The poachers bring out high-powered flashlights and sweep the ravine floor as they search. I can hear them still bickering with each other, although their words are muffled by the howling winds.

How long are they going to keep this up? Probably as long as it takes for them to accomplish their objective. They want me dead because I can identify them to the authorities.

Poor Ray. My boss is going to be beside himself when he finds out what's happened.

It becomes clear pretty soon that I'm vastly underdressed for the weather that's rolling in. Snow is accumulating on the floor of the ravine, and I estimate it to be close to a foot already, in just a matter of hours. Who knows how deep it will be by morning?

I'm chilled to the bone, my muscles shivering despite my long-sleeved shirt and insulated jacket. My bare hands are numb from the cold. I search my jacket pocket for my gloves, but they're long gone. Those assholes must have removed them when they secured my wrists with the zip tie. All I can do is wrap my arms tightly around me and tuck my hands under my arms for warmth.

In the waning light, I shrug off my backpack and dig around inside it as I search for food and water, and anything else useful. I find a small thermal blanket, a pocket-sized flashlight, and a can of bear spray. I don't dare turn on the flashlight in case the poachers see the light, and if I find myself in need of bear spray down here, I'm in far worse trouble than I ever imagined possible.

Because my water bottle is stainless steel, it fortunately survived the fall. The protein bars are smashed, but they're still edible. I fish a folded pocketknife out of my pack and tuck it into my jacket pocket, just to have it handy in case of an emergency. I know full well there are plenty of predators wandering these forests.

I unscrew the cap off my water bottle and immediately guzzle a third of it. I didn't realize how thirsty I was until that cold water hit my tongue. Then I rip open a chocolate protein bar and devour it.

I can still hear them up above the ravine, their muffled voices carrying on the wind. I have no choice but to wait them out. The way the snow is falling, wet and heavy, and as the temps continue to drop, I figure they'll get tired eventually and move on. At least I hope so.

I try to move my left ankle, but the joint isn't cooperating, and the pain is unbelievable. I can't tell if it's broken or just badly sprained, but either way, I know it's not going to hold my weight. I can't even rotate my ankle without wanting to scream.

I settle back against the ravine wall and pull my knit hat down as low as it will go, managing to cover my ears and forehead. Then I hunker down beneath the thermal blanket I pulled from my pack and try to conserve as much heat and energy as I can.

When darkness falls, the only sound I hear is the wind whistling through the ravine... no more human voices. Either they've moved on or they're more patient than I gave them credit for and are waiting me out.

But I can be patient, too. Unless they rappel down into this ravine—which I doubt they'll try in this weather—I'm safe for the night. Unless the cold gets me first.

Try as I might, I can't sleep—my nerves are too raw. Instead, I worry about Scout. It's well past six now, and Maggie already knows I didn't make it to dinner. Hopefully they'll come to my cabin and check on him. Maggie has a key. She'll take care of Scout. She's one of the most reliable people I know.

She won't give up looking for me. Once she realizes something must have happened, she'll call the sheriff's office as well as my brother Shane. She has his contact information for just such an emergency.

And when Shane knows I'm missing, he'll send in the cavalry. Security—taking care of people—is what he does. It's not just his job, it's his calling in life.

Maybe he'll send Killian, who's an expert at tracking in the wilderness.

Just thinking about Killian sends a pang of longing and regret through me. I'd give anything to have him here with me right now. The man's a force of nature. He wouldn't let a freak mountain snowstorm or poachers stand in his way.

Shivering uncontrollably from the cold, I close my eyes and picture Killian as he looked just a few days ago at my brother's estate. Like the rest of us, he'd come to celebrate little Ava's birth.

I can still picture how he looked in the airport, standing head and shoulders above the crowd. My heart nearly stopped beating when I saw him waiting for me in the arrivals lounge.

I don't think I've ever known such a good-looking guy—broad shoulders and chest, huge biceps, tattooed arms, dark hair and eyes, and a trim dark beard. His smile makes me weak in the knees, and that Cajun accent of his, which he slips in and out of, according to his mood—*damn*. It makes me melt.

But unfortunately, he lives in Chicago—where he works for my brother's security company—and I live here in a remote section of the Rockies, far from bustling cities and towns. I don't do cities, so it would never work out between us. That's why I shut him down every time he tries to make an overture, even though it kills me to brush him off.

I close my eyes and try to ignore my pounding headache. My ankle is throbbing, and my wrists sting from where the zip ties cut into my skin. Whoever invented zip ties should be shot. They are nasty, wicked devices of torture.

On top of the sound of howling wind comes a different kind of howl—the forlorn cry of a wolf. His plaintive cry is soon followed by a chorus of howls. In an odd way, hearing their cries gives me comfort. I know I'm not alone out here in the cold and snow. My friend Ruth would tell me it's a good omen.

I settle beneath my blanket and hope that when morning comes—as long as I don't freeze to death in the night—I'll find a way out of this ravine.

Eventually, when I can't keep my eyes open any longer, I lean my head back and succumb to the inevitable. I can only hope my predicament looks better in the morning.

4

Killian Devereaux

Getting called into the big boss's office isn't something that happens every day. In fact, it's never happened to me. So when I get the call early this morning during a high-priority surveillance job, I know something's up. Something serious. As soon as my replacement arrives, I head straight for the office and take the elevator up to the twentieth floor of the McIntyre Security office building, curious to find out what the hell is going on.

Getting called to the CEO's office feels an awful lot like getting called to the principal's office—something that happened to me quite a lot when I was a kid growing up in Lafayette, Louisiana. Back then, I'd much rather have spent my time huntin' gators with my grandpapa or scouring our family's pond for crawfish than sittin' in a classroom. Still would prefer it.

But my rebellious days are behind me. The Army matured me, combat as a Ranger hardened me, and life in general has seasoned me.

As soon as I walk into the executive suite, Shane McIntyre's administrative assistant, Diane, waves me on to his office. "Go right in, Killian. He's expecting you."

Shane McIntyre—CEO, boss, and friend.

And Hannah's big brother.

Damn it, stop thinking about her.

I rap my knuckles on the partially open door, then push it wide and walk in.

Inside the high-rise corner office, Shane sits behind a fancy executive desk in an expensive black leather chair. I'm surprised to see him dressed in blue jeans and a white button-up shirt. He's usually wearing a dark suit and tie at work, looking like a million bucks, which is fitting as he's worth that many times over.

"I thought you were out on paternity leave," I say. His wife, Beth, gave birth to a baby girl just a few days ago. "Is everything okay?"

Shane frowns. "Something urgent came up early this morning." He nods curtly at the pair of chairs parked in front of his desk. "Have a seat, Killian."

I study my boss, noticing the unusual tension in his posture, the flat set of his lips, and the way he's fidgeting with the pen he's holding. Instantly, I go on alert. "What's wrong?"

Another man barges into the office—a big man with the arms of a former heavyweight boxer, dressed in black jeans and a black T-shirt that molds itself to his big chest. His expression is equally dark. *Jake McIntyre.* My team leader and one of Shane's three brothers.

Jake nods to me in greeting. He doesn't seem one bit surprised to see me here.

Shane glances distractedly at his phone and takes a moment to read something. "Sit, both of you."

Neither one of us takes Shane up on his offer. Instead, we both stand at attention. When the chips are down, our military training kicks in. Jake's a former Marine.

"What do we know so far?" Jake asks his brother.

Shane glances up at us, failing miserably to conceal the stark pain radiating from his bright blue eyes. "There's not much to go on, unfortunately."

My heart starts pounding. Nothing ever shakes these two, so something has to be *very* wrong. I look from one brother to the other. "What the hell's going on, guys?"

Shane inhales a heavy breath, as if he needs a minute to collect his thoughts.

When his gaze lifts to *me*, my internal alarm goes off, and I feel an unfamiliar sinking sensation in my gut. "Just say it, Shane."

Shane's jaw tightens. "Hannah's missing."

"What?" I feel a chill as the blood drains from my face. I couldn't have heard him correctly. I just saw Hannah here in Chicago two days ago.

Shane nods. "The last time anyone saw her was yesterday morning around zero eight hundred hours, at a grocery store in Bryce, Colorado. She hasn't been seen since. She apparently hiked up a trail yesterday afternoon into some high country to do reconnaissance on a bald eagle, but she never returned. Her friend Maggie Emerson called the cops to report her missing. The local sheriff investigated and found her Jeep last night, abandoned in the parking lot at the trailhead. He and his people searched the trail all the way up to the ridge but found no sign of her."

For a moment, I stand as still as a statue while my mind processes the pertinent information. *Missing. Abandoned Jeep.* My pulse races as I grapple with the implications.

Hannah.

My Hannah.

Missing.

My mind starts to race with all kinds of horrific scenarios until I shut it down hard. It won't do Hannah any good for us to start fearing the worst.

Shane looks as bad as I feel when he addresses me directly. "Killian, I want you to lead a search and rescue team. Find her. Find my sister. Jake will come with you to manage the logistics."

My breath catches in my chest as I nod. Already, my thoughts are racing as I mentally prepare a checklist of what we'll need.

"You're our best tracker," Shane continues. "And our best bet of finding her. Take whomever you need, whatever you need. All of my resources are at your disposal."

"Are you coming?" I ask, surprised that Shane isn't already on a plane.

He nods. "I'll fly out with the rest of the family as soon as Hannah's located. I need to be here with Beth, who's recovering from surgery. Most everyone is coming except for Beth, Annie, and all the kids. Sam and Cooper will stay behind and help take care of Beth and our kids."

At the sound of a heavy knock, we all turn just as Shane's brother-in-law Dominic Zaretti walks into the room. "I just got word from Sophie," he says in his deep bass voice. *Hannah's eldest sister, and Dominic's wife.* "You'll want to send in Owen Ramsey. He's a damn good tracker. I've already given him a heads-up, and he said he's a go."

I nod, impatient to get going and happy to get all the qualified help I can. "We need to move fast. Time is working against us."

Shane nods. "The jet's being prepped now. You fly out of O'Hare in one hour. It's a two-hour flight to Denver International, and then a ninety-minute drive to Bryce."

"I'll grab what we'll need," Jake says as he heads for the door. Dominic follows him.

Shane stares up at me and bites out the words, "Find my sister, Killian." It's not a request.

"I will." *There's no other acceptable outcome.*

Shane nods. He knows how I feel about Hannah. I haven't gone out of my way to hide my feelings for her. Unfortunately, she doesn't feel the same. But that doesn't matter. If she needs help, I'm there.

"I'll make arrangements to get Owen out there on the next available commercial flight out of his location in Tennessee. Anyone else you need?"

"No. We'll move faster with a small team."

"I'll have all-wheel drive vehicles waiting for you in Colorado."

I pause as I study Shane's bleak expression. His family means the world to him, but he's especially protective of his three sisters. "We'll find her, Shane. Don't worry. I give you my word."

"I'm counting on it."

* * *

Jake and I meet up in the company armory and pack enough fire power to wage a small war—guns, ammo, night vision goggles, tactical gear, Kevlar vests, high-powered two-way radios—everything and anything we might possibly need.

Just shy of an hour later, the company jet is packed with our gear, and Jake and I are on board with the flight crew, ready for takeoff. It's amazing how quickly things happen when money talks.

Jake checks his phone. "Owen will meet us in Bryce. His

flight arrives in Denver an hour after ours. He'll rent a vehicle and meet us in Bryce."

I've heard stories about Owen, Dominic's longtime Army buddy. The man is a recluse, a loner who lives off-grid on a remote mountain in Tennessee. His wilderness and survival skills are legendary. He even saved Dominic and Sophie from a Chicago mafia hit when they were in hiding out in a cabin on Owen's mountain.

I spend the entire flight to Denver staring out my window, lost in thought. I saw Hannah just days ago—in fact, I'm the one who picked her up from the airport and drove her to Shane's estate in Kenilworth, just north of Chicago.

Just thinking about the way she bristled when she realized *I* was her ride to the house still makes me smile. She'd been expecting one of her brothers to pick her up. Instead, she got me. And she wasn't amused.

When Shane asked me if I'd pick Hannah up from the airport, I jumped at the chance. It would give me an opportunity to see her, to talk to her alone without all the curiously prying eyes.

And like a damned lovesick fool who apparently thrives on rejection, I couldn't pass up the chance to spend a few minutes alone with her on the drive. Unfortunately, she acted like she would have rather caught an Uber ride to the house than spend time alone with me.

And now she's missing.

I have to keep reminding myself that Hannah can take care

of herself. That girl is tough as nails. I've seen her spar numerous times on the mat with her siblings. I've seen her go toe-to-toe with her sister Lia, who's a professional bodyguard and trained fighter. I've seen her go up against her brother Liam, who's a martial arts international champion and instructor. Yeah, Hannah can hold her own.

But if someone has hurt her, I'll kill them.

That's a promise.

I glance across the aisle at Jake, who's equally quiet, lost in his own thoughts. Undoubtedly, he's worried about his sister. The whole family is.

༄ 5

Hannah McIntyre

I wake sometime the next morning to find myself buried under a small mound of fresh snow, and it's still coming down. Even with daylight, visibility is so bad I can't even see the opposite side of the ravine, or the top. The poachers could be up there right this minute searching for me, and I wouldn't even know it. I guess the blizzard is a blessing in disguise. If the weather was clear, they'd probably spot me in no time.

First things first... hydration. I won't stand a chance under these conditions if I become dehydrated. After drinking more of my precious supply of water, I eat another protein bar. Water and protein should sustain me for a while. And if I run out of water, I can always try to melt some snow.

It's time to take stock of my injuries, even though there's not much I can do about them.

I shake off the thermal blanket and snow to inspect my injured ankle. I roll up my left pant leg and unbuckle my boot. I open all the buckles as wide as they'll go, stretch the boot open, and finally grit my teeth and pull it off. The pain is like shards of glass digging into my ankle bones.

Gingerly, an inch at a time, I remove my sock. The flesh around my ankle is swollen and horribly discolored. The swelling is so bad I know I won't be able to get the boot back on again. I remember that there's a spare pair of warm socks in my pack, so I pull them out and carefully tug them over my foot. I can only hope that's enough covering to ward off frostbite. I shove my boot into my backpack for safekeeping.

From what I can see of my right bicep, it appears to be a graze—the bullet cut right through the outside of my arm, tearing open the skin, which is ragged and torn. Dried blood is caked on my sleeve, but the bleeding seems to have stopped. The wound is hot and throbbing, though, which isn't good. It's uncovered and liable to get infected.

There's a goose egg on the right side of my skull and cuts on my face, but there's not really anything I can do about those either.

My next order of business is to empty my bladder, which is letting me know that it's full to bursting. By holding onto the sturdy tree branches around me, I manage to haul myself up onto my good foot, unfasten my cargo pants, and shove them and my underwear down to my ankles. I do the best I can to squat, using a thick root protruding from the ravine wall to support myself so I can pee without soiling my clothes.

I finally succeed and manage to redress myself. Then I grab my pack and, using a sturdy stick as a cane, I manage to hobble a few yards down the ravine to find a clean spot to rest.

The ravine is pretty narrow, not more than thirty feet wide. Both sides are practically vertical. I estimate I fell about twenty feet, my descent slowed by densely packed tree limbs. I know there's a spot about a mile and a half down the ravine where it levels out into a valley. There's a hunter's shack in that valley, where I can take shelter until the storm passes. Still, without my satellite phone or a working cell phone, I have no way of summoning help.

But first things first—I need shelter. Not just from the weather, but from the poachers, who might come back any moment now that it's daylight.

I don my backpack, then use my handy walking stick as a makeshift crutch. After just one tentative step, even with the aid of a crutch, the pain is horrendous. I can't put any weight on my left foot. When I try, it's all I can do to keep from screaming. I try another step, but it's useless, so I drop back down onto the ground and crawl beneath an overhang of thick, tangled roots to find shelter again.

At the moment, it's quiet up above the ravine.

Do I think they've given up?

No, not for a second.

I expect them to resume their search as soon as there's a break in the weather. I need to get off this damn mountain, and preferably not in a body bag.

* * *

My ankle continues to swell. I do what I can to elevate my foot, hoping that might help.

The throbbing of the bullet graze on my right bicep has intensified, which I assume means infection has set in. I probably need antibiotics. My head is pounding, but from the blow to my noggin or from the lack of caffeine, I don't know. It could be either.

I'd kill for a large coffee.

I hate sitting here feeling sorry for myself, but there's not much I can do right now.

I need help.

And if Maggie notified my brother, then I know help is coming.

Thinking about Shane reminds me of Killian, of course. Seeing him this past week was hard. He put himself out there, admitting that he had feelings for me, and I shut him down.

I'm sorry, Killian. It's not you. It's me.

What a cliché. And it hurt like hell to say that to him. He was hurting, too. I could see it. But I can't ask him to give up every-thing—his career, his job—for me. And there's no way in hell I can move back to Chicago. My life is here, in the wide-open wilderness, not in a manufactured city of towering skyscrapers, hundreds of miles of asphalt, and over two-and-a-half million people crammed into just over two hundred square miles.

I can't go back there—not to live anyway. And I can't ask him to give up everything for me. We were doomed from the start, and I made the tough decision—I said no. He deserves better. But god, what I wouldn't give to have him here with me now.

As I try moving my right arm, the fire burns something fierce. I peer down at the ragged wound, sickened by the sight of shred-ded muscle. I try to flex my arm, but the pain is unbearable.

The sound of falling rock and dirt off in the distance catches my attention. I freeze and listen intently. It could be anything... animal, human. There are mountain lions in this area, as well as brown bears, bobcats, and coyotes, even wolves. There are hikers, as well, and poachers. But I doubt hikers would be out in this weather. No, they'd have more sense than that. I suppose I should've had more sense than to come out right before a storm was due. But I never dreamed I'd still be up on this mountain almost twenty-four hours later.

Finally, I hear voices—male voices. And they sound like they're coming from the rim on the opposite side of the ravine. Their voices are too indistinct for me to identify. It could possi-bly be a rescue team, which would certainly be preferable to the alternative, which is that the poachers have returned to finish the job.

I do what I can to camouflage myself behind some roots and rocks. Then I cover myself up with the thermal blanket and pile some of the freshly-fallen snow onto me.

Killian.

I can almost hear his deep, resonant voice in my head—his sexy Cajun drawl. *"What the hell trouble have you gotten yourself into, love?"*

I lean my head back and close my eyes, indulging for a moment in the mental image in my head—a tall, muscular man with dark hair and eyes, sun-kissed brown skin, and strong tattooed arms.

I'm struck by how much I wish things could have been different between us. "I'm sorry, Killian."

Lethargy takes me over, and I can barely keep my eyes open. As snowflakes fall on my cheeks, they melt instantly and water runs down my face in little rivulets. I touch my good hand to my face, to my cheeks and forehead.

Shit.

I'm outside in a blizzard, and yet I'm burning up.

Fever.

Infection has definitely set in.

ᯤ 6

Killian Devereaux

When our plane lands in Denver, just before noon, there are three four-wheel-drive SUVs waiting for us—all rugged, off-road vehicles. Jake and I will each take a vehicle, and the third one is on standby for Owen, who's due to arrive at the airport in an hour. But we're not waiting for him. Every minute counts.

Jake and I unload our gear from the company's private jet into our respective vehicles and head northwest to Bryce, Colorado, which is about a ninety-minute drive. We agree to meet up at Emerson's Grocery store on the main road in town, which is where we'll find Hannah's best friend, Maggie Emerson. Ms. Emerson was the last person to see Hannah yesterday, so we'll start our investigation with her.

We arrive at the grocery store at nearly the same time, both of us parking in the lot behind the store. When we come in through the rear entrance, we find Maggie unpacking a box of canned goods and setting them on store shelves. I guess her to be in her late thirties or early forties. She's dressed casually in faded blue jeans and a blue flannel shirt, a pair of well-worn boots on her feet. Her brown hair is pulled back in a ponytail.

"Maggie Emerson?" Jake asks as he scans the store.

The woman stands and faces us, hands on her hips. "That's right. You must be the men Hannah's brother sent."

Jake steps forward and offers Maggie his hand. "Yes, ma'am. Jake McIntyre. I'm also Hannah's brother." He nods to me. "This is Killian Devereaux. A third man, Owen Ramsey, will be here shortly."

Maggie looks me over, a curious expression on her pretty face as she studies me. "So you're Killian."

I nod, wondering how she knows my name. "Yes, ma'am."

She tucks a wayward strand of hair behind her ear and nods toward the sales counter. "I'll show you on a map where my boys and I found her Jeep last night."

Maggie is prepared, I'll give her that. She has a detailed map of the local area spread out on the sales counter, areas already marked on the map.

She points to a spot at the start of a marked trail, which she circled with a red marker. "Here's where we found her Jeep. It was well after dark, and the snow had already started. There was no sign of her, though. Hannah was supposed to join us for dinner last night, but she never showed. I tried calling her, but my calls kept going straight to voice mail. When we couldn't reach her, my sons and I drove to her cabin to see if she was there, but she wasn't. That's when we went looking for her.

I knew where she was headed that morning, to hike up a trail to check on a bald eagle's nest. We found her Jeep Wrangler parked at the trailhead. My sons and I hiked about a mile up the trail, calling her name, but we got no response. And we didn't see anyone else up there. Later, the sheriff and some deputies hiked up there, as well, but they had no luck finding her either."

I study the map, noting where the trailhead is located in relation to the store. I glance at Jake. "That's where I'll start," I say, tapping the spot where the trail starts.

"It's pretty rough terrain," Maggie warns, her eyes on me. "But I'm guessing you're an experienced hiker."

I nod.

"He's an excellent tracker," Jake says. "So is Owen, who will be here soon."

"I'm not waiting," I tell Jake. "I'll head up there now. When Owen arrives, send him after me."

Jake nods. "Roger." Then he looks to Maggie. "Got any suggestions for where we can stay in town?"

She points to her right. "There's a motel two miles north of here, on the main road. You can't miss it. It's pretty dated, but it's clean."

"That'll do fine," Jake says. Then he turns to me. "Go check out Hannah's Jeep and start on the trail. I'll secure rooms at the motel, unload our gear, and wait for Owen to arrive. I'll contact the sheriff's office to let him know we're here."

I glance at Maggie, whose brown eyes are shadowed. "Don't worry. We'll find her."

Maggie nods. "You'd damn well better. She's the best friend I've got in this world."

I leave Jake to set up our headquarters and organize logistics with local law enforcement. While he's doing that, I need to get out in the field and start searching. Hannah was up there just yesterday morning, and she had to have left a trail I can follow.

Following the map, I head up the road toward the trail. As soon as I pull into a small, gravel parking lot, I immediately spot a black hard-top Jeep Wrangler with Colorado plates that match Hannah's.

I hop out and peer inside the Jeep, but there's nothing to see. The interior is spotless, and all the doors are locked. I examine the parking lot, looking for any signs of a struggle, but find nothing. The ground is obscured by a heavy fall of fresh snow, over a foot deep, and it's still coming down hard. Visibility is poor.

I pull out my radio and hail Jake. "I'm here at the trailhead. I looked over her Jeep but didn't find anything unusual. I'm about to head up the trail now."

"Copy," he replies. "Keep me posted."

"Copy that. Out." Armed with my Glock 9mm in my chest holster and a hunting knife in a sheath strapped to my thigh, I pull on my winter coat, hat, and gloves. After strapping on my backpack and grabbing my climbing gear—just in case I need it—I start walking.

It's quiet going up the trail, with the only sounds coming from the wind rustling through the canopy overhead and the crunch of snow beneath my boots. Even though the path is covered with snow, the outline of the trail is visible thanks to the heavy brush bordering each side.

A sign indicates it's a two-mile hike up to Eagle Ridge. Presumably, it was somewhere on this trail that Hannah disappeared.

I take my time as I study the edges of the trail, looking for indications that someone has recently passed—scanning for broken branches, disturbed foliage, bent limbs, bruised leaves. I look for signs of blood, of course, but I don't even want to think about that.

Hannah's an experienced hiker, so it's not likely that she simply lost her way in the storm yesterday. Something must have happened, but whether that something was caused by man or by animal, I don't know.

The Rockies are inhabited by plenty of wildlife, so it's possible she ran into an animal. But knowing her, she would have been sufficiently armed to protect herself from an animal attack, so I don't think that's likely either.

The most probable scenario is that she ran into trouble with a human—and I don't even want to think about the implications of that.

Not far from the trailhead, I pick up two sets of tracks heading down toward the parking lot—two pairs of boot prints with deep impressions in the snow. Based on the tread size, I'm assuming they belong to two men. The tracks are of equal size—fourteens, if my guess is accurate—and therefore too big to be Hannah's. The impressions are pretty consistent, which implies that neither of them was carrying anything heavy—like a body—and that's reassuring.

The trail is pretty rugged hiking, the elevation increasing quickly. I track the two pairs of boots for a mile and a half, and that's when things get interesting.

The two hikers converged on the main path from two different angles, all coming from the south side of the trail. They'd clearly been in the woods, off the path.

Why?

I follow one set of tracks several hundred yards south of the trail and find myself standing at the edge of a deep ravine. I continue following the boot prints quite a ways along the edge of the ravine, until eventually the tracks meet up with another male's.

They were together at one point, presumably looking for something—or someone—and then they split up. My pulse kicks up.

"Hannah!" I yell. My voice echoes over the ravine, and I wait for a good while, hoping to hear a reply. "Hannah!"

But there's no response.

So I keep walking, and I trace those boot prints in the opposite direction, back toward the trail. Even though the snow is still falling, I can see a hint of impressions in the snow underneath the forest's protective canopy. Soon, I can make out *three* sets of prints—the two males I've been tracking and a third, smaller, lighter set. I see a few broken and bent branches, and even some blood splatters on the foliage and tree trunks. My stomach knots. The smaller prints are partially obliterated by the larger ones—they were chasing her. And someone—possibly Hannah—is bleeding.

"Hannah!" I shout.

I've seen enough. I turn and follow the erratic splatters of blood back toward the ravine. Whoever was injured was heading south, in the direction of the ravine, probably hoping to lose her pursuers in the woods.

Once I make it back to the ravine, I search the edge in both directions until I find a spot where the ground recently gave way. What I don't know is if someone fell into the ravine or was pushed.

"Hannah!"

I peer down into the ravine, which I guess has to be at least a twenty-foot drop. My heart hammers as I imagine her falling that far. Granted, there are plenty of trees growing on the ravine wall, and their limbs would have broken her fall somewhat, but it still would have been a brutal descent. And if she was already bleeding—

"Hannah!"

Still, I hear nothing but the wind in the trees and the sound of my boots crunching on the snow. I pull out my radio. "Jake, do you copy?"

There's some interference, but he quickly responds. "I copy, Killian. What have you found?"

"Plenty. Besides what I presume are Hannah's tracks, I found the tracks of two men, and indications of a scuffle and a chase. But there's no sign they carried her off this mountain, and she didn't walk down on her own. I think I know where she is. I think she went into a ravine that runs parallel to the trail. I'm going to rappel down into the ravine and search for her."

"You haven't made contact?"

"No. Nothing yet. And Jake?"

"Yeah?"

This part makes me sick. "There's a blood trail. I'm pretty sure she's injured."

I can't stand the idea of Hannah being hurt. I'm trying my best to remain stoic and not let my emotions get the best of me, but it's hard. She's not just a missing person—she means the world to me. The thought of her being hurt—or even worse—is more than I can handle.

I hear Jake mutter *fuck* over the line. Then more clearly, he says, "Copy that. Get down in that ravine, Killian. I'll send Owen up to meet you."

Then I hear a woman's voice over the radio—undoubtedly Maggie's. "I'm familiar with that ravine. It levels out into a valley with a stream, which makes it a popular place for the kids to hike and fish."

Then I hear an unfamiliar male voice. "Killian, it's Owen. I see the ravine on a map. I'll come up the ravine from the east side while you search from the west. We should find her somewhere between us."

"I'll go with you," Maggie says. "I know where to pick up the ravine. It's not far from the parking lot, but it's not marked either. I can take you right to it."

"Jake, have paramedics on standby," I tell him. "I'm pretty sure she's going to need medical treatment. It's at least a twenty-foot drop, and she's bleeding. If she weren't injured, she would have made it out on her own already, provided the two males tracking her didn't ambush her in the parking lot."

"Copy, Killian," Jake says. "Owen and Maggie are on their way now."

* * *

I study the edge of the ravine, looking for the best spot to set up my rappelling line. Since this may very well be a one-way trip—down only—I double up my line and wrap it around a sturdy tree trunk that can more than support my weight. This way, if I don't need to come back up, I can still retrieve my line.

With my pack secured on my back, and my climbing harness around my waist, holding an array of carabiners, I get into position, secure my line, and start rappelling. The wall is practically vertical, but there are a lot of trees and roots in my way, so it takes me a few minutes to reach the ground.

Once I'm down there, I don't find anything but pristine, freshly fallen snow. If she is indeed down here—which I believe she is—Hannah must have been on the move already, working her way down the mountain as the snow fell. That's good news. It means she wasn't so injured that she couldn't move. I do, however, find signs of a blood trail on some tree trunks. That isn't so good.

"Hannah!" My booming voice carries down the ravine, echoing loudly. If she's nearby, she'll hear me.

I listen for a response but don't get one. My heart is hammering in my chest, but I try not to let it get to me that I'm not hearing her. There are so many reasons why that could be the case, and I absolutely won't let myself think the worst.

I remove my climbing harness and stow my gear in my pack before I start making my way down the ravine. I've walked barely two hundred feet before I find tracks. Female boot tracks. And an impression in the snow, up against the ravine wall, where someone had stopped to rest.

I crouch down to study the area, and when I find signs of fresh blood, I shoot to my feet, my heart in my throat. She's close. She has to be. "Hannah!"

Still nothing.

Damn it!

I keep moving, following her rather obvious trail. It appears she was hobbling on one foot and using something as a crutch. If so, she isn't moving very quickly.

I radio Owen and give him an update.

"Copy that," Owen says. "We're at the bottom of the ravine, headin' up your way. Nothing on our end yet."

"Keep moving," I tell him. "She's bleeding and hobbling on one foot. We need to get her off this mountain."

"Copy," he answers. "We'll find her."

I pick up speed then, not worrying about trying to maintain the integrity of her trail. She's hurt, and time is of the essence. She's probably cold and wet, and those conditions combined with loss of blood are dangerous. Hypothermia is a real risk. Possibly infection, too.

"Hannah! Can you hear me?" I shout, hearing my own voice echo like thunder down the ravine. I just hope to god she can hear me, too.

$\mathcal{C}$ 7

Hannah McIntyre

I wake from a restless cat nap feeling dizzy and weak. My blood sugar is low, so I grab another protein bar and choke it down. I'm shivering from the cold—icy wet clothes cling to my skin—and I ache all over. I find a bottle of over-the-counter pain meds in my pack and swallow two pills with the last of my water, hoping they'll take the edge off. I'm at risk of hypothermia out here in these conditions.

I try once more to haul myself up onto my good foot, but my head is swimming, and the pain is overwhelming. I grit my teeth to keep from crying out and fall back onto the snow, jarring my arm and my ankle in the process. My right arm is oozing fresh blood again, and I have no idea how much blood I've lost. That explains the dizziness. Between the cold and the pain, I'm having trouble thinking straight.

The wind whistles down the ravine, bringing with it more snow. Visibility is down to maybe ten feet. The good news is that if the poachers do come back looking for me, they won't be able to see me, not from all the way up there. If they come down here into the ravine, I'm toast. With no weapons, I have no way to defend myself.

I hear a male voice shouting in the distance, and my heart stops.

"Hannah!"

That voice.

Jesus, it can't be.

My heart starts pounding double time. "Killian!" My voice is little more than a croak. Mustering all I've got, I try again, hoping to be heard over the wind. "Killian! I'm here!"

Relief sweeps through me when I hear a strong response from off in the distance. "Hold on! I'm coming."

I slump back against a tree trunk, feeling hopeful for the first time in nearly twenty-four hours. Maybe I'll survive this ordeal after all.

A few minutes later, I hear someone approaching. "Killian, I'm here!"

The next thing I know, a tall, dark shape marches through the snowfall, dressed in cold-weather survival gear, carrying a large pack on his back.

Killian drops down beside me, breathing heavily, and pulls off one of his gloves. After a quick cursory glance from my head to my toes, his gaze zeroing in on the gunshot wound and my missing boot, he mutters a curse. With a scowl, he presses his palm to my forehead. "Damn it, Hannah, you're burning up."

I've never been so happy to hear that damn, sexy accent. I gasp as a sharp pain shoots down my arm. Nodding at my torn sleeve, I say, "Gunshot flesh wound. It's just a graze, but I think it's infected."

"What else?" he says, sounding very matter-of-fact. He's a professional through and through as he looks me over. "Besides your ankle."

"My head and arm are killing me, and my left ankle is toast. I'm not sure if it's broken or not."

"Jesus, what happened?" he asks.

"Two poachers. I came across them up on the ridge. I managed to get away from them, but they chased me into the woods."

He frowns. "They shot at you."

"They intended to do a lot more than just shoot. I heard them discussing how they planned to kill me. I saw their faces, and that means I can identify them."

He's already inspecting the lump on my temple and the cuts on my face. He peels back the edge of my torn sleeve and surveys the wound. Then he moves to examine my ankle. "Damn, McIntyre. You're a real hot mess, you know that?"

I've never really understood if that was a compliment or not. Wincing, I laugh. "Gee, thanks. I'll bet you say that to all the girls."

He spares me a quick grin. "Nah. Just to the tough ones who can take it." Finally, he meets my gaze head-on, his long fingers cupping my hot face as he stares into my eyes. "What day is it?"

My head is swimming, making concentration difficult. "What?"

"Just answer the question. What day is it?"

"I don't know," I say honestly. "It's all a blur. Thursday, I think? It was yesterday I fell into the ravine. And the day before that I was in Chicago."

Seemingly satisfied with my answer, he nods and pulls a flashlight out of his pack and shines it into my eyes, first one, then the other, blinding me in the process.

"Ouch," I complain when my eyes water. "Do you mind?"

After stowing the flashlight, he grabs my wrist and feels my pulse. "I need to get you to the hospital. Can you walk?"

I laugh. "Don't you think if I could walk, I'd already be out of here?"

He shrugs. "Good point. For a moment, I forgot who I was dealing with. Do you have any water?"

I shake my head. "I drank the last of it this morning."

He frowns at me as he reaches into his pack and pulls out a stainless-steel water bottle, screws off the top, and hands it to me. "Drink. You're probably dehydrated."

"I'm a lot of things right now." But I'm too thirsty to argue with him, so I drink several good gulps of refreshing cold water before handing the bottle back. He takes a drink after me, and it occurs to me that his lips are touching the rim that my lips just touched.

"How did you find me?" I ask as he stows the water bottle.

He came for me.

The realization makes my throat tighten.

"Shane sent me. He knew I'd find you." He reaches into his pack and pulls out a radio. Pressing the mic, he says, "Killian to Owen. Do you copy?"

The radio crackles, and then a man's deep voice comes over the line. "Yeah, I copy." He speaks deliberately, his voice tinged with a southern accent.

"I've got her," Killian says. "She's injured and needs medical care, but she's stable."

"Copy," says the man on the radio. "Can she walk?"

Killian frowns. "Negative. I'll have to carry her."

"Roger. Head down toward us. We're coming up to meet you. And Killian?"

"Yeah?"

"The weather forecast is talking blizzard conditions. A real whiteout. It's going to get a lot worse before it gets better."

"Shit. Copy that. Do me a favor and let Jake know I have her."

"Jake's here?" I ask, grasping his sleeve. "My brother's here?"

Killian nods to me as Owen says, "Copy. Will do."

Then a familiar voice comes over the radio. "Hannah, thank god. Are you okay? I was so worried."

I grab the radio from Killian, my hand shaking as I press the mic. "Maggie! I'm okay. Where are you?"

"I'm with Owen. We're hiking up the ravine from the trail-head. Hang in there, honey. We'll get you help."

"What about Scout?"

"He's at our place. Don't worry. He's fine."

With a sigh, I lean my head back against a tree trunk. My dog is safe, and I'm in good hands. The situation is definitely looking up.

After Killian ends the call, he studies my ankle. "Where's your boot?"

"It's in my backpack. I took it off, but my ankle's too swollen to put it back on."

He nods, then takes the thermal blanket from me and wraps it around me. "There's not much I can do here in terms of first aid. We need to get you to shelter so I can do a proper assessment."

I laugh. "When did you acquire a medical degree?"

Ignoring me, he gazes up at the dark, overcast sky and the snow that's coming down harder by the minute. "We need to move." He attaches my smaller pack to his with a pair of cara-biners. Just as he lifts me into his arms, we hear a shot ring out from somewhere behind us, followed by the sound of agitated male voices.

I flinch. "Shit, they're back." They sound way too close for comfort.

Killian's expression hardens. "They're the ones who chased

you? Who shot you?"

"Yes. And I'm pretty sure they're coming back to finish the job. They know I can identify them. The penalties for poaching eagle feathers are pretty stiff, including jail time."

Another shot rings out, followed by a shout.

Killian secures me in his strong arms and starts off down the ravine. "Hold on to me. We need to move fast."

On a good day, it's a two-hour hike from where we are to reach the trailhead. In these conditions, with the snow falling so hard and with Killian having to carry me and my pack, it'll take much longer. He's strong, yes, but everyone has their limits.

Killian marches on as quickly as possible, which means he's not moving fast. He can't. I'm holding him back.

The sounds of the men farther up the ravine are getting closer and closer. They're gaining on us.

"I hope you're armed," I say. "They took my gun and knife."

He gives me an eye roll, not bothering to answer.

"Of course you are," I say.

I mentally calculate my weight, plus the weight of his pack and mine, and realize he's carrying at least two hundred pounds on rocky terrain in a blizzard. The poachers are presumably much lighter on their feet.

"They're going to gain on us," I say, "and when they do, we're sitting ducks down here."

He nods with a grunt but keeps ploughing forward. "We need to find shelter, someplace defensible where we can wait out the storm."

My thoughts are fuzzy as I try to think of a solution. We're never going to make it to the parking lot before the poachers catch up with us. "Wait." I grab his shoulder. "The ravine diverges ahead, breaking off to the south and leading into a valley. There's a hunter's shack there. It's not much, but it has four walls, a roof, and a door. At least it will get us out of the weather."

"How far is the shack?"

"About a mile once we reach the valley."

He reaches into his coat pocket, pulls out the radio, and hands it to me. "Radio Owen. Tell him where we're headed. And warn him about the poachers."

"Roger that," I say as I make the call. "Owen, do you copy?"

Killian glances down at me, a grin teasing his lips.

"What?" I say as the radio crackles. "Three of my brothers are former military. I know the lingo."

8

Killian Devereaux

S he's alive, and she's going to be okay. That's what keeps repeating in my head. *She's alive.* And as for the bastards who hurt her, I'll deal with them when the time comes.

I have other things to worry about at the moment. The weather conditions are deteriorating rapidly, and there's no way we'll make it off this mountain before the poachers catch up to us. Occasionally, the wind carries their voices down to us, and we've heard a few more random gunshots. I'm not sure if they're firing blindly into the ravine hoping to hit something or simply trying to scare Hannah. Probably the latter since visibility is practically nil.

Hannah is injured pretty badly—I'm guessing her ankle is broken. I need to sanitize her gunshot wound and wrap it, and I need to splint her ankle until we can get her to a hospital. She's probably dehydrated and definitely underdressed for this weather. And to top it off, she probably has a concussion. She needs rest, hot food, and water—and she needs *not* to be traipsing around on a mountain in a snowstorm.

I move as carefully as I can, focusing on planting my boots on steady ground. The ravine is littered with rocks and fallen logs, as well as roots. The last thing I want to do is stumble and risk dropping her. She's holding onto me for dear life, her face tucked against my coat, and not saying a word. I know this must be hard for her to deal with. She's so damn independent, but right now she's seriously at a disadvantage.

I know one thing—the poachers are moving faster than we are. The shots are getting closer.

It's another forty minutes or so before I see where the ravine branches off. Part of the ravine continues straight down the mountain—toward the trailhead and the parking lot—and part of it veers off to the south.

"This is our exit," I mutter as I head south, where the ravine gradually levels out in a valley. When she doesn't respond, I stop and glance down at her face. "Hannah?"

When there's still no response, I tip her face up to me. She's out cold. My heart catches in my throat when I see blood on her lips, the bitemarks obvious. *Damn it.* She's been biting her lips to keep from crying out. As careful as I've tried to be, this rough terrain has got to be jarring for her. "Jesus, love. I'm sorry."

She never complained once, the stubborn, hard-headed fool.

As carefully as I can, I set off once more, following the stream that runs through the valley. If there's a hunter's shack, it'll be near the stream. I just hope I'll be able to find it in this storm. The snow is coming down in blankets.

Gradually, the valley widens and levels out, making the going a bit easier. I follow the small stream south, hoping it's not too far to the shack. She said it was about a mile. I don't know what to expect, but I doubt it's five-star lodging. Right now, I'll settle for anything that gets us out of this bitter cold wind and snow.

"Hang in there," I murmur, tipping my head down to hers. I brush the top of her head with my nose. "It won't be long now." God, at least I hope not.

My arm muscles ache, and my back is killing me. Carrying this much weight in front of me is hard. I'm front heavy, as our two packs on my back don't weigh nearly as much as she does. Still, I trudge on. I'll keep going no matter what.

Fortunately, I haven't heard any sounds coming from behind us in the last twenty minutes or so. No voices, no gunshots. My hope is that they won't think to follow this branch of the ravine.

Almost an hour later, I come across the shack. It's exactly that, little more than a woodshed with a rickety door hanging loosely on rusted hinges, one small, dirty window pane, and a potbelly woodstove with a smokestack rising straight up through the roof.

I lay Hannah and our packs on the rickety porch, withdraw a flashlight and my 9mm, and open the door, revealing a small one-room cabin.

I do a quick sweep of the space to make sure it's empty—it is, thank god. No squatters, no vermin. I was prepared for anything—human, mountain lion, raccoons, a brown bear. But there's nothing here, and it doesn't look like it's been occupied in a while. The wood floor is littered with dirt and leaves, and the bed doesn't look much better. Besides the bed and the pot-belly stove, there's a small rocking chair in front of the only window. Across the room, by a rudimentary kitchen, is a wooden table with four chairs.

After quickly checking the bed for vermin, I lay Hannah on the mattress and bring our packs in and set them on the floor beside the bed. She's still out cold. I take a moment to check her pulse and respiration rate—both stable. She's shivering, though, despite having a fever.

What she needs most right now is heat—we need a fire in the woodstove. At the foot of the bed is a folded sheet and a dingy wool blanket. They'll have to do. I shake them both out to check for anything crawling around and cover her before I head outside to find firewood. Hopefully, there's a ready supply nearby, otherwise I'll be hunting for wood.

Armed with my handgun, I grab the radio and carry it outside with me. Pressing the mic button, I say, "Owen, do you copy?"

The line screeches, and then Maggie's voice comes online.

"Killian, it's Maggie. How's she doing?"

I smile but refrain from laughing. Of course it's Maggie on the line. Who else would it be? "She's been unconscious for a while now, probably from a combination of the cold and pain. I'm gathering wood for a fire now. How far out are you guys?"

"We made the turn toward the valley, so we're not too far from you. We should be there in twenty minutes."

Owen comes online. "How defensible is this shack?"

"It's not. A strong wind could blow it over."

"Any sign of the poachers?"

"Not for the past hour or so. I'm hoping they gave up."

"We heard a couple of shots coming from up the mountain, so don't rule them out," he says. "We'll be there soon. Over and out."

According to my watch, it's late afternoon, but the sky is already so dark that it seems much later.

I make a quick circuit around the shack and find seasoned firewood stacked beneath a tarp about twenty yards from the structure. Fortunately, the wood is dry. I grab an armful, along with some kindling, and head back inside.

Hannah's still out cold—and that worries me.

But first things first.

A fire.

She needs to warm up.

After throwing some dry kindling into the stove, I retrieve my lighter from my pack and ignite the twigs. I coax the flames until they catch enough that I can add some small logs.

There's an oil lantern sitting on a bedside table, and I find a supply of oil in a small cupboard in the kitchen area, if you can call it that. Once I light the lamp, I do a more thorough investigation of the cabin.

It's pretty bare bones, with just the one room. There's a rustic countertop with a sink, but no running water. Instead, I find an empty bucket and a ladle. The few hooks on the wall are bare. There's no bathroom, but I do find a portable potty chair in the only closet, along with a broom and dustpan. Maybe there's an outhouse somewhere outside.

I'm all for roughing it—and if it were just me, these accommodations would be fine. But Hannah needs more than this. We need to get emergency services up here as quickly as the weather will allow so we can transport her to the nearest hospital.

Once the fire is well underway, I take a seat on the bed beside her sleeping form. Already, I can feel warm air wafting up from the top of the woodstove, where an old kettle sits. I'll fetch some water from the stream shortly and boil it so I can use it to clean her wounds and make her something to eat. I brought some freeze-dried rations with me, so a hot meal is on the menu.

Gently, I brush the tangled strands of hair back from her hot face. "Hannah? Can you hear me, love?"

Her poor face is so battered I almost don't recognize her. Fury wells up inside me. I can't believe someone would do this to her—to anyone. One way or another, I'm going to track down those motherfuckers. Part of me hopes they do catch up to us, so I can deal with them myself.

Now that she's safe, and the shack is starting to warm up, it's time to get her out of her wet clothes. I remove her knit hat and unzip her coat. There's no sign of any gloves—she must have lost them at some point. I check her fingers for signs of frostbite—it's a miracle I don't see any damage.

She cries out restlessly as I try to pull off her right sleeve. Fresh blood is oozing from the gunshot wound, so I work slowly and carefully. Once her jacket's off, I take a quick look at the nasty gouge in her arm. The flesh is a jagged bloody mess revealing some muscle, and anger floods me once more. I'm going to kill the bastards if it's the last thing I do.

I do my best to tamp down my emotions as I continue my rough triage. Using a pair of scissors from my pack, I cut off the bottom portion of the left leg of her cargo pants to get access to her ankle. It's horribly swollen, the skin an angry shade of red, but fortunately, there's no puncture wound and no bones are sticking out. My guess is it's broken, but we won't know for sure until we get her to a hospital. Gently, I attempt to rotate her ankle, but the joint's not cooperating at all.

Her eyes flash open, and she sits up and screams.

I grab her shoulders and try to hold her still. "Hannah! It's okay. You're safe."

When she stares at me with wild eyes, her face flushed from fever, I give her a little shake. "Hannah, look at me."

It takes a moment before recognition settles in. "Killian? Are you really here?"

"Yeah, love. It's me."

"You came for me," she says as if she can't believe it.

A knot forms in my throat. *Hell yes, I came for her.* "Of course I did." I gently brush her hair back from her hot forehead. "Lie back down, please."

She lets me lower her to the mattress, her gaze locked on me.

I grab my pack and pull out the first-aid kit. "I'll treat your injuries as best I can with what I've got. We'll get a medical transport up here as soon as the weather breaks."

Her brow wrinkles in confusion. "We?"

"Yeah. Jake's here, remember, and so is Owen Ramsey—he's a friend of Dominic's."

She doesn't know Owen, but her eyes widen at the mention of her brother. "Jake's here?"

I told her he was here, but she doesn't remember. "He's in town, coordinating with the sheriff's office and the medics. Owen and Maggie are on their way up here. They should be here soon."

Hannah slumps back onto the mattress as if she's expended what little reserve of energy she had left. Tears flood her eyes. "I can't believe you're here."

Gently, I cup her face, careful not to touch any of the cuts and bruises. "Where else would I be? You think I'd let you be out there all alone and hurting? Over my dead body."

She looks away, guilt written plain as day on her poor battered face.

I can guess what she's thinking. She's kept me at arm's length since we first met last summer at the baby shower for Shane's son, Luke. I've seen her a few times since then and tried repeatedly—and failed—to connect with her.

It's not you, Killian, she told me just a few days ago when I picked her up from the airport on her most recent visit to Chicago. But she wouldn't say much more than that. She just shut me out.

I can't help feeling that there's some real chemistry between us. I've seen the way she looks at me when she thinks I can't see her. I've seen flashes of longing—even desire—in her beautiful big brown eyes. And I'm not ready to give up on her—on the possibility of *us.*

"Let's get you out of these wet clothes. I have some dry clothes in my pack." I dig into my backpack and pull out a clean T-shirt and a pair of gray sweats with a drawstring waistband. "They'll be too big for you, but you'll be more comfortable once you're warm and dry."

She nods gratefully, but when her eyes meet mine, I see a flash of panic.

"I can help you," I offer hesitantly. "Or, if you think you can manage it yourself—"

"I can do it," she says hastily.

"Okay." I rise from the bed and walk over to the kitchen area, my back turned to give her some privacy. I listen to her huffing and groaning in pain as she wrestles with her wet clothing, which is undoubtedly clinging to her skin and making removal difficult.

"Killian."

"Yes, love?"

She sighs in defeat. "I need your help."

I know it's a blow to her pride to admit she needs help, so I try to be as matter- of-fact as I can. I undress her quickly, doing my best to avert my gaze. Her shirt comes off first, then her pants. I see a lot of smooth, supple skin and beautiful curves, but I try not to fixate on it.

"My bra, please," she says, as she leans forward.

I reach behind her and unclasp the straps, letting the garment fall into her lap. Before I'm in any danger of seeing her bare breasts, she pulls the T-shirt I laid out over her head and slips her good arm into the sleeve. I help her with her other arm.

"Lie back now," I advise. When she does so, I reach up beneath the T-shirt, grip the waistband of her underwear, and slide them down her long legs. Then I hold the sweatpants for her and help her slip them on and pull them up to her waist. I cinch the drawstring to keep them from falling off her.

She lets out a relieved sigh. "Thank you."

"I'll need to splint your ankle," I tell her as I cover her back up again. "It'll feel better once it's stabilized. But first, let's get you some food and something to drink. Then you can take some pain meds."

I rise from the bed and gather my coat, hat, and gloves, as well as my 9mm, which I tuck into my chest holster. Then I retrieve the empty wooden bucket from the kitchen counter. "I'll be right back. I'm going to the stream to fetch some water."

Her eyes follow me to the door, and I swear I see a tinge of panic lurking there.

"I'll be back in ten minutes," I tell her. "The stream is just twenty yards straight out this door."

She nods and closes her eyes.

For a moment, I stand there at the door, just watching her as I let out a tight breath. Finally, I can allow myself to feel a little bit of relief knowing she's alive and not in any immediate danger. I'll keep her safe from here on out, no matter what those assholes try. I'm not leaving her unprotected—not for a second. If they come for her, they'll be in for a surprise because it's *me* they'll be dealing with.

I unbar the door and push it open. The cold, biting wind sweeps inside, so I rush out and close the door behind me to keep what little heat we have inside the shack.

The snow is still coming down, and visibility is so poor I can't even make out the stream from the cabin porch, although I can hear the rushing water. Not wanting to leave her alone for long, I race down to the water and fill the bucket and then head back up to the cabin and step inside, barring the door behind me.

She eyes the door with a wary gaze. "They took my gun."

"Don't worry. I'll be your gun."

⁀ 9

Hannah McIntyre

I lie back on the bed and close my eyes, unsure what to think. Killian's here, risking his own life for me when I don't deserve it. I don't deserve *him*.

I listen to him moving about the small cabin as he takes off his outer gear and hangs it up. He pours water into a kettle and sets it on the stove to boil. The stove is relatively small, but it's putting out a good amount of heat. I already feel warmer.

He sits on the edge of the bed and pulls two small pouches out of his pack. "Pot roast or chicken and rice? Take your choice."

It takes me a minute to realize he's holding up pouches of freeze-dried food. "Either is fine. Thank you."

"I think you're a pot roast kind of girl," he says as he opens one of the packs. He carries it to the woodstove and picks up the kettle, which is whistling now, and pours water into the bag. Then he closes the bag and lets it sit for a few minutes. "Won't be long now," he says as he digs around in his pack and pulls out a set of stainless-steel cutlery wrapped in plastic. "Dinner is served."

While I eat, he heats up the other pouch for himself and wolfs it down. Then he locates a bottle of over-the-counter pain medication and sets it on the little table by the bed.

There's a noise outside the door, like boots stomping on the wooden porch, and I freeze.

Killian drops what he's doing, grabs his handgun, and moves to the small window overlooking the front of the cabin to peer outside. The tension in his body immediately eases. "It's Owen and Maggie."

There's a knock on the door, then a man's deep voice says, "Killian."

Killian opens the door, and two snow-covered figures come inside.

"Hannah!" Maggie rushes toward me.

"Wait," Killian says as he bars the door. "Take off your wet gear first. I'm just now getting her thawed out."

Maggie pulls off her knit hat, then her gloves, and finally her coat. She hangs everything up on hooks near the kitchen and returns to the bed to sink down on the mattress. Her expression falls as she gets a good look at me. "Oh, Hannah. Your poor face."

"I'm all right," I say as I try to sit up.

"No, don't," Killian says as he picks up my discarded meal and pokes around inside the bag with my fork. "You missed some," he says. "You need to eat it all."

"I can't eat lying down." I slowly and painfully push myself into an upright position, grimacing at the pain in both my ankle and arm.

Maggie arranges two pillows behind me so I can lean against the headboard. After she helps me settle into place, she brushes my hair back, careful not to touch the goose egg on my temple or the cuts on my face. "You poor thing. Is that better?"

I nod. "Thanks." *Not really. Everything hurts.*

Killian hands me a fork and the pouch of food, which is still quite warm to the touch. "You need to finish it. Sorry, but you'll have to make do without any seasonings. We don't even have salt or pepper. When we get out of here, I'll cook you a proper meal."

I catch Maggie eyeing Killian with a curious smile on her face. "You cook?" I ask him, surprised.

He nods. "I do. *Ma mère* made sure I knew how to feed myself." At the look of confusion on Maggie's face, he says, "My mother."

"Oh, right. It's French." Maggie winks at me. "He speaks *French.*"

Killian nods. "I was raised in a French-speaking household. I didn't speak a lick of English until I started grade school."

"You got any more of those MREs?" the other man asks. He nods toward Maggie, who's undoubtedly hungry too.

Killian motions toward his pack. "Help yourself. There's plenty for both of you."

Owen digs around inside Killian's pack and pulls out several pouches. "We've got chicken and rice, penne with marinara sauce, and chili mac. What'll you have?"

"I'll have the penne," Maggie says, smiling at Owen before she turns to me, speaking volumes with her eyes.

I take a moment to get a good look at Owen Ramsey. He's a big guy, like Killian, with a broad chest and huge biceps. He has blue eyes, long ash-blond hair tied up in a bun, and a full beard. From the efficient way he moves—with purpose—I imagine he's former military as well.

I don't know him, but I do know that he was there in Tennessee when Sophie and Dominic were attacked by a mafia hit squad that had come down from Chicago to find them. My sister and her future husband were vastly outgunned, and Owen likely saved their lives.

Owen makes up Maggie's pasta and hands it to her, along with a fork. Then he pulls on his hat and heads for the door. "I'll do rounds," he says to Killian.

Killian nods.

"Don't you want to eat something first?" Maggie asks Owen as he unbars the wooden door.

Owen shakes his head. "No, ma'am. I'm fine. I'll patrol. The poachers are still out there, so we need to be on alert."

Owen closes the door behind him, and Killian bars it shut.

"Do you know anything about first aid?" Killian asks Maggie.

She laughs as she mixes her pasta and sauce and sets it aside to rehydrate. "I have two teenage boys. I *invented* first aid."

"Good. I'm going out to find some wood we can use to splint Hannah's ankle. If you could wash her face and apply antiseptic, that would be great." He drops a first-aid kit on the bed.

Maggie salutes Killian. "Yes, sir."

As Killian bites back a grin, his gaze drifts to me. "I won't go far. Yell if you need me. I'll hear you." And then to Maggie, he says, "Make sure she finishes her food and takes some of that pain medication there on the table. And bar the door behind me."

Once he's outside, Maggie jumps up to secure the door. Then she returns to sit with me and lays a gentle hand on my thigh. "I was so worried when we couldn't find you last night. What happened?"

"I inadvertently stumbled upon a couple of poachers up on Eagle Ridge. I think they were scoping out Betty's nest. One of them got the jump on me, knocked me unconscious, then tied me to a tree. The bastards took my gun and my knife. I was able to escape, but in the process I fell into the ravine." I glance down at my left foot. "My ankle's probably broken, and"—I turn to show her my right bicep—"they grazed my arm."

"Oh, my god, they shot at you?"

"Yeah, I think that was the goal. They wanted to kill me."

Maggie pales. "And they're still out there?"

"We think so. I saw their faces, Maggie. I can identify them. They're not going to just give up."

"And the guys are out there, walking around in the dark as if nothing's wrong." Maggie rolls her eyes. "Spare me. I've never been around so much testosterone in my life."

I laugh, despite the pain it causes. "Yeah, they're something, aren't they? And you met my brother Jake, too, right?"

"I did. Tell me again why you wanted to leave Chicago?"

"Oh, god, please don't make me laugh. It hurts too much."

"I'm sorry. None of this is funny." Maggie grabs the first-aid kit and pulls out gauze and antiseptic solution and starts gently dabbing at my face.

"I'm so sorry," she says when I flinch. "I'm trying to be gentle."

"It's okay."

When she's done cleaning my face and applies a bandage to the worst of the cuts, I tell her to eat her food.

She takes a bite of her pasta and makes a face. "I'd kill for some spicy Italian sausage to go with my pasta, but some salt definitely wouldn't hurt."

"Me too." But in all honesty, the food's really not that bad. And it's hot, which is a blessing. "Kudos to Killian for bringing food."

"He's quite the Boy Scout." Maggie levels her gaze on me. "You didn't tell me he was so fucking hot."

"Who, Killian? Yes, I did."

"You said he was *hot*, sure. But you didn't say he was panty-melting, mind-blowingly hot. And his friend Owen? Oh, my god."

I try not to laugh, because it hurts, and end up gritting my teeth.

"I'm sorry," Maggie says, patting my hip. "I shouldn't make you laugh." She takes another bite of her pasta and makes a face as she swallows. "How are you feeling?"

"Like crap." I pop two pain pills and swallow them down with a bite of food. "My arm wound is just a graze—it'll heal. The cuts on my face will heal. I just hope my ankle's not broken. That would really suck because I can't do my job if I'm hobbling around on crutches for six weeks."

Maggie gingerly uncovers my ankle and studies it. "It's swollen and bruised, but at least no bones are sticking out."

When she touches my ankle lightly, I flinch. "Gee, thanks for the visual."

"Sorry. I'm just saying, there's no obvious sign that it's broken, so keep thinking positively that it's just sprained."

When a strong gust of wind rattles the glass panes in the window, we both jump.

"Do you think they're still out there?" Maggie asks.

Of course she means the poachers. "I'm not sure. They were following the ravine down the mountain for a while, and we heard gunshots occasionally. I hope they gave up because of the weather."

"At least we have armed guards," she says, nodding toward

the door.

"Yeah, but I hate for them to be out there in this weather."

There's a brisk knock on the door, followed by Killian's voice. "It's me, Maggie. Open up."

Maggie lets Killian in. "Any sign of the poachers?"

"I heard gunshots way off in the distance. Could be them. But don't worry. Owen's patrolling the perimeter as we speak. They won't be able to sneak up on us."

He's carrying two flat sections of tree bark, both about eight inches long and two inches wide. "These should do the trick," he says as he lays them down at the foot of the bed. He pulls a roll of tape from the first-aid kit.

"Hold these, please," Killian says to Maggie as he positions the two pieces of bark on either side of my ankle. While she holds the splints in place, Killian tapes them tightly. "How does that feel?" he asks me when he's done.

I try moving my leg just a bit. It hurts, yes, but not nearly as bad now that my ankle is stabilized. "That's better."

"How much better?" he asks. "How's your pain on a scale of one to ten?"

"It went from an excruciating ten to a six."

He nods. "Good. Did you eat your food? All of it?"

"Every bite."

He eyes the bottle of pain medication sitting on the nightstand. "And you took your pain meds?"

"Yes, *mom*."

He arches his brow at me. "I am definitely not your mother." Then he grabs my empty water bottle from my pack and fills it with water from the kettle, which has cooled off quite a bit. "Drink this. I just wish I had some antibiotics on me. That's what you really need."

Killian fills his own water bottle, then asks Maggie if she brought one in her pack. "Everybody, drink up."

"What about Owen?" Maggie asks. "He didn't eat anything."

"He has protein bars on him and a water bottle. He'll be fine."

Maggie drifts over to the window and peers outside at the falling snow. "I can't see anything beyond the porch. Shouldn't we check on him?"

Killian chuckles. "We don't need to check on Owen, trust me. Quite the opposite. He periodically checks on us."

Maggie pulls her winter coat tight around her and takes a seat in the rocking chair by the window. Killian adds more wood to the stove and covers me with the wool blanket. Then he sits at the table, positioning his chair so that he can watch both the door and me at the same time. It's pitch-black outside, so I figure it must be late evening.

"I spoke to Jake via radio a little while ago," Killian tells me. "He's got an emergency medical team prepared to come up here and evac you in the morning, as soon as the snow lets up."

"*If* they can get up that ravine," Maggie says as she glances at the window. "I wouldn't be surprised if there's over two feet of snow on the ground now. Navigating the ravine in the morning is going to be a nightmare."

"Jake'll figure something out," Killian says. He picks up his handgun, checks the magazine, and then lays his gun on the table within easy reach. "Our job is to stay put and keep Hannah warm, fed, and hydrated."

I watch Maggie as she stares out the window, concern written all over her face.

"Are you worried about Riley and Brendan?" I ask her.

Maggie shakes her head. "Ruth is staying with them tonight. They'll be fine. And they've got Scout to keep them occupied." She peers out the window. "Stupid man. I don't know why he thinks he has to stay outside all night. It's freezing out there."

"He's fine, Maggie," Killian says. "Stop worrying. No one will be able to sneak up on us in the night with Owen keeping watch."

"You could take turns with him, give him a break," she says.

Killian shakes his head as he looks my way. "I'm not leaving Hannah."

He says that with such finality, I feel a shiver ripple down my spine, and I don't think it's because of the cold.

Killian's here.

He came for me.

He comes over and lays his hand on my forehead. "You still have a fever." He frowns as he lowers the light on the oil lamp. "Try to sleep, love."

My chest tightens at the comforting sound of his deep voice. I hate having to rely on anyone, but right now, he's exactly who I need.

✎ 10

Killian Devereaux

As night falls, so does the temperature. The cabin is dark and quiet when I put on my winter gear and step out onto the porch. It's well below freezing. I glance out at the yard around the cabin and see nothing but snow with a few tracks to and from the porch.

Owen is doing his rounds and making sure no unwanted company sneaks up on the shack.

A moment later, a dark figure drifts up onto the porch to stand beside me.

"All clear?" I ask him unnecessarily.

He nods. "I checked the ravine. The snow is over two feet deep in places. The rescue crew's going to have a hard time getting a gurney up here."

"I was afraid of that. We need some other way to get her off this mountain."

"How's she doing?"

"She's hanging in there. That woman is tough, I'll tell you that. She's in a lot of pain, but she tries not to let it show."

The cabin door opens and Maggie stands in the doorway, a blanket wrapped around her, over the top of her coat. Her gaze connects with Owen's first, but she doesn't say anything. Then she turns to me. "You need to come back inside, Killian." Frowning, she glances back toward the bed. "She's not doing so well."

With a curt nod, Owen steps off the porch and disappears into the darkness. I step back inside and close the door behind me, barring it.

I hang up my coat and stand beside the bed to assess Hannah. There's a painful tightness in my chest when I watch her clutching the wool blanket to her chest. Her eyes are closed tight, but what worries me most is how badly she's shaking. "Damn it." I lay my palm on her forehead. "She's burning up. We need those damn antibiotics."

Hannah's shaking so badly, I'm afraid she's going to hurt herself. She could be cold—after all, this rickety shack isn't airtight. Frigid wind blows through multiple loose wall boards and beneath the door. Or, it could be hypothermia setting in, or fever.

Hell, I wouldn't be surprised if she was in shock.

Making a quick and practical decision, I strip down to my boxer-briefs. Then I climb onto the far side of the bed, behind Hannah, and slip beneath the wool blanket and the sheet. I press my body against hers and wrap my arm around her waist, careful not to touch her wounded arm or jar her ankle, and basically spoon her from behind. I tuck my Glock under the edge of my pillow in case I need it.

"I've got you, love," I murmur against the back of her head. "I'll keep you warm."

My body heat, combined with the insulating properties of wool, helps raise the temperature beneath the blanket considerably. Maggie puts more wood in the stove and uses the poker to stir the coals and stoke the flames.

She smiles as she watches me holding Hannah. "I'm glad you're here. Hannah talks about you a lot."

"She does?" That surprises me.

Maggie nods. "I think you've made quite an impression on her."

I chuckle. "Could'a fooled me."

"Hannah's a complicated one, you know? But she's worth it."

I nod. "I come from a family of strong, complicated women, so I can respect that."

Maggie glances out the window. "I hope Owen's okay out there."

"He's a tough one, so doan you worry."

She doesn't look happy.

"Maggie?"

"Hm?"

"We need to find another way to get Hannah off this mountain in the morning. Owen says the snow is piling up in the ravine. It's doubtful the medics will be able to get a gurney up here. I could carry her out, but it's risky."

Maggie stares off at the window, lost in thought, before she snaps her gaze back to me. "I might know a way. Micah—my friend Ruth's brother—owns a helicopter tourism business. There's a flat area just downstream where he might be able to land his chopper. It'll be risky because of the snow, but Micah's a damn fine pilot."

"How far downstream?"

"Half a mile or so."

"Grab the radio and hail Owen. Tell him you know someone with a chopper."

She calls Owen and gives him the information.

Owen confirms, saying, "I'll contact Jake and let him know to set up the exfil."

Sharing my body heat with Hannah has definitely helped her sleep more comfortably. She's not shaking quite as badly now. She's still out of it, though. As I hold her against me, I try not to enjoy the contact. I've never been this physically close to her before, and I doubt she'd appreciate it if she weren't impaired. Occasionally, she stirs with a pained moan, and that reminds me of how much she's suffering.

I press my lips to her hair and whisper, "Hang in there, love.

It's gonna be all right." And I swear to god, she clutches my arm and holds it to her chest.

Sometime later, the radio crackles with an incoming call. "Killian, do you copy?" It's Jake.

Maggie hands me the radio. "Yeah, I copy. Over."

"Micah will fly his helo into the valley at first light to pick up Hannah and transport her to the hospital. He'll bring a medic with him. Seating is limited, so some of you will have to hike out."

"Copy." I damn well plan to be on that helo, too. I'm not leaving Hannah's side until she's stable.

"The sheriff has had his men up and down that ravine all night," Jake says, "and they haven't seen anyone else up there."

"They were close by earlier. We heard gunshots."

Jake mutters a curse as he ends the call.

Maggie makes decaf tea with the water in the kettle, and after it cools, we succeed in getting Hannah to drink some.

After Hannah's had enough to drink, Maggie returns to the rocking chair and dozes off while I stand guard.

It's just after midnight when a shot rings out in the distance. Maggie jerks awake in the rocking chair, and I'm already climbing out of bed, careful not to disturb Hannah, who's still sleeping. I dress quickly and pull on my outer gear before grabbing my handgun.

"Stay here," I tell Maggie as I unbar the door. "Lock this after I'm gone and see to Hannah."

"Will do," Maggie says as I slip out the door.

The moonlight is blocked by an overcast sky. I walk to the end of the porch and listen. Another shot rings out, and although the sound reverberates in the valley, I think it's coming from the ravine.

I step off the porch and melt into the shadows beside the shack. I can't leave the women undefended, but I need to know what's going on.

Owen signals his presence as he slips up behind me. "Two men to the north," he says, his voice low and succinct.

"The poachers?"

"I'd bet money on it."

"Have they seen the shack?" I ask him.

"Unlikely. They're still at least a klick away. After I spotted them, I hustled it back here to give you a heads-up. I think they're mostly stumbling around in the dark."

The temperature is brutal cold, and Owen's been out here for hours. Every man has his limits. "Why don't you go inside and warm up? I'll take watch."

Owen shakes his head. "It's better if I stay out here."

I'm not sure what he means by that, but I don't press him. He's a grown man, and he knows his own business. If he wanted to come in, get warmed up, and eat or drink something, he would. "The offer stands. If you change your mind, let me know."

As I pass the front window, I catch Maggie's eye. At first, I can't tell what the hell she's doing. She's leaning over Hannah, helping her to sit up. I watch for a moment, honestly curious, until I see the portable potty chair beside the bed.

Oh.

When Maggie helps Hannah transfer to the bedside commode, I turn my back on them to give Hannah some privacy.

Of course she needs to pee. I've been plying her with fluids all night. Thank god Maggie's here. As hard as it must be for Hannah to need help to perform basic bodily functions, she'd be mortified if she'd had to ask me.

✏ 11

Hannah McIntyre

Despite the fact that my bladder feels like it's about to burst, it's not coming easily. Nerves probably. That and the fact that I can't stop shaking. It's hard to relax enough to pee when your body is shivering so violently your teeth are chattering.

It's also damn cold in here. After coming out from beneath the warm wool blanket, my skin feels like I just took a dip in an icy pond.

Maggie rubs my back. "Try to relax."

I glance toward the door, thinking Killian could return any

moment and catch me with my underpants down. Maggie said he left the cabin to investigate after hearing some gunshots. I doubt he'll be out there long.

Finally, through force of will, my body relaxes sufficiently that I can pee. "This is so embarrassing," I mutter at the sound of the waterfall hitting the bucket.

Maggie chuckles. "I've raised two boys, Hannah. Trust me, this is nothing."

Once I'm done, Maggie hands me a sheet of paper towel and I wipe myself. Then she helps me stand long enough for me to pull my clothes up and crawl back into bed.

"I'll be right back," Maggie says as she removes the bucket. "You just rest." She dons her coat and removes the bar from the door. Just as she's about to step outside, a gloved hand reaches in and grabs the handle from her.

"I'll do it," Killian says in a low voice.

Oh, my fucking god. Just kill me now.

I don't think I've ever been so embarrassed in my life.

Maggie closes the door and turns to me with an amused expression. "It's official, Hannah. He's a keeper."

Mortified, I press my hot face into the pillow.

But Maggie just laughs. "I'm serious. Doing what needs to be done without complaint—that's hot as hell."

A moment later, the door opens again and Killian walks inside saying nothing about the fact that he just dumped my pee bucket. I swear, if he makes a joke about yellow snow, I'll clobber him.

But he doesn't. He bars the door, then retrieves the portable potty chair and takes it back to the closet where it came from. He's incredibly circumspect, which I appreciate.

"Thank you," I say when he returns to sit on the edge of the bed.

He pats my leg. "Anytime."

"So, who fired the shots?" Maggie asks him.

"Someone's firing in the ravine. They haven't come into the valley, so we're fine. Owen's monitoring their location."

Maggie glances out the window, a worried look on her face. "He must be so cold."

Killian shrugs. "He's a tough one. I offered to trade places with him, but he said no." He glances down at me. "How are you feelin'?"

"About the same. My head hurts, my arm burns, and my ankle is throbbing."

"Let me take a look," he says as he lays the covers aside. He unwraps my ankle, studying it with a neutral expression. He checks the splints to make sure they're holding.

I have to admit, the splints do help. "How bad is it?" I ask him.

"About the same. Maybe a bit more swollen."

Maggie comes over to look, too, but she's not as good at schooling her features as he is. She winces just before she looks away.

"That bad?" I ask her.

She gives me a guilty smile. "Hopefully it's just a bad sprain."

Killian wraps my ankle once more and covers me with the bedding. Then he checks beneath the bandage on my arm. Studying the flesh wound, he frowns.

The bitterly cold wind outside rattles the glass panes of the window and shakes the door on its hinges.

I shudder and pull the blanket tighter around me. "Is it still snowing?"

Killian nods. "But don't worry. Come morning, if the snow has stopped, we're getting you to a hospital."

"How? I can't walk off this mountain."

"Micah's going to fly his chopper up here in the morning," Maggie says. "There's a flat area just down the stream."

Wincing, I laugh. "Micah's been pestering me to take a ride on his precious helicopter since I moved here. Now he's going to get his way."

Frowning, Killian moves to the stove and adds more wood. "Want more tea? Or some water?"

"No, thanks," I groan. "What goes in must come out."

He grins. "Don't let that stop you. You need to stay hydrated."

I follow Killian's gaze as he notices Maggie nodding off in the rocking chair.

Killian walks over to her and touches her shoulder. "Why don't you lie down with Hannah? I'll keep watch."

Maggie stands and nods, looking guilty. "I'm sorry. I'm exhausted."

"No need to apologize," Killian says. "Go rest. Share your body heat with Hannah."

After Maggie climbs in bed with me and we huddle together, both of us shivering, Killian takes a seat in the rocking chair, gun perched on his lap. "Get some sleep, ladies. Sunrise will be here before you know it."

He glances toward the bed and catches my eye. I meet his gaze head-on, and we watch each other for several long moments, neither of us looking away. There's so much emotion there in his dark eyes. I think I see yearning and longing, but it might be wishful thinking on my part. I don't know what to make of him. He's bigger than life. He's courageous, kind, and selfless.

"Need anything?" he asks quietly when I continue watching him.

When I shake my head, he nods and then turns to watch out the window.

Once in the night, I wake from a fitful sleep to find Killian stoking the fire in the woodstove.

After he closes the stove door, he walks over to press his palm to my forehead and frowns. "Need anything?"

"A drink of water?"

He hands me my water bottle and, while I take a few sips, he shakes a couple of pain pills into his palm and offers them to me. "You can take more now."

I swallow the pills and hand the water bottle back to him. "Thank you."

"My pleasure."

As Killian returns to the rocking chair—and his look-out

post—I close my eyes and find myself wishing he was the one in bed with me, sharing his body heat. When he lay with me before, I dozed in and out of sleep, and I was fully aware of his presence. I felt his hard body pressed up against mine. I sensed his heat. I felt his warm breath on the nape of my neck. I smelled him—his maleness—and it did wonderful things to my body. His nearness made my belly flutter. And despite all my aches and pains, I felt a rush of desire coursing through me. My breasts felt heavy, and tingles rippled down my spine. My sex felt flushed and aching.

I don't know how long he'll be here in Bryce, but when he leaves, it's going to hurt.

After this closeness—after what we've shared—I don't know how I'll manage without him.

$\wp$ 12

Killian Devereaux

J ust after dawn, Owen steps onto the front porch and catches my gaze through the window.

"It's stopped snowing," he says. "The helo will be able to fly in."

I nod, then hail Jake on the radio. We coordinate the evacuation, then sign off.

The women are still sleeping, and I hate to wake them, but I need to get Hannah ready to travel. She'll need her outerwear on, and then I'll wrap her in the wool blanket and carry her to the exfil site.

I wake Maggie first. She jolts awake, sitting up in confusion.

"It's about time to go," I tell her. "You should eat something first. You'll need the energy. There are protein bars in my pack. Help yourself. Or you can heat up one of the freeze-dried meals."

There won't be room for everyone in the helicopter, so some of us are hiking out. I'm just not entirely sure who yet.

After Maggie gets herself ready, she wakes Hannah. I step out of the cabin for a short time to let both women use the potty chair.

When they're done, Maggie sets the bucket out on the porch, and I take care of it.

When I return to the shack, Hannah is sitting up in bed, fully dressed and eating a protein bar. "Ready to go?" I ask her. I nod toward the door. "Owen says the helo's ETA is thirty minutes. We should head for the exfil site."

Hannah finger combs her shoulder-length brown hair and ties it back in a ponytail. Then she pulls on her hat and coat. "Ready as I'll ever be."

Before we leave the shack, I slip my gloves onto her hands and wrap her in the wool blanket.

"No, you keep the gloves," Hannah says. "You'll need them."

"You need them more," I tell her. "This isn't negotiable."

"But I'll be wrapped up in a blanket, and your hands will be bare. Killian, please—"

I reach down to cup her left cheek, which is free of cuts. "No arguments."

"You're wasting your time arguing with him, Hannah," Maggie says as she puts out the fire in the stove. "I know a stubborn man when I see one."

"Well, I'm stubborn, too," Hannah says, glaring at me in the process.

After I make sure Hannah is wrapped securely in the blanket, I lift her into my arms and carry her out the door. Maggie closes it behind us.

Owen is waiting in the yard. "Ready to travel?"

I nod as I readjust my grip on Hannah. "Let's go."

Owen leads the way, with Maggie behind him, and I take up the rear. Maggie and I follow in Owen's footprints through the snow, making the going easier.

When we arrive at the designated rendezvous site, I brush the snow off a fallen nearby log so Hannah has a place to sit while we wait for the chopper.

It's not a long wait. We hear the chopper before we see it, the familiar *whup, whup, whup* sound of the blades filling the quiet morning air.

Owen had already marked the landing site clearly with some fallen branches, and we stand back as the pilot lands right on the designated spot.

The pilot remains in his seat, keeping the blades running, but the medic jumps out of the front passenger seat, and Jake McIntyre jumps out of the rear. Three of them flew up here, which means there's only room for one more to fly back with them: Hannah. The rest of us will have to walk out.

Jake heads straight for his sister, crouches down in front of her, and cups her poor battered face. Then he leans forward and kisses her forehead. "You about gave us all heart attacks," he says as he scans her face. "Please tell me you're okay."

Hannah smiles at her brother. "I'm okay." Then she glances my way. "Thanks to Killian."

"They didn't *hurt* you?" Jake asks.

Hannah knows exactly what he's asking. She shakes her head. "My injuries are all superficial, except for my ankle. I'm afraid it's broken."

"We'll find out as soon as we get you to the hospital." He brushes her hair back as he examines her face. "Mom and Dad are on their way from the airport. Most of the family is. They'll come to the hospital as soon as they arrive."

Jake stands and approaches me, his hand outstretched. We shake, and then he pulls me close for a bear hug. "Thank you, Killian," he says, his voice shaking. I don't think I've ever seen him so emotional before. "I'm in your debt. My whole family is."

"No need to thank me." I glance at the medic, who's now assessing Hannah. "I'm glad I could help."

"Let's get her into the helicopter," the medic says.

Beating me to it, Jake steps forward and scoops Hannah into his arms and carries her to the chopper. After sitting her gingerly on the rear passenger seat and buckling her in, he climbs in to sit beside her. The medic climbs up into the front passenger seat.

Yep, it looks like I'm walking.

I swallow my disappointment hard, like it's a rock lodged in my throat. I have no claim over Hannah. Jake's her brother; of course he should fly out with her and see her to the hospital.

I approach the chopper and glance up at Hannah one last time. She's looking right at me, her eyes wide. She looks a bit lost as she reaches out to me, and I take her gloved hand in mine. She squeezes my hand hard. "You're not coming with me?"

I shake my head. "Sorry, but there's no room. I'll hike out with Maggie and Owen."

She whips off my gloves and offers them back to me. "You take these. You'll need them to get down the mountain."

I step back. "Keep them. Your hands will get cold."

Her eyes fill with tears. "I can't take them." She extends them farther toward me. "Killian, please."

Jake pulls his own gloves off and hands them to me. "Here, take mine."

Before I can decline his offer, he nods toward his sister and gives me a hard look. *Take the damn gloves.*

I nod to Jake. "Thanks." To Hannah, I say, "I'll see you soon, okay?" My heart's pounding, and I hate the idea that she's about to be taken away without me.

I step back from the rotors, and the chopper lifts into the air.

Hannah waves at me as they ascend.

I don't know how long I stand there, watching the helo bank and head toward town. I don't snap out of it until Maggie comes up beside me and pats me on the back.

"She'll be fine," she says.

I suck in a deep, frigid breath, hating how bereft I feel. For once, even for just a short time, I mattered to Hannah. And now she's gone, and I can't help fearing that I won't matter again.

"Let's go," Maggie says. "The sooner we leave, the sooner we can get to the hospital." She grabs my sleeve and pulls me back in the direction of the shack. "Come on, Romeo."

I glance up to see Owen already leading the way. Maggie follows him, and I take up the rear. We can't let our guard down. Those poachers are still out there, and they're looking for blood.

ᘓ 13

Hannah McIntyre

The chopper shakes and shudders as we lift off, jarring my ankle something awful. Not meaning to, I cry out at the sharp twinge of pain.

Jake reaches for my gloved hand and holds it tight as he turns to me, concern etched into his dark expression. "Hang in there, sis. We'll have you at the hospital in no time."

Biting my lip to keep from making noise, I glance down at the ground. Killian, Maggie, and Owen are all down there, watching as we ascend into a cloudless, bright blue sky. The storm has passed and already the temperatures are steadily rising. That's so typical of the weather here at this time of year. There's a blizzard one day, and the next day the sun is shining and the snow is gone.

Killian raises his hand to block the glare of the sun and stares right at me until we turn east and head toward town.

Killian. I hated leaving him behind in that valley. He's been with me for nearly twenty-four hours, right by my side and taking care of me, and now he's not. I feel an emptiness inside without him.

Jake's talking into a radio headset, speaking loud enough to be heard over the sound of the rotors.

Leaning back in my seat, I close my eyes and force myself to breathe slowly—in, out, in, out—taking steady breaths as I try to manage the pain. The helicopter's rough vibrations are killing my ankle.

It's not long before our chopper hovers over the rooftop landing site at the county hospital. I see two people dressed in scrubs standing beside a gurney, waiting for us. As soon as the chopper lands and the rotors slow to a stop, the hospital staff members push the gurney next to my open door. Jake hops out first. He unbuckles my harness, lifts me out of the helicopter, and lays me on the gurney.

My head is spinning now as I battle the pain and some lightheadedness.

Jake follows us into the building, and the guy pushing my gurney guides me into an oversized elevator. He pushes the button for the emergency room on the first floor, and soon we're descending.

I wonder how far Killian and the others have gotten. God, I hope they don't run into any trouble hiking down that mountain. What if the poachers are still up there? I know Killian and Owen are trained for this sort of thing, but I hate the idea that they're risking their necks for me. And as for Maggie—she's not trained for this. Still, I know the guys won't let anything happen to her.

Jake stays with me as I'm wheeled into the emergency room treatment area. A nurse—Shelly—takes my pulse and temperature. Shortly after, a doctor comes in to assess me.

My brother stands across the small room, leaning against a wall, and quietly observes everything going on. I see him typing periodically on his phone, and I imagine he's sending messages to family members. My poor parents must be worried sick.

"Are Mom and Dad okay?" I ask him.

With a rueful smile on his face, he nods. "As well as can be expected under the circumstances. They're chomping at the bit to see you. It shouldn't be long now. They're about a half hour away."

"Tell them I'm okay."

Jake's gaze shoots over to the physician, Dr. Lundquist, as she unwraps my ankle and begins to examine it. "I can tell them that until I'm blue in the face, but they'll still want to see you with their own eyes."

After she takes my vitals, a nurse helps me undress and change into a hospital gown. Someone comes into my room and hooks me up to an IV. Something about needing fluids and an antibiotic. The wound on my arm looks horrible, the flesh red and angry, torn to shreds. It hurts so bad I can't bear to move my arm. After it's cleaned and treated, Dr. Lundquist stitches me up herself.

I'm shipped off to the Radiology department. Then I'm back in my treatment room, and we wait for the radiologist to look at the X-rays and give us the news. Is it broken or not? *Please not.*

My brother parks himself on a chair beside my bed.

"Why don't you go eat something?" I ask him. It's been a long morning, and he's probably hungry.

Jake shakes his head. "I'll stay with you until Mom and Dad arrive."

"Coffee, then. You don't have to sit here and babysit me. I'll be fine."

"Give it up, sis. I have my orders." He tries not to smile.

"Mom told you to stay with me until she gets here, didn't she?" When he doesn't deny it, I say, "Jake, go. I'm fine." I nod toward the IV. "I feel better already."

He laughs. "Nice try, sis, but antibiotics don't work that fast." His phone chimes with an incoming text, and he reads it, then replies.

"Who was that?" *Killian? Are they back yet?*

"Shane. They're about to arrive at the hospital."

My chest aches when I think about my family. I hate knowing I worried them.

But what about Killian? Jake hasn't said anything about him. Or about Owen and Maggie. "Are they back yet? Killian and Maggie and Owen?"

"Yeah. They arrived at Maggie's place about an hour ago. They're fine. There were no mishaps on their hike out of the ravine."

I wish he'd be more forthcoming. What about Killian?

Before he can say more, his attention is diverted to his ringing phone. He checks the screen. "It's Annie," he says eagerly as he rises to his feet. He nods toward the door. "Do you mind?"

"Of course not. Go talk to your wife."

Jake takes his wife's call out in the hallway. I'm glad he has her. I'm glad they finally reconnected after so many years apart. Better late than never, right? It's just too bad that Annie had to endure so much suffering before she and Jake got their second chance.

For the first time since arriving at the hospital, I'm alone with my thoughts.

Where's Killian? Will I see him again before he heads back to Chicago?

I realize I didn't get to say thank you or goodbye. If he up and leaves, I swear I'll kill him the next time I see him.

When there's a knock at the door, my heart leaps into my throat. *He's here.* Jake wouldn't knock.

"Come in," I say, my gaze glued to the door.

It swings open, and Maggie walks in, her expression tentative. "Can I come in?"

"Of course you can," I say, extending my good arm. She comes to the side of my bed and leans down to gently hug me. "Are you okay?" I ask her. "Did you guys have any trouble getting down to the trailhead?"

She drops down into the vacant chair beside my bed. "We made good time getting out of there."

"And you didn't have any trouble with anyone?"

"No, but we did hear a few stray shots. Owen said they were likely still on the ridge, searching. But the parking lot was empty, and we didn't see anyone."

"Owen's okay? He doesn't have a frostbit nose or toes after staying out all night in the freezing temperatures?"

Maggie chuckles. "No frostbite. He looked mighty fine to me. After we hiked out, we drove back to my place so we could take showers and get cleaned up. Scout is fine. Riley and Brendan are spoiling him rotten."

"Glad to hear it." I force a smile. She hasn't mentioned Killian, and I don't know what that means. I'm afraid to ask, not sure if I want to know the answer. If she tells me he's already on his way back to the Denver airport, I'll be crushed. At least he could have said goodbye in person.

"How's your ankle?" Maggie asks as she lays her palm gingerly on my left thigh. "Is it broken?"

"I haven't heard yet. I'm still waiting on the radiologist's report."

She stands and takes a peek at it. It's currently immobilized in a proper splint pending a diagnosis.

"Did you see Jake out in the hall?" I ask.

She nods. "I think he's on the phone talking to his wife." Then she glances toward the door, which is only half-closed. "Owen's out there, too. He was hesitant to come in. He said he didn't want to intrude." Maggie leans close and whispers, "He's shy."

"He seems like a good man." *Like Killian. Why won't she tell me anything about Killian?*

She's pensive for a moment, and then her face lights up with a smile. "Yeah, he is." She hands me a shopping bag from a store in town. "I stopped on the way to pick up some things I thought you'd need—flannel PJs, underwear, and a bra. I figured you'd need something to wear when you go home."

"Thank you!" I motion to the lovely hospital gown I'm currently wearing. "I arrived wearing Killian's clothes. I'll need something to wear when I leave the hospital."

There's another knock on the door, and I say, "Come in."

The door opens just a few inches, and Owen pops his head in. "Hey, Hannah. I'm glad to see you're doing all right. Any word on your ankle?"

"Nothing yet. I'm still waiting to hear."

"I hope it's good news." Then he looks at Maggie. "You should eat something."

I grasp her arm. "You haven't eaten yet? You should go, definitely. The cafeteria's just down the hall. Go get something to eat."

She frowns guiltily. "You don't mind?"

"Of course not. Go." And then I turn my gaze on the big, blond mountain man standing hesitantly in the doorway. He could do with a haircut and a beard trim. "Owen, I can't thank you enough for helping me, for helping Maggie and Killian, and for keeping us all safe last night. I owe you."

He shakes his head dismissively. "It's nothing. Glad I could help."

I give Maggie a nudge. "Go eat something, and feel free to bring me some coffee."

Smiling, Maggie stands. "All right. We won't be long," I promise.

And then with a wave to me, she walks out the door, leaving me alone with my aching ankle and throbbing arm.

When I hear a quiet knock on my door, my pulse starts racing. "Come in."

The door swings open and Jake walks in, tucking his phone into his pocket. "Annie and Aiden send you their love. Aiden says he's glad you're all right. He said he knew you would be because you're tough, like Aunt Lia."

That makes me smile, because my little sister is tough as nails.

Jake's phone rings again, and he takes the call. "It's Mom," he says, handing the phone to me.

"Hi, Mom," I say as my mom bursts into tears. "Please don't cry. I'm okay, I promise." I can hear my dad in the background, peppering her with questions.

"We just arrived at the hospital. Your father is parking our rental, and then we'll be right up to see you. I just wanted you to know."

My dad comes on the line. "Hey, kiddo. We're coming up. I hope you feel like having visitors."

"I'm looking forward to it."

That's my family for you. When one member is down, the rest circle the wagons and prepare for war.

After we hang up, I force myself to accept the fact that Killian's left without even saying goodbye. I have no one to blame but myself. I pushed him away one too many times, it seems, and he's taking me at my word. I told him repeatedly that there was no future for us, so I guess he listened.

ꙅ 14

Killian Devereaux

After the radiology report came back that her ankle was indeed broken, Hannah was taken to orthopedics to have her bones set and a cast put on. Fortunately, it was a clean break and the doctor said it should heal well. Surgery wasn't needed, thank god. But she does have to stay overnight in the hospital for observation because she has a concussion, and they want to make sure the antibiotic is effective against the infection in her arm.

I'm grateful to Jake for keeping me updated on her prognosis. And to Maggie and Owen, who also filled me in on how she's doing just before they left the hospital.

Hannah's family arrived at the hospital about an hour ago—the whole McIntyre clan—her parents, her brothers, and two sisters, along with a number of spouses.

I've intentionally kept my distance from Hannah and stayed on the periphery, because I don't want to intrude on her privacy and recovery. She needs her family more than anything. All morning, I've been camped outside her hospital room, standing guard more or less, just to be safe. We still know next to nothing about the assholes who attacked her. It's possible they could try again.

I'm also killing time wondering when Jake's going to send me back to Chicago.

I watch as various family members come and go from her room in small groups, starting with her parents. Her mom's a wreck, her eyes red and swollen from crying. When Bridget sees me, she runs into my arms and hugs the daylights outta me. She's pretty strong for a petite little thing. Now I know where Lia gets it.

Calum McIntyre, Hannah's dad, pats me on the back. "Well done, son. Thank you for saving our little girl."

Hearing Hannah referred to as a *little girl* makes me smile. She's more of a wildcat, I'd say. But who am I to argue with her kin? "I'm glad I could help, sir."

Hannah's parents go into her room, and from the hallway, I can hear her mother crying and both Hannah and her dad trying to console the woman. Then her sisters, Sophie and Lia, come in to see her. Then the rest of her brothers have a turn—Shane, Jamie, and Liam. Jake's been in and out of her room all day.

Many of the significant others are here as well—Sophie's husband, Dominic; Jamie's girlfriend, Molly; and Lia's husband, Jonah, who's wearing a pair of dark aviator sunglasses and a hat as part of a disguise. The last thing we need is for news of Jonah's whereabouts getting out on social media. This small hospital would be overrun in no time by screaming fans.

Eventually, the family congregates in the waiting room.

Jake's the last one to leave her room. "She's sleeping finally," he says to me as he closes the door quietly. He makes no move to join the rest of the family, instead loitering in the hallway with me.

My heart starts pounding as I straighten away from the wall. *Is this it?* Am I about to get reassigned? The idea of returning to Chicago guts me. I don't want to leave her. "I'm sure she's exhausted after the past forty-eight hours."

Jake nods. Then he offers me his hand. "On behalf of my entire family, I want to thank you, Killian. If we'd lost Hannah, we would never have recovered."

I swallow against the lump in my throat. *This is it.* He's sending me home—and I have no justification for staying. "Happy I could help."

Jake looks away, staring off down the deserted hallway. It's clear there's something on his mind, and I wait him out. I'm certainly not in any hurry to rush this conversation because

I'm afraid I know what's coming. I just hope he's not sending me back tonight. I'd like to stay a few more days at least, long enough to make sure she's okay, and to see her home safely.

And how in the hell is she going to manage on her own with a broken ankle?

I'm a patient man, so I wait for him to say whatever's on his mind.

I can't count the number of times my grandpapa told me, "Patience wins the day, son." Of course he was referring to fishing, but I still think it's good advice.

Jake finally breaks the silence. "She's not going to be able to take care of herself while she's got that cast on. For one thing, she lives in a remote cabin in the woods that's heated by a woodstove—I don't see her out in the snow chopping and hauling wood anytime soon. And for another, her Jeep has a manual transmission, which means she won't be able to drive until she gets the cast off. And most importantly, there are the poachers to consider. We have to assume we haven't seen the last of them."

I nod.

Patience.

"My parents tried their best to convince her to come back to Chicago with us so she can recuperate there," he continues, "but she refused. You know Hannah—she's decidedly pigheaded."

Smiling in agreement, I nod but don't say anything. He's not done talking.

Patience.

There's a reason he's telling me all this, and it's not to share his family's business.

Jake turns back to face me. He looks deceptively casual, leaning back with one black boot propped against the wall behind him, but I know better. He's wound tight as a drum. He's worried about his sister. He's *afraid* for her.

"Shane and I discussed it, and—" He breaks off.

My pulse kicks up. "Yeah?"

"We'd like for you to stay here with Hannah until the poachers are caught and she gets that cast off. Would you be willing to do that? Consider it a temporary reassignment."

It's all I can do not to laugh in the man's face. *Is the Pope Catholic?* "What does she think about this plan?"

Jake glances back at her closed door. "I haven't brought it up with her yet."

"Don't you think you should ask her before you go making plans on her behalf?" One thing I know about Hannah—she's not one to be run roughshod over.

"Why don't we ask her together when she wakes up?"

I nod. "Fair enough." My heart's pounding. I thought for sure I'd be on a plane headed back to Chicago this evening, and for the life of me, I can't stomach the idea of leaving her.

My head may tell me I'm wasting my time where Hannah's concerned, but my heart tells me somethin' different.

* * *

Late that evening, once visiting hours are over, and after assuring themselves she's not going to die, the McIntyres leave for their hotel where they'll stay the night. They're coming back in the morning to see her again before they fly back to Chicago around noon.

I'm sitting in the cafeteria staring at a half-drunk, cold cup of coffee when I get Jake's text.

Jake: She's alone. Come now and we'll ask her.

After tossing my cup in the trash can, I head back to her room and knock quietly on her door.

"Come in," Jake says.

When I step into her room, her brown eyes go wide.

"You're still here," she says in a slightly accusatory tone.

"I am."

"I thought you'd already gone home, without saying goodbye."

She sounds a bit pissed about it, which I take as a good sign. "Why would I do that? Of course I'm still here."

Before she can get another word out, Jake breaks into the conversation. "Hannah, you can't stay alone in your cabin. Not with a broken ankle. You won't be able to take care of yourself and keep that place running. And you can't drive that stick shift with a cast on."

Hannah looks at her brother, suspicion clouding her eyes. "And?"

"And..." Jake nods in my direction. "Killian's agreed to stay with you until your ankle is healed."

She sucks in a breath. "That's six weeks from now."

Jake nods. "It's an extended assignment."

Her gaze bounces from me back to her brother. "When you say with me..."

"In your cabin," her brother says. "He'll be living with you temporarily."

Her focus shifts back to me. "And you're okay with this plan? With being away from home that long?"

Chicago's not really my home—it's just the place where I live and work. "I'm happy to do it." I keep my tone light. I figure that's a better option than saying, Hell yes, I'm okay with it. I don't want to leave you.

"I could stay with Maggie," she counters, glancing back at her brother. "I'd hate to impose on her and her sons, but I'm sure they wouldn't mind."

"It's not just your ankle, Hannah," Jake says. "The men who attacked you are still out there, and if they find out who you are and where you live, you're a target. You don't want to draw that kind of danger to your friend's house. Until we know more, you need protection."

Hannah frowns. "Can I speak to Killian alone for a moment?"

Jake nods toward the door. "Sure. I'll go grab some coffee in the waiting room."

As soon as Jake's out the door, Hannah nails me with a curious gaze. "When I didn't see you today, I thought maybe you'd left."

"I've been here the entire time—mostly standing outside

your room. I didn't want to intrude on your privacy."

"Killian, you shared your body heat with me in that shack, half-naked in a bed. You emptied my pee bucket, for crying out loud. I think we're well past worrying about my privacy, don't you?"

I grin, happy to see a glimpse of the Hannah I know and love. "Hard to argue with that."

"And if you're going to stay with me while I'm recuperating—help *take care of me*—there will be a lot more privacy violated, don't you think?"

"Without a doubt."

"And you're totally okay with this? With putting your own life on hold for me?"

"I'm fine with it. Perfectly fine." Glancing down at her bright green cast, I realize all the things she'll need help with. Not just the obvious things—like chopping wood for the stove, fetching and carrying, cooking, cleaning, taking care of her dog—but also personal things, like dressing and undressing, and perhaps bathing. But most of all, what she truly needs from me is protection in case those motherfuckers come looking for her. If they want her, they'll have to go through me first. "Yeah, I'm definitely fine with it."

"My cabin's small," she warns. "There's only one bedroom."

"That's all right. You have a sofa, right? That'll do me just fine."

"Well, yes, there's a sofa, although I'm pretty sure it's not long enough to accommodate you."

"It'll be fine. Don't worry."

She looks far from convinced. "All right then. If you're sure. I'd be grateful for your assistance."

"Then it's settled. I'm staying."

* * *

When I step out of her room, Jake's standing in the hall with a vending machine coffee cup in his hand.

"It's settled," I tell him.

He finishes off the last of his coffee and crushes the paper cup in his hand. "Well, that wasn't too hard," he says, sounding surprised.

I suppose I'm a bit surprised, too. The woman who has refused to give me the time of day for quite a while just agreed to let me move in with her, at least for the next six weeks. "Now what?" I ask him. "Are you going back to Chicago?"

He nods. "I hate leaving my sister at a time like this, but my wife's at home taking care of two sick babies. I need to get back."

"What about Owen? When's he heading back to Tennessee?"

"He hasn't decided." Jake's gaze bores into mine. "My gut tells me this situation isn't resolved yet. The poachers are still out there. You're on Hannah's full-time security detail until further notice. We have to assume she's still in their crosshairs. As for Maggie, we don't think she's at risk, but Owen's going to hang around a little longer to be sure."

"Understood," I say. These poachers are wildcards, and that makes them unpredictable. "I won't let anything happen to Hannah."

Jake grips my shoulder hard. "I know you won't." Then he returns to Hannah's room to have a private conversation with her. I assume he's telling her why he needs to get home. She'll understand.

I wait in the hallway, giving them some privacy.

Just before Jake leaves, we shake hands one last time. "Thanks, Killian. I'll arrange to get your rental back to the agency. You might as well use Hannah's Jeep, as she won't be driving anytime soon. I'll arrange for someone to bring it here to the hospital."

He glances back at his sister's door, indecision clearly written on his face. He nods curtly to me, then heads down the hallway and steps into a waiting elevator.

Just as the elevator doors close, a second elevator's doors open and a man steps out, pausing as he glances up and down the corridor. He starts walking in my direction, clearly checking out the patient room numbers.

"Can I help you?" I ask him when he nears Hannah's room.

He glances at me briefly but doesn't answer. Instead, he continues on his way, glancing at each patient room door as he passes. I'd follow him, but I can't leave Hannah unprotected. And by the time I call someone for backup, he'll be long gone.

I never got a look at the poachers, but Hannah certainly did. It looks like she and I need to have a talk.

15

Hannah McIntyre

After a brief knock, the door to my room swings open and Killian walks in, his expression guarded as he stands just inside the room. His posture is rigid, and the firm set of his jaw tells me something's up.

I meet his gaze. "What is it? What's wrong?"

He walks to the foot of my bed. "Did you get a good look at the men who attacked you?"

I shrug. "Pretty good. They were bundled up in winter gear, so what I saw was limited, but I got the basics."

"Describe them to me."

A chill runs down my spine, and I don't like where this is going. "Two Caucasian males, both around five-ten or so, average weight. One had blond hair, and the other had black. Why?"

"Any facial hair?"

"No. They were both clean shaven."

"How about facial marks? Tattoos? Scars? Piercings?"

"Yes. The guy with blond hair had a crooked nose, as if it had been broken and not set right. His right eyebrow was pierced with two gold hoops, and he had large black plugs in his lobes."

"And the other guy?"

"The other guy had a scar running down his face." I trace a line from the top of my right cheek down to my lip. "Why?"

"And they got a good look at you?"

"Unfortunately."

He glances back at the closed door. Then he crosses the room to grab a guest chair and positions it at the foot of my bed, facing the door.

That's a little unnerving. "What are you not telling me?"

He shrugs offhandedly, like he's discussing something as mundane as the weather. "I might have seen someone scoping out the patient rooms just now. He matches the description of the first guy. The blond with the piercings."

My heart contracts painfully. "Shit. What do we do now?"

"*We* don't do anything," he says, reaching for his phone. "You need to focus on healing. Leave the rest to me."

I roll my eyes. "Hello, Killian. This is me, remember? I'm not going to sit on my ass while you take all the risks."

One corner of his mouth lifts. "Sorry, I forgot who I was talking to." He punches a button on his phone, then says, "We may have a problem. I saw someone here canvassing the patient rooms. He meets the description of one of the tangos." Killian listens a moment and then says, "Copy. I'll keep you posted."

"Who did you just call?" I ask when he tucks his phone into an inside jacket pocket.

"Owen. He's staying in Bryce a while longer—with Maggie—just as a precaution."

I sit up, instantly on guard. "You don't think those bastards would go after her, do you? They didn't even see her."

"We don't know what they saw, Hannah. We don't know what they know or what they're willing to do to get leverage on you."

Immediately, I feel sick to my stomach. "My god, if I've put Maggie in danger—"

"You didn't do anything. Besides, she's not alone. Owen's with her, and he's not going to let anything happen to her."

It dawns on me that Killian is wearing his jacket, which in the security business means he's armed. I have no doubt there's a Glock tucked into his chest holster. "Are you carrying?"

He gives me a look. "What do you think?"

"Are weapons even allowed in this hospital?"

He grins like he doesn't care. "Nope."

* * *

A middle-aged nurse with red hair comes to my room that evening to check my vitals. My fever is gone, which of course is a good sign. She changes the bandage on my arm and inspects the sutures.

"Looking good," she says as she redresses the wound. She refills my water bottle and sets it on the bedside table. "Do you need anything else, hon?"

"No, thanks. I'm good." That's not entirely true, but I hate being fussed over.

After she leaves, Killian gets up to close my door. When he returns to his guard post—the chair positioned at the foot of my bed, facing the door—he sits.

I stare at the back of his head—at thick hair the color of fine dark chocolate—and sip my water. Before I know it, I've drunk half of it, which turns out to be a mistake because my bladder is suddenly complaining.

Crap.

I glance with dread at the bathroom door, which seems so far away from the bed. I need to pee. I also need to brush my teeth before I fall asleep.

I reach for the pair of crutches leaning against the nightstand. It's been a while since I've used crutches—not since I broke my leg at the age of ten when I crashed my bike into a tree. I smile when I remember how my siblings rallied around me, helping me carry my books to school, helping me up and down the stairs at home. It was a real family ordeal.

Quietly, I sit up and slowly swing my legs to the side of the bed. After my good foot settles on the cold tile floor, I reach for the crutches and position them beneath my armpits.

How hard can it be, right?

As I rise up to stand on my good foot, pain shoots from my broken ankle straight up my leg, making me suck in a sharp breath. "Damn it." I fall back onto the bed.

A second later, Killian's there beside me. "Why didn't you call me first?" He helps me to stand and steadies me when I sway. "Easy does it." Standing this close, he towers over me. "How badly does it hurt?"

Gritting my teeth, I do my best to shake off the pain. "It's fine. I'm fine."

"Hannah." His tone is laced with disapproval.

"What?"

"Since we're going to be spending a lot of time together over the next couple of months, we need to establish a few ground rules, okay? One, don't lie to me. If you're hurting, then say so. And two, stop pretending you're invincible. I'm here to help you, so let me do my job."

"Fine. But I have some ground rules of my own."

He chuckles. "Such as?"

"One, don't patronize me. And two, don't baby me. Despite what it looks like at the moment, I'm not helpless."

He grins. "You are the farthest thing from helpless. Now, where do you want to go?"

"To the bathroom. I need to pee and brush my teeth."

His lips flatten as he suppresses a smile and nods toward the bathroom. "Okay. Shall we?"

Killian walks behind me as I hobble across the room, his hands at my sides as if he's waiting to catch me. It takes me a few tries to get the hang of using the crutches, but eventually it comes back to me. It's like riding a bike, right? Once you learn, you never forget. Of course, riding a bike was never this painful.

When I make it to the bathroom, he reaches around in front of me and opens the door. "After you." He motions me inside.

"Thanks, but I've got this." I block him from following me inside. There's no way I'm letting him come into the bathroom with me. I have to draw the line somewhere.

He frowns. "If you fall, you could do serious damage to that ankle."

"Let me worry about that. Your job is to protect me from bad guys, not supervise my bathroom activities."

He laughs. "*Sha*, my job entails doing whatever da hell needs ta be done. If ya need help pulling down your britches so you can take a piss—"

I love it when his Cajun accent slips out.

Sha. Sweetheart.

The endearment makes me smile. "I don't need your help pulling my britches down, but thanks for the visual." I swing myself into the room and turn to close the door.

"I'll be right out here. Holler if you need help."

"Roger that."

I manage to make it over to the little sink, beside which is a small cabinet that holds a basket of complimentary toiletries—a cheap plastic comb, a bar of soap, tiny bottles of shampoo and conditioner, a toothbrush and toothpaste. A shower is definitely beyond my capabilities tonight, but I make good use of the comb, soap, and toothbrush. At least I can wash away most of the two days' worth of grime coating my skin.

After I empty my bladder, I make my way back to the door.

As expected, Killian hasn't moved from his spot outside the bathroom, where he's leaning casually against the wall, his arms over his broad chest. "Everything okay?" he asks as I step out.

I swing my way past him. "I'm still standing, as you can see."

He chuckles. "Easy there, McIntyre. This isn't the Indy 500."

His warm laughter follows me across the room, and I have to admit I like the sound of it. He stays right behind me, ready to jump to my rescue at a moment's notice.

"Look, I admit I'll need help at the cabin, but I don't need a nursemaid. I'm perfectly capable of taking care of my basic needs, broken ankle or not."

He nods. "Got it. No nursemaiding."

I suspect he's really enjoying this. Even I'm having a hard time keeping a straight face. I have to admit, the situation is a bit preposterous. It's like we're characters in a rom-com, suddenly thrust together in a time of crisis, both of us secretly lusting after the other. Well, he's not so secretive about it. But this is reality. It's not a movie or a romance novel. And the truth is, I do need him. Well, I need *someone*, and right now he's the only one offering to do the job. Beggars can't be choosers.

But more than that, I *want* him. At least I'm willing to acknowledge that much, if only to myself.

Once I'm safely settled in bed, Killian opens the door to my room and scans the hallway before closing it again. Then he returns to his post at the foot of the bed.

"You can go get something to eat if you like," I suggest. "Go grab a coffee, or take a smoke break. Whatever."

"I don't smoke."

"You do eat, though, right?"

He chuckles. "I'm fine. Doan worry 'bout me."

Honestly, I'm not worried about him. Not one bit. I'm worried about myself and the risk of my ovaries exploding. Having him near me all the time is going to drive me nuts. I don't think my hormones can take it.

* * *

Morning comes bright and early—too early, as I don't think I slept more than a couple of hours. My ankle kept me up most of the night—throbbing and aching—and I kept having these weird flashbacks to what happened up on Eagle Ridge. The slightest noise in the hallway outside my room woke me. I even heard Killian get up a couple of times in the night, once to slip into the bathroom, and once to open the door and scan the hallway.

I think we're both on edge, but maybe for different reasons.

When I wake up to discover a breakfast tray sitting beside

my bed, I force myself to eat cold scrambled eggs and dry toast, even though I have zero appetite. When Maggie and Owen stop by for a visit, Killian and Owen step out into the hall and close the door behind them. I think they're trying to give me and Maggie some privacy.

"So," Maggie says with a grin as she pulls the guest chair beside the bed and sits. "Killian's staying, too? That's what Owen said. Is it true?"

"He is. My brother assigned him as my full-time bodyguard while I'm recuperating, in case my attackers show up again."

"Do you think they will?"

"I have no idea. But since I saw their faces...." I shrug. "You do the math."

Maggie frowns. "You should talk to the police. Give them their descriptions, and maybe they'll know who they are. Or maybe you can look at a binder of suspect photographs or something, like they do on in TV shows."

I don't even want to think about criminals coming after me. "What about you? Killian said Owen's going to stay with you for a while."

She smiles. "He is. Apparently, your brother Jake decided that you and I both might have attracted some unwanted attention. Killian and Owen are going to hang around Bryce for a while to make sure there's not going to be any more trouble."

"Where's Owen going to stay?"

Maggie shrugs innocently. "With us, in one of the spare bedrooms. Goodness knows we have plenty of room in that big ol' farmhouse." Her eyes light up. "Trust me, I'm not complaining. It'll be nice having a man around the house for a change—you know, for the boys' sakes. I'm sure they'll benefit from having a positive male role model around. God knows their father failed miserably in that department. But enough about us. How's your ankle?"

I glance down at the neon green cast that runs from mid-shin to the ball of my foot. "Same as usual. It still aches, and walking with crutches sucks."

Maggie laughs but then catches herself. "I'm sorry. I know it's not funny. I broke my leg once, and I remember how that felt. At least you have a handsome stud to keep you company while you're healing." She lowers her voice, as if she's afraid the guys can hear us through the closed door. "He's seriously hot."

Maggie knows all about my crush on Killian Devereaux. Each time I returned home from a visit to Chicago, I talked her ear off about him.

"Yeah, and he lives in *Chicago*," I remind her, just as quietly. "You know I don't want to move back to the city. Visits are one thing, but moving back permanently—no."

"I don't want you to move back either. I'm not saying you have to relocate. Just have a little fun while he's here. It's not like you're making a lifelong commitment. He's going to be living under the same roof as you for *weeks*, Hannah. A lot can happen in that amount of time. Just go with it."

I glance down at my cast. "Not likely. There's nothing remotely sexy about a cast."

"Hey, sister, you can do a lot of fun stuff with a cast on. Trust me."

* * *

My family comes back to visit me after breakfast. They take turns sitting with me in my room, in small groups. Around noon, after lots of hugs and tearful goodbyes, they head back to Denver to catch their return flight.

My mom calls me from the road on her way to the airport. "Hannah, please reconsider coming back to Chicago for a while. You can stay with me and your dad, or with one of your sisters. Or, if you prefer to have a place of your own, I'm sure Shane will let you use one of the furnished apartments in his building."

I sigh heavily. We had this discussion already this morning. "I'll be fine, Mom. I promise."

"But until those men are caught, you could still be in danger, sweetheart."

I hear my dad's cajoling voice in the background. "Bridget, honey, please. Hannah's a grown woman. You have to let her make her own decisions. Besides, Killian's gonna stay with her. You know that boy won't let anyone hurt her."

I hear a soft sniffle over the phone. Then Mom says to me, "Let me know as soon as they release you from the hospital, okay? And let me know the minute you get home. Killian's staying *in* your cabin with you, right? Under the same roof so he'll be close at all times?"

"Yes, Mom. He'll be staying with me *in* my cabin."

And lord help me, I don't know how I'm going to survive having him under the same roof as me for *weeks*. It's a small cabin, with only one bed and one bathroom. We'll practically be on top of each other.

And for some reason, the thought of that makes me a little giddy.

$\wp$ 16

Killian Devereaux

Once Hannah's doctor releases her, a nurse brings a wheelchair to the room. It's hospital policy—she has to be wheeled out. Her Jeep is waiting for us in the parking lot, and I have a set of keys.

I hold the wheelchair in place as she transfers herself from the bed to the seat. I'd offer to help her, but *je ne suis pas couyon. I'm not stupid.*

If I so much as tried to help, she'd bite my head off. Instead, I stand there ready to catch her if she falls. She sways a bit, but she manages just fine.

Once she's safely settled in the wheelchair, she holds her crutches while I wheel her down to the front entrance. Her Jeep is parked halfway across the visitor lot, thanks to Owen and Maggie dropping it off for us this morning. I wrangle a young hospital staffer to follow us out there so that, after I put her in the vehicle, he can return the wheelchair to the hospital for us. I'm not leaving her alone for a second.

My Spidey senses are on overload, and Owen didn't help matters when he told me he spotted a suspicious individual in the parking lot this morning who matched the description of the blond guy I spotted scoping out hospital rooms.

If those poaching motherfuckers come after Hannah, they'll have to deal with me.

"Ready?" I ask Hannah as she buckles her seat belt. She's in the front passenger seat. I'm driving, of course, since she can't shift gears with a cast on her foot.

She nods. Then she tells my phone where we're headed. According to the navigation app, we have a twenty-two-minute drive to her cabin in Bryce.

"Anything you need to pick up on the way home?" I ask her. I'm thinking food, medicine, beer. Okay, the beer is for me.

As she scans the parking lot, I wonder if she's feeling a bit exposed out here.

"No, I'm good," she says, sounding distracted.

I reach over and clasp her hand. "Relax, love. You're safe."

"I'm fine," she says, clearly lying.

"Didn't your doctor give you a prescription for some pain

medicine? Do you wanna fill it?"

"Nope. I have over-the-counter pain medication at home."

"That's not quite the same thing."

"I'm not taking prescription painkillers." She shakes her head. "It's fine."

"Maybe just for a few days—"

She shoots me an irritated scowl. "Are we going to argue about every little thing?"

I try not to smile. "Probably." *God, I love her fire.* I try not to think about how that would play out in bed. If I ever got so lucky as to be in her bed, she'd have me by the balls in no time.

"Killian, just drive, will you?"

I start the engine and throw the Jeep in gear. "Fine. No pain meds, but don't come crying to me when you're suffering needlessly."

As we pull out of the parking lot, I notice she's typing a message on her phone.

When she spots me watching her, she explains. "I promised my mom I'd let her know as soon as I was released from the hospital."

I pull out onto the main road and turn right. We drive through a small suburban town until the houses quickly disappear, and the road is bordered on both sides by pine forests. It sure feels good to be out of the city and back into the wilderness. Even though I've been gone from Cajun country for seventeen years, it's still a huge part of me—the language, the people, the food and music. It's still who I am at my core—a Cajun through and through.

I'm reminded that I need to call *my* Mama. She knows where I am and why, and she'll want to know if I found the *jeune fille*—the young lady. She's heard me talk about Hannah plenty times before. Even though she's never met her, she'll be worried.

Twenty minutes later, we pass Emerson's Grocery store in Bryce. Owen's rented SUV is parked out front in plain sight. I imagine he did that on purpose—making his presence known to scare off potential intruders.

Hannah glances at the store, and I wonder if she's missing her friend. "Do you want to stop?"

She shakes her head and sighs. "I'm tired. I just want to get home."

"Sure thing." I know she's probably hurting as well. A little rest will do her good, as well as a hot, homecooked meal. I'll see what she's got in her pantry.

I turn off the main road and drive up a paved lane that leads to the turn off to Hannah's place. Her driveway is at least a half mile up a winding gravel road, bordered on both sides by dense, pristine forest. "Beautiful place."

She nods. "I fell in love with it the moment I saw it."

The lane brings us to a clearing in front of a modest one-story log cabin with a front porch. There's a small shed off to the side. But other than that, it's pretty bare-bones.

She checks her phone, reading a text message. "Maggie and her sons will stop by this evening to bring Scout home."

"Your dog?"

She nods. "He's just a year old, but already, he's a wonderful watchdog. He won't let anyone sneak up on us."

I step out of the Jeep and walk around to the front passenger door to help Hannah out, but she's already got her door open, both crutches planted on the ground, and she's in the process of stepping down from the vehicle with her good foot aimed at the ground.

"Slow down, *fille*," I say as I reach out to catch her. "Let's not break your good ankle before you even get inside."

"Did you just call me *girl*?"

I laugh. "No. It can mean woman, too."

She looks skeptical. "I warn you, you better watch what you say. I took two years of French in high school and two years in college. I remember quite a bit. And for the record, I can get out of the Jeep on my own."

She lowers herself to the ground, landing on her good foot and nearly falling forward in the process. I catch her and set her upright. Her jaw clamps shut as she refrains from crying out.

She's a stubborn one.

"What'd I tell you?" I swing her up in my arms and carry her toward the porch.

She holds her crutches tightly. "I can walk, Killian," she insists.

I ignore her. "Where's the key?"

"In my backpack." She fishes it out once I set her down on the smooth oak boards.

I take the key from her and unlock the door. Then I reach

inside my jacket and pull the handgun from my chest holster. "Wait here while I check the inside. It'll just take a second."

Leaving her leaning against the exterior wall, I step inside and flip the light switch, which turns on a small pendulum light fixture hanging over a small square table with four chairs. There's not much else to see—a small kitchen with white appliances, an even smaller pantry; and a living room with a sofa, rocking chair, woodstove, and stone hearth. It's sparsely furnished, but it's tidy and homey looking. There's a good-sized dog bed in front of the hearth. That must belong to Scout. Lastly, a rear hallway leads to a bathroom and the only bedroom.

"All clear," I say as I join her on the porch. Before she can say a word, I swing her up in my arms and carry her inside, setting her down gingerly on the sofa, lengthwise. I tuck a throw pillow under her cast. "Doctor said you should elevate it to reduce swelling."

"Thanks."

I help her shuck off her coat, gloves, and hat, and then I take those things to the small closet and hang them up, along with my own. "Are you hungry or thirsty?" It's well after lunchtime.

"Thirsty," she says, sitting up and swinging her good leg to the wood floor.

"Hold your horses, McIntyre," I say when she reaches for her crutches. "Where do you think you're going?"

"To the kitchen."

"I'll get your water."

"Killian, you're not here to wait on me. I can—"

"If you say you can manage on your own, I'll take you over my knee and spank you. You've been out of the hospital for less than an hour. It won't kill you to let me fetch and carry for you." I locate the glasses in a cupboard over the kitchen counter. "How do you want it?"

"There's a water pitcher in the fridge."

I pour her a glass. "Do you want ice?"

"Yes, please."

I pull an ice tray out of the freezer, dump in a few cubes, then return the tray. "Here," I say as I hand her the glass. "That wasn't so hard, was it?"

She tries not to smile. "Thanks."

I allow myself a moment just to drink her in. Never in my wildest dreams did I think I'd be here with her, in her home, just the two of us. "You're welcome." I take a seat on the sturdy wooden coffee table in front of the sofa. "Now let's go over the ground rules."

Her brown eyes narrow on me. "We already did that in the hospital."

"I have a few more. Just some basic safety issues. One, you stay off your foot for a few days and give it a good head start on healing. Two, you stay inside the cabin. If anything needs to be done outside, I'll do it. Three—"

"*Three*, you stop babying me," she says. "Remember, that was one of *my* rules."

"*Three*, you stop arguing with me about every little thing. I'm here to help you, McIntyre, so let me do my damn job."

She starts to come back at me with some undoubtedly witty retort, but she stops herself. I'm sure this isn't easy for her. She's used to doing for herself.

"It's not a weakness to accept help when you need it, Hannah."

"Fine. I'll let you help me."

"*C'est bon.*" That's good.

"I've never heard you speak so much French."

"That's 'cause you're hardly around me more than a few minutes at a time. It slips into my vocabulary a lot, especially when I'm irritated."

Wisely, she doesn't comment on that. "I guess there's a lot I don't know about you."

I smile. "Looks like we'll have plenty of time to rectify that over the next couple of months."

She surprises me by reaching out to take my hand, her expression suddenly serious. "Thank you, Killian, for everything. For finding me, for getting me to safety. I don't know what I would have done without you. I could have died in that ravine."

My heart stutters painfully for a moment, and then I shake it off. "You're too ornery to die. And there's no need to thank me. I was just doin' my job." I pat her good leg before standing. "I'm parched. I think I'll get some water, too."

As her gaze follows me across the room, I wonder if she knows I just lied my ass off. She's a lot of things to me, but a *job* sure as hell isn't one of them.

ℒ17

Hannah McIntyre

I jump when Killian's phone rings. He looks at the screen and answers. "*Salut, Mama.*" Then he listens. "*Oui. Elle va bien. Elle s'est cassé la cheville.*"

My French is rusty, but I can follow some of what he's saying. *Hi, Mom. Yes, she's fine.* "What was that last bit?" I whisper.

"She broke her ankle," he whispers back.

The rest of his conversation is lost on me. Maybe if he spoke slower I could follow some of it, but it's way too fast.

He laughs and says goodbye. "*Au revoir, Mama. Je t'aime aussi.*"

That last bit I understand. *Goodbye, Mama. I love you, too.*

"That was your mom."

"Yeah. Mama and my grandparents. They were all on speaker phone."

"Where do they live?"

"Lafayette, Louisiana. Right in the heart of Acadiana."

"And that is?"

"The Cajun heartland."

"Your dad, too?"

"No." His expression flattens. "He died while serving in the Army, when I was a baby. That's where my name came from. He named me Killian after his best friend in the service."

"Your dad was Cajun, too?"

"Nah. He was Creole, from New Orleans. Mama's Cajun. When my dad died, Mama took us back to Lafayette to live with her parents. That's where I grew up. I worked a fishing boat with my grandpapa until I was eighteen. That's when I enlisted in the Army."

We both grow silent as we hear a vehicle approaching the cabin. Killian jumps up to look out the front window, but his posture quickly eases. "It's Owen and Maggie," he says, the tension in his shoulders relaxing. "Along with two boys and a dog."

"Scout!"

Killian opens the door for our guests. Scout rushes inside and runs straight for me, jumping up on my lap and eagerly licking my face. He's sixty-five pounds of unbridled affection.

"Whoa, pal," Killian says as he grabs Scout's brown leather

collar and pulls him off me. "On the floor before you squash her."

Scout sits beside the sofa and rests his head on my lap, gazing up at me with big dark eyes that beg for attention.

I scratch behind his ears. "Hello, sweet boy. Did you miss me? I sure missed you." I glance up at Maggie's sons. Riley, the eldest, is seventeen. Brendan is fifteen. They're both tall, lanky boys, not quite done growing. "Thanks for taking care of Scout for me, guys. I hope he was well-behaved."

"He was the best," Brendan says with enthusiasm. "I taught him some new tricks."

"He's a fast learner," Maggie says. She sits down at the far end of the sofa, careful not to jostle my ankle, and pats my good leg. "It's so good to see you home again." Then she glances at Killian, who's standing by the door conversing with Owen. "I'm also glad to see you have a houseguest."

"Do you want us to take Scout back home with us?" Brendan asks, his expression hopeful. "Just until you get your cast off? He's a handful."

I lean down to kiss the top of Scout's head. "Thanks, Brendan, but I think I'll keep him here. I've really missed him."

"Okay, sure," the kid says. "But if you change your mind, just let me know."

Maggie catches my gaze. "So, how do you feel? Are you in pain?"

"It's getting better." I carefully flex my right arm. "The arm's doing well. Mostly it's my ankle that still bothers me."

"If there's anything you need—anything at all—you just holler. You know we're here for you."

"I will. Thanks."

"Hannah?"

I glance back at Killian, who nods toward the door.

"Owen and I are going to step outside for a few minutes. Call if you need me."

As soon as they're out the door, Maggie says, "Boys, why don't you take Scout outside and throw the ball for him?"

"Can we take him through the agility course, too?" Brendan asks.

"Absolutely," I say, grateful because I know Scout needs the exercise. "He'd love it."

Brendan whistles for Scout, and they all race out the door.

Once we're alone, Maggie moves to sit on the coffee table, facing me. "How are you *really* doing?"

I laugh. "Fine, honestly." I pat my cast. "It'll take time, I know that."

She nods toward the front of the cabin. "And your handsome shadow? How's he working out so far?"

"Killian's been wonderful."

"This is your chance, Hannah. It's just the two of you holed up inside this cabin—two people who both have crushes on each other—you know where that leads. Passions erupt and things just happen."

"Maggie, be serious." I'm tempted to tell her I don't have a crush on Killian, but that would be a lie.

"I am being serious! And please, don't bother trying to kid me. How can you *not* have a crush on that man? He's sex on a stick."

I laugh. "Yes, he is. But he also has a good heart, and that's even more attractive than his looks."

Maggie grins. "So, you *do* like him."

"Of course I like him. But it's pointless. You know that."

"Yeah, yeah," Maggie says, easily dismissing my argument. "So you keep saying. But I think life here in the Rockies would suit him just fine. Have you thought about *asking* him?"

"Ask me what?" Killian says from the open doorway.

Maggie and I both jump. *Shit!* Neither one of us heard the door open. My face heats because I have no idea how much he heard.

"Ask you what you want for dinner," Maggie says quickly. "I brought some steaks—they're outside in a cooler. I was thinking we could grill them."

"That sounds great," Killian says, not missing a beat. His gaze locks on mine, and I can't tell if he believes Maggie or not. "Sound good to you?" he asks me.

Hoping I don't look as flushed as I feel, I nod. "Sure."

"Then I'll start the grill." Then he heads back outside, closing the door behind him.

"Do you think he heard us?" I ask.

Maggie's brow arches in contemplation. "Honestly, I have no idea. But if he did, he's a damn good actor. And I'd call it a good omen that he didn't run in the opposite direction." She walks over to the front window and glances out. "I think you should give it some thought, Hannah. His answer might surprise you." She looks back at me, eyeing the couch. "What are the sleeping arrangements?"

I frown. "He's sleeping on the couch."

Maggie laughs. "He's not going to fit."

"I know. I told him he's welcome to take the bed, and I'll sleep on the couch, but of course he refused."

"You two could *share* the bed."

"Trust me, that would create more problems than it would solve."

Maggie purses her lips and resumes watching out the front window.

When I swing my feet to the floor and reach for my crutches, she says, "Where do you think you're going?"

"To see what's so fascinating." I heave myself up onto my good foot, catch my balance using the crutches, then slowly make my way to the window.

Outside, the sun is shining, and much of the snow has melted. It's hard to believe we had nearly two feet of snow just over twenty-four hours ago. I still haven't gotten used to the weather in Colorado. Back in Chicago, this much snow would last for weeks.

Owen and Killian are standing in front of the gas grill as Killian fires it up. Riley and Brendan are tossing the tennis ball back and forth, playing a game of keep away with Scout. Scout jumps straight up, at least six feet into the air, and intercepts the ball. He runs off with it into the woods, and both boys shout as they give chase.

"You should get a dog," I tell Maggie.

"I suppose so." Maggie laughs. "But I can guarantee you I'll be the one who ends up taking care of it." She points at the sofa. "Go sit down. I've got a baked potato casserole and a salad in the car, as well as a plate of brownies. I'll bring in the food and set the table. You get off your ankle and rest."

* * *

While the food is cooking, the sheriff and a deputy show up to ask me some questions about the men who attacked me up on the ridge. Jake had already given them a detailed rundown of what had happened, but they want to hear it from me.

Sheriff Christopher Nelson is a handsome man, in his mid-forties, with blond hair and blue eyes. He's nearly as tall as Killian, with a broad chest and a bit of a dad bod. The deputy with him is a young woman around my age, with jet black hair pulled up in a tight bun. I've seen her with her girlfriend playing pool at Ruth's tavern. They ask me to tell them the whole story, from beginning to end, which I do. Killian is never far from me, practically hovering as I recite the tale.

The sheriff asks me for a description of the two men, and I tell him what I told Killian. Their descriptions don't ring any bells, but he promises he'll do everything he can to identify them.

After the police leave, Killian announces that the steaks are ready. The four guys eat at the kitchen table, while I eat on the sofa, and Maggie sits on the floor across the coffee table from me. Scout scarfs his meal in the kitchen.

After dinner, Maggie, Owen, and the boys say goodbye and head back to Maggie's farm. It's not really that late, but I can barely keep my eyes open.

"Sit tight," Killian says as he clears the table and sets the dirty dishes by the sink. "I'll clean up the kitchen and take Scout outside. Then we'll get you in bed. You must be exhausted."

"Killian, wait. About that."

"About what?"

"The sleeping arrangements. You're too tall for the sofa. Why don't you take the bed, and I'll sleep out here?"

"Don't be silly. I'm not kickin' you out of your own bed."

"This isn't just for one night, Killian. We're talking *weeks*. You can't sleep crammed on the sofa."

"You got a sleeping bag? I'll sleep on the floor with the dog."

I bite my lip, trying not to smile. "Actually, the dog sleeps with me. In my bed."

The silence that follows is deafening.

Then he laughs. "It'll be fine, Hannah. Stop worrying." He brings me a glass of water and a pain pill. "Here. It's time for you to take another pill."

I pop the pill in my mouth and swallow it down with a gulp of water. Killian's supposed to be here for my protection, but he's doing far more than that. He's taking care of me—like a partner would—and it's unsettling.

Frustration eats at me. *He thinks I'm stubborn?* That's like the pot calling the kettle black.

Killian, just share the damn bed with me.

༄ 18

Killian Devereaux

Hannah's one stubborn young woman. She hates that I'm waiting on her, and fetching and carrying, but I don't mind. In fact, I'm kinda enjoying it. Just wait until I help her get into bed—that'll be interesting. As for the sleeping arrangements—yeah, the sofa's too small for me, but I'll get over it. I imagine it won't be long before she suggests that we share the bed—platonically, of course. She's very pragmatic.

At least then I won't rate below the dog.

She's quiet while I do the dishes and clean up the kitchen. I'm just glad she's not over here insisting on helping. When I'm done, I dry my hands on a kitchen towel and whistle for the dog, who jumps up from his bed by the hearth and comes right to me.

It's dark outside, so I grab the heavy metal flashlight hanging on a hook by the door, just in case. It wouldn't do for me to lose her pet in the dark. Scout heads out the door and down the steps, and I follow him out, leaving the door ajar so I can hear Hannah if she needs me.

"Last call, pal," I tell the dog. "Go do your business."

Scout races across the yard, finds a nice tree at the edge of the clearing, and lifts his leg. When he's done, he starts to meander into the woods, but I whistle for him to come back. "Time to come inside, you lucky dog. You get to sleep in your mistress's bed."

Scout runs back into the cabin, but I linger on the porch a short while longer, doing a visual sweep of the clearing around the cabin and listening for any sounds that shouldn't be there. But I don't hear anything other than the wind rustling the tree branches, insects calling to each other, and an owl hooting off in the distance.

When I step back inside the cabin, the sofa is empty. Hannah's gone. So's the dog. For a moment, my heart stops. There's no other door, so unless someone came in through a back window— "Hannah!"

"In the bathroom."

Jesus. I suck in a deep breath. "Don't do that to me, woman," I mutter beneath my breath as I head down the hall toward the bathroom.

"Did you say something?" she asks, her voice garbled.

The bathroom door is open, and she's standing at the sink brushing her teeth, her crutches propped against the wall. Hannah's leaning against the counter, while Scout sits beside her, gazing up with pure adoration. I can certainly relate.

"You should have waited for me," I say, trying to sound like I didn't almost just have a heart attack. My gaze locks on her reflection in the bathroom mirror. Even though her face is marred by scratches and a cut from her ordeal, she still takes my breath away. She's perfect—like the girl next door. Smart, funny, big brown eyes, an expressive mouth that's quick to smile and quick to backtalk, and shiny hair the color of sable that reaches just past her shoulders when it's hanging loose. And when it's up in a ponytail, like it usually is, all I can think about is grabbing hold of it and—*fuck.*

Don't even go there.

Hannah's everything I'd want in a woman—loyal, strong, family-oriented, resilient, courageous, funny. She's able to hold her own and not afraid to push back.

"Killian, relax," she mumbles around her toothbrush. "I can manage."

This woman's going to be the death of me. "Fine, but next time wait for me. You could have fallen and hurt yourself."

She gives me the stink eye. "I fell nearly twenty feet into a ravine. I think I'd survive taking a tumble in my own house."

I shrug begrudgingly, as she does have a point. "Maybe.

There's no need to take chances."

Hannah spits in the sink, rinses her mouth, and wipes her face on a tissue. Pivoting to face me, she leans against the cabinet for support. She stands there eyeing me expectantly, her brows shooting up. Finally, exasperated, she looks pointedly at the toilet. "Do you mind? I need to go."

"Do you need help?" Of course I'm just kidding. I know she doesn't want that kind of help from me.

"I think I can do it myself."

"Sure thing." I step outside the bathroom and close the door.

A few minutes later, I hear the toilet flush, the faucet runs, and then the door opens. Ignoring me, Hannah swings herself out into the hallway, managing the crutches much better now as she propels herself the few feet to the bedroom. I follow her inside the room.

She grimaces as she sinks down on the bed and lets out a heavy sigh.

"Be careful not to overdo it," I warn her.

She rolls her eyes at me. "Gee, thanks, Mom."

I try not to laugh but fail miserably. Why does she make everything so fun? Even teasing her—getting her riled up—is fun. "Is there anything I can help you with?"

She lifts her good foot in the air. "Actually, yes, there is something. Unfasten my boot, please?"

I catch her boot in one hand and unbuckle it with the other. Then I tug it off and set it on the floor. "Anything else?"

She falls back on the bed with a weary groan. Begrudgingly,

she says, "I think I'll need your help getting my pants off." She's still wearing the red-plaid flannel bottoms that Maggie brought to the hospital.

I approach the bed like I might approach a female mountain lion, wary of getting scratched or bit. I'm as pragmatic as I can be as I grab the elastic waistband of her pants and work them over her hips. She's wearing pale blue cotton bikini underwear, which I do my best to ignore. I motion toward her upper half. "What about the rest of it?" She's still got a long-sleeved shirt on and, presumably, a bra.

"Oh, right." She holds her hand out to me. "Help me sit up?"

After I pull her into a sitting position, she attempts to reach behind her back and up beneath her shirt to unfasten her bra, but she winces in pain. "Ow." She drops her arms and leans forward. "I can't reach the clasp. Do you mind? Just unfasten my bra and let the straps slip down my arms. I'll sleep in the T-shirt."

"Sure," I say, trying to sound nonchalant, as if the girl I'm crazy about didn't just ask me to remove her bra. I pull up the back of her shirt and focus on undoing the clasp. I make a pointed effort not to catch a glimpse of her breasts. Instead, I focus on the bandage on her arm. "Now would be a good time for me to check your sutures."

While she sits there with her T-shirt draped in front of her, covering her bare breasts, I grab the first-aid kit and quickly change the bandage on her arm. "The stitches look good. No redness or swelling."

When that's done, I help her slip both arms back into the sleeves of her shirt, and she lies back. After I cover her with the sheet and comforter, Scout jumps up on the mattress, circles a spot at the foot of the bed, then curls up like a fox with his nose tucked beneath his tail.

Lucky bastard. He gets to sleep in the bed.

I check the lock on her bedroom window to make sure it's secure. "If you need anything in the night, just holler. I'll hear you."

"I will, thanks."

"Anything else before I go?"

"Would you turn off the light on your way out, please? Oh, and there are sheets and blankets in the hallway linen closet. And a couple of extra pillows. Help yourself."

I nod. "Don't—"

"Yeah, I know—don't worry, you'll be fine." She sounds far from convinced. "Good luck fitting your six-foot-two frame on a five-foot-ten sofa."

"Actually, I'm six-three, but who's counting? And how do you know exactly how long the sofa is?"

"Because I'm five-eight, and I can stretch out on it with a couple inches to spare. That's how I know."

I chuckle as I turn off the light. "Goodnight, Hannah." Then I pull her door closed.

I take my pack into the bathroom with me and set out my toiletries—toothbrush, toothpaste, deodorant, shampoo, razor and shaving cream. I don't know where I'm going to store this stuff. It's a tiny room with hardly any storage.

I open the top of three cabinet drawers and find it filled with Hannah's stuff—lotions, hair ties, hairbrushes, and make-up. I open the middle drawer and get an eyeful of tampons and pads. *Okay next.* The bottom drawer is empty except for a blow-dryer. It looks like this one will have to do.

I grab a quick shower, then dress in the last pair of clean boxer-briefs I brought with me. Looks like I'll be doing laundry in the morning. After I brush my teeth, I head to the living room.

I add wood to the stove and stoke the fire, hoping it will last most of the night. Probably not. I'd love a cold beer—I've been wanting one all day—but I can't drink when I'm on duty, and technically, I'm now on duty twenty-four-seven.

After checking the locks on the door and all the windows, I find the spare bedding right where she said it would be and make up the sofa. I figure if I sleep on my side and draw my knees up, it just might work.

It takes me a while to find a suitable sleeping configuration. And once I'm halfway comfortable and just starting to doze off, I hear a loud thump and a muffled cry, followed by a string of curse words that would impress even my grandpapa.

What the hell?

I jump off the couch and turn toward the hallway just as Hannah comes swinging her way into the living room. She's wearing just that T-shirt, and her gorgeous long legs are bare.

"What's wrong?" I ask, trying not to stare at all that skin. "Are you hurt?"

"I'm fine." She huffs in irritation. "This is stupid, Killian. You take the bed. I'll sleep out here."

I can't help smiling. "It's cute that you think you need to worry about my sleeping comfort." I head over to her, ignoring the fact that I'm wearing even less than she is. I'm especially ignoring the fact that her gaze is locked onto my body. Her eyes widen as they skim my bare chest, moving slowly down my abs to finally rest on my damned cock, which is taking this opportunity to make its presence known. I sigh. A man can only take so much. "Please go back to bed."

"I'm serious, Killian. We should trade—"

I stalk over to her, swing her up in my arms—ignoring the clatter of the crutches as they hit the wood floor—and carry her back to her bed. I lay her down, cover her up, and scowl down at her. "Not another peep out of you, *jeune femme. Bonne nuit.*"

…young lady. Good night.

I turn to leave, but she grabs my hand. "Wait."

I turn back to face her. "What?"

"At least share this bed with me. I'm not going to be able to sleep knowing you're out there trying to cram yourself onto that sofa. Be practical, please."

She nods to the empty side of the bed and pulls the covers down. "There's plenty of room, and we're two grown adults. We can share the damn bed."

As I contemplate her offer, I come to the conclusion that I'd be an idiot to turn it down. One, at least she'll stay in bed and be less likely to hurt herself getting up; and two, I'm a selfish bastard.

Yeah, I want in her bed.

Even if it's just to sleep.

"Fine," I say as I walk around to the other side of the bed. I slide beneath the bedding and lie on my back, staring up at the ceiling with my hands clasped on my belly. Immediately, I realize this wasn't such a bright idea after all. I'm only inches away from her, and she's practically naked. My cock hardens even more. "Goodnight, Hannah."

She sighs. "Goodnight."

I feel the warm, comforting weight of the dog's head on my ankle as he settles down for the night.

ᶜᵉ 19

Hannah McIntyre

Killian's presence in my bed is electrifying, and I can't sleep. It's like there's an electromagnetic field crackling between us, and my skin is covered in goosebumps. With a groan, Scout stretches out between us. He's clearly in heaven. Me, not so much. This is more like torture.

And it's not just my awareness of his proximity that's keeping me awake. My ankle is killing me. As the night rolls on, the discomfort worsens to the point that I have to work at hiding it so I don't disturb Killian. I squeeze my eyes shut and breathe carefully, in and out, as I try to distract myself from thinking about the pain.

"Hannah."

Shit! I guess I wasn't doing a very good job of hiding it. "Yeah?"

"How about we prop your ankle up on a pillow? That might help."

"Okay," I gasp. "It's worth a try."

Killian sits up. "I'll grab one of the spares from the sofa." He gets out of bed as carefully as he can, so as not to jar my leg, and heads to the living room.

He's back a moment later, lowering the bedding and gently slipping a pillow beneath my cast. "This should help."

"Thanks."

He sits beside me and reaches out as if he's going to brush back my hair, but he stops himself. "*Tu es une femme courageuse.*"

I got part of that. "I'm a *what?*"

He smiles. "A courageous woman."

I frown. "Not courageous enough. I ended up in the bottom of a ravine and couldn't even get myself out."

"That's because you were injured. If you hadn't broken your ankle, you would have gotten out of that ravine all by yourself."

I smile. "True."

He reaches for my hand, this time bringing it to his mouth and kissing the back of it. The feel of his lips against my skin sends a shiver up my arm. God, what I wouldn't give for him to really kiss me. I've imagined what it would be like—his lips on mine. His strong hands on me... giving and taking.

He checks the digital clock on my nightstand. "Try to get

some sleep."

Squeezing his hand, I nod. "Goodnight."

* * *

Fortunately, I do fall asleep, and I manage to stay that way until the sun is shining brightly through my sheer bedroom curtains and into my face. I'm alone in bed, and there's no sign of Scout or Killian. But the aroma of something delicious wafts into the room, making my stomach growl.

"I hope you're hungry," Killian says from the doorway, a spatula in his hand.

"What smells so good?"

"Breakfast. *Pain perdu et le bacon*. French toast and bacon."

"I didn't know you cooked."

He laughs. "Oh, Grandmama made sure I knew how to feed myself. When I get the chance, I'll make you some beans and rice—Cajun style, of course—and maybe a gumbo. Or jambalaya, if I can get the ingredients."

"I'd like that."

The kitchen timer goes off with a loud *ding*.

He points down the hall. "That's my cue. You need anything?"

"I need the bathroom." My bladder is screaming at me.

Killian offers me his hand and pulls me up into a sitting position. As I swing my feet to the floor, he hands me my crutches. "You take care of business and come eat," he says, and then he walks out the door, leaving me to manage on my own. The man is learning.

By the time I wash up in the bathroom and change into a pair of knit shorts and a University of Denver hoodie, I hobble into the kitchen and take a seat at the table, which is already set with plates, silverware, and coffee cups.

Killian's standing on the other side of the kitchen counter holding a hot cast-iron skillet in one hand and a spatula in the other. "Perfect timing," he says as he walks around the counter to the table and lays two slices of French toast on my plate. I can smell the cinnamon.

"Coffee?" he says.

"Yes, please. I'm in dire need of caffeine."

He pours me a cup first and then himself. He grabs a small pitcher from the counter and pours milk into his. "*Café au lait.*"

"Is that cream?"

"Boiled milk. Want some?"

"Sure, I'll try it." I glance back into the kitchen. "Where's the sugar?"

"I'll get it." He reaches across the counter with his long arm and grabs the white ceramic sugar bowl that my mom gave me as a housewarming gift when I bought this cabin—she bought me a whole set of kitchen wares. He sets the bowl in front of me, then hands me a clean spoon. "Eat, before it gets cold."

I spoon sugar into my coffee and stir. "I hope my brother is compensating you adequately. I doubt cooking for your client is a regular part of your job description."

"It's not, I'll admit. But usually my clients aren't so pretty, and I'm not so eager to impress them."

His blunt admission surprises me. "You want to impress me?"

He ignores my question as if he realized he said too much. "So, where can a guy get fresh seafood around here?"

I laugh. "Not in Bryce, that's for sure. Maybe in one of the bigger towns, but it'll be quite a drive."

He nods. "Maybe, when you're feeling up to it, we can take a road trip and stock up."

I slather butter on my French toast, then drizzle maple syrup over top. I cut off a piece and slip it into my mouth... and groan with delight. "Oh, my god, that's so good. I haven't had French toast in ages. My mom used to make it for us kids on Sunday mornings." Then I take a bite of the bacon, which is crispy and perfect. Another groan. I could really get used to this.

"Tomorrow I'll make you some *coosh coosh* for breakfast. You need some good home cookin'."

"*Coosh coosh*? What's that?"

"Fried cornmeal with milk, with warm honey drizzled on it. My mama used to make that for me every morning before school."

"Why did you leave home? I mean, leave Louisiana?"

He shrugs. "After the Army, I didn't know what to do. I couldn't envision going back to Lafayette and selling cars or helping my uncles operate the fishing boats. I was hooked on the adrenaline. A buddy of mine had taken a job with your brother in Chicago. He said I should come check it out myself. I've been with McIntyre Security ever since."

"Do you get home often to visit your family?"

He chews a mouthful and swallows. "I visit as often as I can. It'll always be home to me—da food, da music, da people. Dey're fierce and proud, and I'm proud to be part of dat community."

Hearing him slip into his Cajun accent makes me smile. I love seeing this part of him. "Your mom and grandparents must be very proud of you."

He smiles as he raises his coffee cup to his mouth and takes a sip. "*Sha*, she'd like you, dat's for sure."

* * *

After breakfast, Killian insists on doing the dishes—again. "It wouldn't do for you to stand at the sink. Go sit down on the sofa, put your leg up, and read a book. I'll finish up here, and then I promised Scout I'd take him outside for a while."

I do as he says, sipping a fresh cup of coffee and trying to concentrate on reading while Killian does the dishes. I'm not having much luck, though. He's singing something in French, and I can't help listening to the sound of his voice. It's hypnotic.

When he's done in the kitchen, he whistles for Scout, and the two of them head outside. Already, I feel his absence.

My phone rings. It's Maggie.

"I've got Killian's order together," she says. "Riley will bring it by after school."

"He placed a grocery order?"

"Apparently your pantry is inadequately stocked because he called in this morning with quite a list."

"What did he ask for?"

"Black-eyed peas, shrimp, paprika, beans, rice, grits, real crab meat, bacon, Worcestershire sauce, corn, jalapeños, three different kinds of peppers, cayenne, sausage, and hot sauce. It was an impressive list. I had most of what he wanted, but not any fresh seafood. I asked him if frozen would suffice, and he said no." She laughs.

Killian's culinary ambitions bring a smile to my face. "When he made breakfast for me this morning, he admitted he was trying to impress me."

Maggie squeals over the phone. "I told you! He's got ulterior motives, girl. He *likes* you."

Hearing her say that, my heart swells with anticipation. But I just don't see it happening. He has his life—his career—back in Chicago. His family is in Louisiana, and obviously they're very close.

"Ruth wants to see you," Maggie says. "She wondered if you'd feel up to stopping by the tavern sometime soon. She said drinks are on the house."

"I'd love to. Maybe Micah can join us. I didn't get a chance to properly thank him for flying up to get me. If it weren't for Micah and his helicopter, I might still be up there on that mountain."

"When have you ever known Micah to miss a party? I'm sure he'll join us."

The sound of boots stomping on the wood porch makes me jump. Then the door swings open, and Scout races inside. His tongue is hanging out, and he's breathing hard. He runs to me and licks my hand.

"Did you have fun?" I ask him, just as Killian closes the door and slides the lock in place. Man and dog both look like they just had a good workout. "I have to go," I tell Maggie. "I'll talk to you again soon."

Scout runs straight to his dog bed beside the woodstove and crashes, panting heavily as he tries to catch his breath.

"Who was on the phone?" Killian asks as he pours a glass of cold water and practically guzzles it.

"Maggie. She said you ordered groceries."

He twists the lid off the bottle and sits in the rocking chair. "I did. Your pantry is a little bare. Did she mention anything else? Any problems?"

"No. But she said Micah's sister, Ruth, wants us to meet up with them at her tavern. Sort of a little party."

"Micah's the helo pilot?"

"Yes."

Killian takes a long draw on his drink. "Okay. If you're up for it."

"Killian, about the food—the cooking. I don't expect you to cook for me. And you certainly don't need to impress me."

He frowns. "No point in it? It's a hopeless cause?"

"No, it's not that."

"Then what?"

"I'm saying you don't need to *work* at it. I'm already impressed."

He grins. "You are? My plan is working?"

I nod. "I've been impressed, for a long time."

His dark eyes widen. "Then why the hell did you give me all those cold shoulders back in Chicago? Why did you always shut me down when I tried to talk to you?"

I shrug. "I just didn't think anything could come of it. It seemed pointless—for both of us."

He sets his drink down on a coaster on the wooden coffee table and stands, coming near to lean over me. "And now? What's changed?"

He's so close, my heart is pounding, and I can't catch my breath. I want to reach up, grab him, and pull him in for a kiss. I want to— "Oh, to hell with it." I grab the neckline of his T-shirt and pull him to me for a kiss.

He responds instantly, his mouth hungrily covering mine. He threads the fingers of one hand through my hair and holds me for his kiss.

Pleasure shoots through my body to the heated, aching spot between my legs. Everything's tingling—my lips, my breasts, my sex, my skin. Everything feels hot and tight.

"Damn, woman," he says when he finally breaks the kiss and catches his breath. He falls back to sit on the coffee table. He looks a bit flummoxed. "One thing is sure, you never fail to surprise me."

ᥱ᧹20

Killian Devereaux

That kiss changes everything. And I mean *everything.* Damn, if she wasn't the one to make the first move. She about pulled the rug out from under me when she grabbed my shirt, sending my brain reeling and my heart thundering.

I sit here staring at her, probably lookin' like a dumbstruck fool.

Did that just happen?

Did Hannah McIntyre actually put her lips on mine?

I lean forward and take her hands in mine. "Tell me what

just happened, love, so I don't go off half-cocked and make a damned fool of myself." I've wanted this too long to risk fucking it up now.

She raises an eyebrow. "Seriously? I have to explain to you what a kiss is? I *kissed* you, Killian."

"Yeah, that part I know. But what did it *mean*? Were you just bein' nice? Like, '*Hey, Killian, thanks for makin' me breakfast dis morning. Or, Gee, Killian, thanks for carryin' me outta dat ravine.*' Like that?"

She shakes her head at me. "It means—"

Without warning, Scout rockets to his feet and runs to the window, his hackles standing straight up and his teeth bared. A deep, throaty growl reverberates in the room.

"Fuck." I shoot to my feet and grab my gun, which is lying on the kitchen table. I point down the hallway. "Hannah, get in the bathroom and lock the door."

But she ignores me, watching instead as I move into position by the window so I can see out into the yard.

From her spot on the sofa, she cranes her neck as she tries in vain to see who's here.

"Hannah, go!"

Instead of listening to me, she grabs her crutches and hobbles toward me. "It's probably just Maggie, or maybe Ruth."

"Black SUV, tinted windows," I say as I peer out the window. "Male driver, Caucasian, dark hair. He's wearing sunglasses and a baseball cap." That certainly fits the description of one of the poachers. "Hannah, will you just go?"

"I'm not hiding in the bathroom."

A second later, there's a soft knock at the cabin door. "Hannah? It's me, Ray. Sorry for stopping by unannounced. I hope it's not a bad time."

Hannah's posture relaxes. "It's okay. That's my boss."

I beat her to the door and open it slowly to reveal a man in his early thirties. His sunglasses are off now, hanging from the neckline of his dark green sweatshirt bearing the logo of the Bryce Wildlife Rehabilitation Center. He takes off his baseball cap and smooths his short black hair.

"Hannah," he says, a bit breathless as his gaze drinks her in. Then he glances at me and frowns. "I'm sorry. I didn't realize you had company."

"Come on in, Ray," she says. "This is Killian, my... temporary bodyguard."

Ray smiles in obvious relief. "Bodyguard? Oh, good."

I scan him from head to toe—sweatshirt, khaki trousers, scuffed hiking boots. No weapon in sight.

As Ray closes the door behind him, he eyes me curiously before offering me his hand. "Ray Calhoun. I'm the director of the wildlife rehab center where Hannah works."

I tuck my gun into the back of my waistband and shake hands with him. "Killian Devereaux. McIntyre Security."

Ray's gaze returns to Hannah. "I'm so sorry, Hannah." He steps close and hugs her, his arms slipping around her waist as he pulls her against him. His face nestles against the side of her hair, and I swear to god, he's inches away from kissing her temple.

What the fuck?

There's no way she has a boyfriend and forgot to tell me.

He pulls back so he can see her face. "This is all my fault. I'm the one who sent you up there in the first place." He shudders. "My god, honey, you could have been killed."

Honey?

What the double-fuck?

Hannah extricates herself from his embrace and steps back. "It's not your fault, Ray."

She takes a step back, away from him, and in the process ends up teetering on her crutches. I automatically reach out, ready to catch her if she falls.

"You had no idea they'd be up there," she continues.

He smiles gratefully at her—probably relieved that she's not pissed at him. Then his gaze bounces from her to me and back to her, then down to her cast. He frowns again. "So, it's broken?"

She sighs heavily. "Yeah."

"I guess you'll be out of commission for a while."

She nods. "The doctor told me to take off work for at least a month. I should be able to come back then, although I won't be able to do any field work."

"No, of course not," Ray says. "Anything you need, Hannah. You've got to take care of yourself, first and foremost."

"Can I get you something to drink?" she asks him, acting the perfect hostess. "Coffee? A soft drink? Beer?"

Ray shakes his head. "Thank you, but no." Then his gaze

darts to me. "I should go. You're probably busy."

If he's waiting for me to invite him to stay, he's fresh outta luck. My gut tells me dis guy wishes he was more than Hannah's boss, and he's not going to get any help from me.

Hannah gives him a smile. "Thanks for stopping by, Ray. I appreciate your concern."

Ray nods, his head bouncing like a bobblehead. He frowns when he looks my way again. "Are you expecting trouble?"

"You never know," I say, not wanting to share any information with this guy. "It pays to be prepared for anything."

His eyes widen as if he's finally just catching on. "You mean they might come looking for Hannah?"

Not wanting to drag out this scintillating conversation any longer, I open the door wide. "Like I said, Ray, it pays to be prepared."

Ray hugs Hannah once more, holding her far too close for my comfort. "Call me if you need anything," he says. "Anything at all." He hesitates as if he wants to say more, but he doesn't. After glancing at me one last time, he walks out the door.

I close the door and lock it. "Well, that was interesting."

Hannah starts shuffling on her crutches to the kitchen. "What was interesting?"

I take hold of her shoulders to halt her progress. "Where do you think you're going?"

"To the kitchen."

"What for?"

"More coffee."

I turn her back toward the living room. "Back to the sofa and put your foot up. I'll get you some more coffee."

I watch her swing her way back to the sofa and sit, making sure she makes it all right. Then I grab a clean mug and pour her a cup from the coffee maker. After locating the sugar and the creamer she likes, I make it up and carry it to her.

I sit on the coffee table and watch her take her first sip. "What's with you and Ray?"

She peers up at me from beneath dark brown lashes. "Ray? What are you talking about? He's my boss."

"Only your boss?"

Her brow wrinkles in confusion. "Yes."

"You sure about dat?"

"Yes. Killian, what in the hell are you getting at?"

"The man likes you."

"Well, sure. We're friends."

"No, I mean he *likes* you. As in a man liking a woman and wanting to be more than her friend."

She gives me a bit of an eye roll. "You're nuts."

"Nah." I shake my head. "It was pretty obvious to me, the way he held you. Do you like him, too?"

"You're being silly. Ray's just a touchy-feely kind of guy. He's like that with everyone."

"You didn't answer my question, Hannah. Do you *like* him?"

Her eyes flash with indignant fire. "No. Do you think I would have kissed *you* if I was crushing on my boss?"

"I sure as hell hope not."

Now she's mad at me. "No, I wouldn't have. I would have been on the damn phone to Ray telling him to get his ass over here."

I smile, partly from amusement, but mostly from relief. I'm not afraid of a little competition, but I want to know where I stand. "All right, fine. I believe you."

She huffs out an irritated breath.

"Now, back to what we were discussing before we were so rudely interrupted by your secret admirer."

She snorts out a laugh, then winces as she clutches her leg. "Oh, god, don't make me laugh, Killian. It hurts."

My smile evaporates. "Shit, I'm sorry." I stand. "I'll get you a pain pill. It's time."

I jump up from my seat and head for the bathroom to grab her a pill. As I'm popping off the cap, I hear Scout barking up a storm, a deep growl rumbling from his throat. Then I hear the thump of Hannah's crutches hitting the floor as she stands. "Hannah, wait!"

"Someone's here. It's probably just Ray coming back."

Shit!

Dat man tucked his tail and ran; he's not comin' back. "Hannah, no! Stay away from the door." My heart's pounding as I drop the pill bottle on the bathroom counter and race back to the living room, reaching behind me to grab my gun.

Hannah's standing in the middle of the living room, halfway to the door. "I'm sure it's—"

I motion her back as I position myself beside the front

window, gun raised. There's a black SUV parked in the lane, half-hidden by trees. The windows are heavily tinted, so I can't see who's in the driver seat or even how many hostiles there are.

Fuck.

This situation has wrong written all over it.

"Toss me the radio, Hannah. Then get in the bathroom."

Hannah's just a couple of feet from the table. She grabs the two-way radio and tosses it to me.

I press the mic. "Owen, this is Killian. Do you copy?"

There's static on the line, and a moment later a voice comes through loud and clear. "Owen here. I copy. Over."

"We've got company here," I tell him. "A black SUV staying well outta sight."

"On my way. Over and out."

I set the radio down and nod toward the bathroom. "Go."

Scowling, she shuffles down the short hallway.

"Close the door and lock it. Don't come out unless I tell you to."

I scan the yard and see no one—just that ominous black SUV parked where it shouldn't be. I move to the kitchen windows to see what I can—again, nothing. No sign of any tangos approaching the cabin. Scout's pacing, his hackles up as he grows quietly.

"You and me both, pal," I tell him as I return to the front window.

A few minutes later, the SUV backs out of sight and reverses down the lane.

I radio Owen back. "They're leaving. See if you can get a visual and follow them. I want an ID."

"Copy that," Owen says. "I'm on it."

When the yard is clear, I pull out my phone and dial my boss's direct number.

"Killian?" Shane says, his voice guarded. "How's it going?"

"I think we have a problem, Shane."

21

Hannah McIntyre

I swallow a pain pill with my lukewarm coffee and sit on the sofa with my leg propped up on a pillow while Killian talks to Shane. As the oldest of my four brothers, Shane's the one who personally takes responsibility for everyone in his sphere. He's the ultimate caretaker. The protector.

After a short conversation, Killian hands me his phone. "He wants to talk to you."

"Hey, bro," I say, doing my best to sound unfazed by what just happened. "How are Beth and the kids?"

"They're well." He sighs. "The pertinent question is, how are *you* doing?"

"I'm okay. I'm recuperating."

"How's your ankle?"

"It aches, but I'm managing."

"How's it going with Killian?"

I have to remind myself that Killian can only hear my side of the conversation. "Pretty well, actually."

"Really?" He sounds skeptical. "I know he's the last person you wanted to see, but—"

"No, really. It's fine."

"Hannah." His voice makes it clear he doesn't believe me. "You're sure?"

"Yes."

"Good. I just wanted to be sure you were okay with this arrangement. If you're not, I can send someone else out—"

"Nope, it's fine. No need."

"Okay." Shane chuckles. "Are you sure you're Hannah? You're not being coerced?"

I laugh, then groan. "Stop. It hurts when I laugh."

"Sorry." His voice grows serious. "Please, don't take any chances, Hannah. Let Killian do his job."

"I will. I promise."

"Good. Now put him back on the phone."

I hand the phone back to Killian, who walks toward the kitchen as he continues his conversation. "I agree," he says. "I don't think it's a coincidence that an unidentified vehicle arrived at our location just ten minutes after Hannah's boss stopped by for a visit. Ray Calhoun is either working with the poachers, or they tailed him to discover her location. Owen just missed them, or we might have gotten at least a plate number." He pauses. "Yeah, I will. But I'm not leaving her alone. I'll have Owen and Maggie stay with her while I do a bit of reconnaissance." Another pause. "Sounds good."

Killian ends the call and pockets his phone. "Can I get you anything?"

"My coffee's cold. How about topping it off?"

He brings the pot to me and pours some into my cup. "Better? You need more sugar or cream?"

I take a taste. "No, this is fine. Thanks. When we were kids, my dad always told us that drinking coffee black would put hair on our chests. My brothers insisted on drinking theirs black, but not me and my sisters. The last thing we wanted was hair on our chests. We used liberal amounts of sugar and creamer."

Killian chuckles as he sits beside me. "Thank god you heeded your dad's warning." He gently rests my cast on his lap, laying his hands on top of it to hold it steady. "How does it feel?"

"A little better. The pain meds help."

He nods, seemingly satisfied. "In a few days, the aching should stop. Just hang in there." His hand sweeps up my cast to settle on my knee, his palm and fingers warm and rough against my skin.

I allow myself to imagine that hand sliding up my leg, between my thighs, closer and closer still to that aching spot. My entire body heats up at just the idea. Reflexively, I clench the muscles between my legs, the nerve endings down there sending tingles up my spine. I shiver.

"You cold?" he asks me, nodding toward the woodstove. "Want me to stoke the fire?"

"No, I'm fine." I'm not cold. Far from it. I'm heating up inside in anticipation of something that may or may not ever happen. *Yes, I want him.* I always have. I just never thought it could be an option. It's not fair of me to lead him on if we don't have a future.

Carefully, so as not to jar my leg resting on his lap, Killian turns to face me. He lays one arm along the back of the sofa cushions, and the other cradles my cast to ensure it doesn't slide off his lap. His gaze is locked on me, his expression just as heated as I feel.

As I swallow nervously, my belly flutters in anticipation.

He meets my gaze head-on. "I realize this isn't the best time to say this—"

"No, it's fine. Just say it. You and I have been dancing around each other for over a year now."

He nods. "I want you to know I didn't come here expecting *anything.* You're not beholden to me because of what happened on that ridge. I would have come for you no matter what. And I'll stay and do my job—protect you—no matter what. Are we clear on that?"

I smile at him. "Yes."

"I want to make that perfectly clear."

"It's clear. Crystal." I guess now it's my turn to make a gesture. I lay my hand over his as I work up my courage to be up-front with him. "When we first met, you made one hell of an impression on me, but I didn't see how anything could come of it. You know how I feel about the city. Moving back to Chicago isn't an option for me."

"I've always known that, Hannah." He turns his hand so that his palm is pressed against mine, and he links our fingers. "And I would never ask—or expect—you to do something that would make you unhappy."

I stare at our hands, mesmerized by the differences. His are so masculine, with short, crisp brown hairs on the backs of his hand and fingers. I can feel the callouses on the pads of his fingers and on his palm. "Killian, I can't ask you to uproot yourself just for me."

He reaches out and brushes back my hair. "Don't you think that's my decision to make?"

"Well, yes, but—"

"There aren't any *buts* about it, love. I'm a grown man; I make my own decisions. Chicago wasn't the first place I would have chosen for myself, but the offer at the time was too good to pass up. And I've never regretted it. I've loved working for Shane. I couldn't ask for a better boss. But my point is, darlin', I'm not tied to Chicago." He frees his palm, presses it to his chest, and stares pointedly at me. "I'd rather be tied to *you*."

The air rushes from my lungs and my pulse races. "You risked your life for me."

"It was nothing. I'd do it again a thousand times over." He

grabs my hand and kisses the back of it, his lips clinging to my skin for a long moment. "All I'm asking for is a chance to prove that we'd be good together. That I can make you happy."

"I always felt it would be unfair to you—" I don't get a chance to finish because he leans in and kisses me.

Unlike the last time, this kiss is soft, gentle, teasing—a flick of his tongue against my bottom lip. "I'm a big boy, Hannah. You don't need to worry about my poor little feelings. Be unfair to me, please. Walk all over me and expect me to pick up my life and adjust it to fit yours."

Laughing, I smack his chest playfully. "Be serious."

He catches my palm and holds it to his chest, right over his heart. "I am being serious. I've known a lot of girls in my life, Ms. McIntyre, but never once did I meet one who made me wanna throw myself to da wind and see where life takes me. You do. In spades. And we'll never know how we feel about each other, and if we work, unless we give it a try. Dat's what I'm asking for. A chance."

I smile as that little bit of Cajun sneaks into his speech. It comes and goes at random, and when I hear it, my heart melts. "Okay."

His dark eyes widen. "Okay? It's dat easy?"

"Yes, but don't come crying to me if you get your feelings hurt."

He laughs. "Oh, *ma belle jeune fille*, doan you worry one bit about my feelings. Like I said, I'm a big boy."

His choice of words makes me smile. *My beautiful young*

woman.

"So, *oui?*" he asks, confirming.

I nod. "*Oui.*"

"You want this?" He leans closer, moving slowly as if giving me time to change my mind. I sit frozen in anticipation. *Hell yes, I want this.* Are you kidding? He's the star of my daydreams. He has been for a long time. When I'm alone and need a release, it's his face in my mind, his voice and touch I'm imagining. Aching for.

I glance down at my cast. "What about my ankle?"

"I won't hurt you," he says.

"I mean, it's a bit of a party crasher, don't you think?"

He gives me a mischievous grin. "Believe me, I know lots of delicious ways to pleasure you that don't involve your poor ankle."

Of course I believe him. I believe this man can do absolutely anything he puts his mind to. "Yes, I want this."

He shakes his head in disbelief. "I've dreamed of havin' the right to touch you—to know that you want me to. You have no idea how badly I've wanted that right—since the first time we met, when you would hardly look at me."

My chest tightens as I recall the first time I saw him. It felt like the bottom fell out of my world—he stole my breath, my ability to think straight. And now we're here, like this? How is that even possible? "I think you need to kiss me right now, Killian—*really* kiss me."

"Oh, I mean to kiss you and a whole lot more."

Carefully, he extricates himself out from beneath my cast, pushes the coffee table aside, and kneels beside the sofa, right next to me. His long fingers thread through my hair, and for a moment he holds me there, gazing so deeply into my eyes that I swear he can see all the secret needs and desires I've been keeping from him. When I nervously lick my bottom lip, his gaze locks onto my mouth. He licks his own bottom lip, and I know what we're both anticipating.

Touch.

Taste.

God, I want to taste him.

"I've waited a long time for you," he says quietly as he leans in. "An embarrassingly long time." He brushes his lips gently against mine. "You were all I could think about. No one else measured up."

"Are you saying you haven't dated—"

"I haven't so much as looked at another woman since I met you. It's been a long dry spell."

"Same for me," I admit. "In the back of my mind, I kept thinking, *maybe*, just maybe, one day it could work out for us."

He chuckles. "I've never worked so hard for a kiss." And then he closes the distance between us, his lips settling over mine, nudging them open, wider and wider as he creates the most delicious suction molding our mouths together.

My nipples tighten in response to his touch, tingling almost painfully. Pleasure shoots down my spine, to my core, hot and teasing. The ache between my legs intensifies, and I can feel my body softening in anticipation.

His hands slide forward to cradle my face, and he holds me for his kiss. His breath mingles with mine, and we're both breathing hard. I'm not sure how far this is going—I certainly wasn't prepared for this—but I don't want to even think about stopping him.

One of his hands slides down my throat, then across my shoulder and down my arm. It slips to my torso, his fingers searching. When his thumb brushes the side of my breast, I shiver as a breathy whimper slips out. His hand tightens on me, and he groans deep in his throat, the sound so raw and masculine that it makes me melt.

Killian is honestly the sexiest man I've ever met in my life. I don't say that lightly—I've met a lot of good-looking men here in Colorado. They're everywhere, in fact. Rugged, outdoorsy types that drive Jeeps or ride motorcycles. They hike to mountain peaks and solo climb rockfaces. They hang out every single Saturday night at Ruth's tavern, and I've had more than my fair share of male attention. But none of them have haunted my imagination the way Killian has. None of them have tempted me like he does.

He coaxes my head back onto the sofa cushion and rises up over me, holding himself inches from my body. He's being so careful with my ankle—so careful with me—and I love him for it. As he trails kisses along my jawline and down the sensitive curve of my neck, his thumb brushes my already peaked nipple. The result is electrifying pleasure. With a cry, I arch my back and press my chest against his.

That little movement is enough to send a streak of pain shooting up my leg, catching me off guard. A cry escapes me before I can squelch it, and immediately he draws back with a curse.

"Shit, I'm sorry," he says as he reaches down to lay his hand on my knee. "Too soon."

"No," I protest, grabbing his hand. I don't want this to stop. Even if we can't do more than make-out like desperate teenagers. "It's okay. I'm fine."

He pulls away and sits on the coffee table, his expression contrite. "I shouldn't have done dat."

"Oh yes, you should have," I say. "And I want you to do a lot more. *I* want to do a lot to you."

He laughs. "You'd be more comfortable stretched out on a bed, *oui?*"

Yes?

"*Oui.*" That idea sounds perfect to me.

He raises his index finger. "But…" He draws out the word as if he regrets what he's about to say. "We'll have to pick this up later. There's something I need to do first."

"What?" I have a suspicion I know. I heard his half of his conversation with Shane.

"I need to go pay a visit to your boss. I have some questions for him. Later tonight, if you're feeling up to it, we'll pick up where we left off, only this time in a proper bed where you'll be more comfortable."

The idea of *bed* and *Killian* in the same sentence makes me a little dizzy.

22

Killian Devereaux

Hannah grabs hold of my shirt. "I promise you Ray's not involved with them. He has dedicated his life to wildlife conservation. He'd never get involved with poachers."

"Maybe not by choice. They might have coerced him somehow. I need to look into it. It's too much of a coincidence that a mysterious vehicle shows up to case this place just *minutes* after Calhoun stopped by for a visit. Care to explain that?"

Hannah frowns. "I can't."

"Okay, then. I have to check it out. I wouldn't be doing my

job if I didn't."

At the sound of tires crunching on the gravel drive, Hannah's whole body flinches. She bites her lip, suppressing a cry of pain.

"It's okay, love," I say. "It's just Owen and Maggie. I asked them to come stay with you while I go out for a bit."

She grabs my hand. "Where are you going?"

I give her a look but don't answer.

She huffs in exasperation. "I'm telling you, Ray's not involved with the poachers. I'd bet my life on it."

Scout's back on his feet, pacing at the door as a low growl reverberates deep in his throat.

I head for the door. "It's okay, boy." I reach down and pat him on the head. "Good dog. Now sit."

Scout sits at my heel as I open the door.

A moment later, Maggie strolls inside, followed closely by Owen. Maggie's holding two grocery sacks.

Owen's carrying a weapons bag, which I imagine is well stocked with everything from handguns to a rifle to plenty of ammo. It wouldn't surprise me if there was a semi-automatic or two in there as well.

He sets the bag on the table. I unzip it and snoop around inside. Sure enough, there's an AR-15. *Nice.*

"What?" he asks, sounding almost offended that I'm looking over his inventory.

Grinning, I shake my head. "I'm glad to see you're prepared."

Seemingly satisfied with my reply, Owen nods. "Maggie knows how to shoot a rifle. The AR-15 is for me."

Scout goes from guard dog to welcoming committee as he wags his tail eagerly.

"Hi, Scout," Maggie says as she sets several bags on the table. She reaches down to pat the dog's head. "We brought you guys some groceries. I'll just put these away."

Owen and I shake hands. "Thanks for coming." I've already updated him via text message. He knows the score.

Owen nods. "Not a problem. Maggie's brother, Paul, is watching the store. The boys are still in school for another hour, and Maggie's sister will pick them up after they get out of football practice."

I strap on my chest holster. "I won't be long. I need to have a talk with Hannah's boss." I walk over to the back of the sofa and peer down at Hannah. "Call me if you need anything."

She nods. "I'll be fine. Just be careful. They could be watching the cabin."

I gaze down at her for a moment, reliving the moment of our first real kiss—the touch of her skin and the shape of her breast beneath my palm. I need more of that. A hell of a lot more. But her safety, and comfort, come first—and that means I need to stop mooning over her like a horndog and do my damn job. I reach down and cup her cheek. And then—to hell with our audience—I lean down and kiss her lightly. "I'll be back soon."

As I walk out the front door, I feel Maggie's and Owen's gazes burning a hole in the back of my head.

Yeah, I kissed her. Get over it.

I hop into Hannah's Jeep and plug the address to the conservation center into my phone's mapping program. It's about a twenty-minute drive.

Hannah's lane is heavily wooded on both sides, making it relatively easy for someone with bad intentions to sneak up on the cabin. The property needs surveillance cameras to make it more secure.

As the lane ends at the main road, I hang a right. Here, the road is paved and much easier to navigate, despite the steep hills and sharp turns.

I put in a call to Jake.

He answers immediately. "Killian, how's Hannah?"

"She's fine. The reason I'm calling is to tell you we need some surveillance on the cabin. We've already had two uninvited guests show up at the cabin. I'd like to know someone's coming before they pull up to the front door."

"Got it. I'll send Cameron out there today with some equipment. We'll put cameras on the exterior of the cabin and partway down the lane so you'll have greater visibility."

"Thanks."

"Now tell me about these uninvited guests."

"The first one was Hannah's boss—Ray Calhoun."

"I'll run a background check on him."

"Good. The other was a dark SUV that came up the lane, didn't make contact, and then left. I think they were casing her home, and I suspect they followed Calhoun to her cabin. Either they followed him or he's working with them."

"Shit."

"Yeah. I'm on my way to see Calhoun now to evaluate how much of a risk he is."

"Good. Report back and let me know. In the meanwhile, I'll get Cameron on a flight out there this afternoon."

"Thanks." Just before I'm about to end the call, I check out the vehicle behind me, quite a ways back. It's a black SUV with heavily tinted windows—what a surprise. It's been behind me for a few minutes, and I've been tracking their speed. It matches mine. Whether I speed up or slow down, they keep pace with me, careful to hang back a bit. They've had a couple of opportunities to pass me if they wanted to, but they didn't, and that definitely raises a red flag. "Gotta go, Jake. I have a tail."

Jake mutters a curse. "Copy that. Watch your six, pal."

"Will do. Over and out."

After the call ends, I shoot an update about the possible tail to Owen so he'll be alert. They might be wanting to make sure I'm heading far enough away from Hannah's before they double back, thinking she might be there alone. I have news for them—she's not.

I slow my speed to force their hand. They'll either have to expose themselves or pass me. They opt for the former. Pulling up beside me in the opposite lane, they attempt to run me into the ditch that runs alongside the road. *Fuck that.*

I slam on the gas and shoot forward, my pulse exploding as I charge ahead of them. They race after me, still running alongside me in the opposite lane, still keeping pace. The driver careens into me, scraping against the rear bumper, and the sound of metal on metal is jarring.

Fuck!

This is Hannah's Jeep they're fucking up.

I think they're just trying to scare me off. If they were serious, they would have shot at my tires—or at me—already.

I speed up again, getting a couple of lengths ahead of them, and when they race after me, I slam on the brakes and drop back behind them. The loss of momentum sends me slamming into my seat.

Now it's my turn. I bump them from behind, then edge over to the center of the lane and tap them harder. Their SUV goes nose first into a shallow ditch, and I continue on my way as they flip me off and curse me to the heavens.

Shit. I'm sorry, love. Looks like I owe you a repair job.

When I arrive at the wildlife center, I hop out of the Jeep and survey the damage to the rear end and the front bumper. *Damn it.* Hannah's gonna kill me.

Since there's nothing I can do about it at the moment, I walk inside the building and am greeted by a pretty brunette seated behind a desk. She's wearing the familiar dark green logo shirt that Ray was wearing when he visited. A large spacious room behind us is filled with the chatter of school kids as they race excitedly from one exhibit to another.

"Ray Calhoun," I tell the woman. "Is he in?"

"He's in his office." She nods toward a closed door to her right. The plaque on the door says DIRECTOR. "Do you have an appointment?"

"Nah, 'fraid not."

"Mr. Calhoun is very busy today." She smiles apologetically. "Perhaps I can schedule an appointment for you later in the week."

"That won't be necessary." And then I head straight for his door and knock sharply."

"Come in," comes the muffled response.

I open the door and walk in. Calhoun looks up from his desk, his expression startled. "I'm sorry—I forgot your name."

"Devereaux."

"Right. Mr. Devereaux." Looking a bit perplexed, he stands. "How can I help you?"

I reach back and close the door a bit harder than I mean to. It slams shut with a satisfying crack. "You and I need to have a little talk."

He's looking a bit pale. "All right. What about?"

"Oh, I think you know."

He shakes his head. "Honestly, I have no idea—"

"Don't bullshit me." I do a quick sweep of the office. It's smaller than I expected, and cluttered. The desk is covered with stacks of papers and files and books. Two of the walls are lined with more books, and the third wall is covered in framed diplomas and photographs. There are stacks of boxes against the wall.

I walk over to the wall of photos, and my eyes go to a candid group shot. It doesn't take me long to spot Hannah standing in the center of the group, with Calhoun right beside her. He's got his arm across her shoulders, and he's smiling at her as she laughs.

The bastard.

My attention goes back to Calhoun. I'm easily almost half a foot taller than he is. He's slender, with black hair and brown eyes. His cheeks are shaved smooth. No scar, I notice. But I didn't expect him to be the man who assaulted Hannah up on that ridge. She would have recognized him. Still, there could be a connection.

He gazes up at me, a bit frozen in place. I don't mind intimidating him a bit. I can be a prick when I want to be.

"What can I do for you—Killian, isn't it?"

"That's right."

He points to a guest chair. "Have a seat."

"No, thanks. I'll stand." I can better survey his office environment on my feet. I spot a large glass terrarium on a stand, filled with plants, rocks, pieces of driftwood, and a ceramic water dish. "What's in there?"

"A ball python. One of our staff members found him on a hike. It's not native to this area, and it would never survive our winters, so now he's one of our full-time residents."

"I see." I've learned that a direct approach gets the best results because the subject doesn't see it coming. "So, what's your interest in Hannah?"

Ray flinches as he sits back in his chair. "Excuse me?" His brow wrinkles as if I've just insulted his integrity. "I don't understand the question. She's a valued member of my staff."

"I'm glad to hear it. But I asked what your interest is in *her*, specifically. Is it professional or personal?"

He sputters. "I don't know what you mean. Of course—"

"Cut the crap, Calhoun. I saw the way you looked at her this morning when you stopped by. That wasn't professional interest on your side. It was personal. Do you have a thing for her, or were you worried that maybe your poaching buddies went a little too far?"

His eyes widen and he suddenly looks even paler than before. "I—I—how dare you!" He sucks in a breath. "My relationship with Hannah is none of your business. But if you must know, it's entirely professional. She's an excellent employee and a valued colleague. And as for the poachers, I have no idea who they are. Poaching is a serious crime with serious penalties, and anyone involved in that practice should be dealt with accordingly, as should any criminal."

"Why did you send her up on that ridge when you knew there was a possibility she could run into criminals?"

His eyes widen again. "I never would have sent her up there if I thought for one second she could run into poachers. I would never endanger her."

"Regardless, it was dangerous. *You* put her in harm's way. She could have been killed. She's injured as it is."

He takes a deep breath. "You're right. I never should have sent her up there alone. In hindsight, I don't know what I was thinking. It's just that she always acts so invincible, as if she's not afraid of anything. It just didn't occur to me. I'm sorry." He shudders, looking genuinely shaken. "Honestly, sending her up there is one of my biggest regrets. If anything ever happened to her, I'd never forgive myself. I'm very sorry. It'll never happen again."

"It had better not." I meet his gaze head-on, unrelenting, and he finally looks away. "Now back to the poachers. Do you know who they are? Their identities?"

He shakes his head vehemently. "Don't be ridiculous. If I knew, I'd tell the police."

"Are you working with them?"

"No, of course not."

"Did you know they followed you to Hannah's cabin this morning?"

The shock on his face is pretty authentic, so I'm inclined to believe him. He's not that good of an actor.

He pales. "Are you sure?"

"I'm absolutely sure. They showed up ten minutes after you left. I hardly think that's a coincidence. And on my way here, they tried to tail me."

"Tried?"

I smile. "They weren't successful."

"Oh, my god. I'm so sorry. You've got to believe me when I say I had nothing to do with that."

"Actually, I do believe you. You're not that good of an actor. However, I'm telling you now, they're using you, so be vigilant. If you *ever* bring trouble to Hannah's cabin again, you'll answer to me. Is that clear?"

He nods. "Yes." He looks away nervously and licks his lips. "Please tell Hannah I'm sorry. Please tell her she can have as much time off from work as she needs to recuperate. I'll make sure she's authorized for paid leave. And I'll be more careful when I come visit her."

"How about you don't visit her? If she wants to see you, she'll make arrangements to see you here. How about that?"

"Of course. That makes the most sense." He turns pained eyes on me, bereft of any guile. He truly looks deflated. "Hannah is such an amazing young woman. I wouldn't do anything to hurt her, I swear."

"I believe you." And I do believe him. It's pretty clear he's smitten with her.

"Keep your distance from her until this whole matter is resolved, all right?"

"Of course. Please tell her—"

I head for the door, taking hold of the knob and turning it. "I'll pass on your regards." And then I'm out the door, closing it behind me.

When I'm back in the Jeep, I receive a text message from Jake.

Jake: Cameron is on his way to your location with equipment. ETA three hours.

Killian: Copy. Thanks.

Fortunately, despite the damage to the front and back of the Jeep, the engine starts right up. The drive back to the cabin is uneventful. I pass the spot where the SUV went into the ditch, and it's gone. Other than some ruts in the ground, there's no sign they were ever there.

I call Owen. "I'm on my way back. My ETA is twenty minutes. Everything okay?"

"Fine," Owen says. "No problems."

"Ask Hannah if she wants me to pick up anything in town on my way back."

Owen mutes the phone for a moment. Then he comes back with, "She said how about hot wings and beer from Ruth's? The tavern is next to the grocery store. Oh, and she said pretty please."

I laugh. "All right. Have her call the order in."

"Copy," Owen says. "We'll see you when you get here."

I end the call and stow my phone. "She can have any damn thing she wants," I mutter to myself with a stupid grin on my face. I'd move heaven and earth to make that girl happy.

౿ 23

Hannah McIntyre

Maggie waits until Owen, with a shotgun cradled in his arm, steps outside with Scout and closes the door. "Oh, my god, he fucking kissed you!" she practically squeals, sounding far more like an excited teenager than a grown woman with two teenagers. "I can't believe it."

I smile. "And, we might have been making out just before you guys arrived."

Maggie looks dumbfounded. "Deets, girl. Give me the deets. I want to know everything."

I shrug. "You know I've had a thing for him for a long time."

"Yes, and he has a thing for you, too. Get to the point—what happened? Did you have sex?"

I laugh. "No, we didn't. But we have kissed, several times. It would have gone further, but I hurt my ankle."

Maggie sits back in the rocker and shakes her head. "I leave you two alone for one day, and you end up sucking face."

"And he copped a feel," I say, remembering how it felt when his thumb brushed my nipple. "Does that count?"

"Oh, my god. This is fantastic, Hannah. The guy's a dreamboat. You need to jump on him."

I glance down at the lovely fiberglass cast that will be with me for the next six weeks. "That would be a bit difficult right now."

Maggie instantly dismisses my comment. "Don't be silly. You can improvise."

When my stomach growls loud enough that Maggie can hear it, we both laugh.

"At least your hunger isn't affected by a broken ankle," she says. "But seriously, now what? Are you two an item?"

I shrug. "It seems that way. I think it's fair to say we both want to give it a try. He knows how I feel about moving back to Chicago, and he said that wasn't a roadblock for him."

"You think he'd move here? To Bryce?"

"It's possible. He said he wasn't tied to Chicago. I hate to have him uproot—"

"Stop right there. If the man is willing to relocate for you, then embrace it. Men like Killian don't come along every day,

Hannah."

"What about you?"

She looks puzzled. "What about me?"

"You and Owen—"

She throws up a hand. "Stop right there. There's nothing going on between me and Owen. Yes, he's an amazing guy. Yes, he's gorgeous and kind and smart, and he has muscles that won't quit. But no. I'm old enough to be his mother."

I snort out a laugh. "You are not! You can't be more than—what—five years older than Owen. Max."

She shrugs. "That's plenty. I'm a middle-aged, divorced woman with two nearly grown sons."

"So?"

"What d'you mean, so? I told you, it's not happening. Come on, Hannah. You've seen the guy. He could have *anyone*."

"If you say so."

"I do. And I don't want to hear another word about it." Maggie makes a face. "Be serious, Hannah. If Owen walked into Ruth's, he'd be instantly waylaid by every single woman in town, and you know it. I'm talking younger, prettier, single girls. They'd be all over him. Why in the world would he be interested in me? I come with teenagers and lots of baggage, including an ex-husband who's in prison."

"Okay. I won't say another word." I mime zipping my lips shut and tossing away the key.

"Thank you," she says. "Now, how about some coffee? I could sure use a cup."

While Maggie's in the kitchen pouring our coffee, the door opens, and Owen and Scout come in. Scout races over to the sofa to greet me, shoving his wet nose into my hands. His tail thrashes back and forth, thwacking the coffee table leg in the process.

Owen hangs his shotgun on the wall gun rack. He looks a bit windblown. Maggie and I watch as he lets his hair down, fingercombs the long ash-blond strands, and gathers them up in a neat manbun, which he secures with a black hair tie.

"It's pretty windy out there," he says, oblivious to the fact that he just had an audience. "We might be gettin' some more bad weather tonight."

"I wouldn't be surprised," she says as she winks at me. "September weather in Colorado is unpredictable."

Owen walks up to the kitchen island counter, which separates him from Maggie. "Anything I can do to help?" he asks her.

She grabs the sugar bowl out of the cupboard. "Want some coffee?"

"Yes, ma'am," he says, sounding grateful. "I'd love some." When Maggie busies herself getting creamer out of the fridge, Owen turns his attention to me. "I'm supposed to tell you that someone named Cameron is on his way here from Chicago to install outdoor surveillance cameras."

While waiting for his coffee, Owen adds more wood to the stove and stokes the fire. When his cup is ready, he sits quietly on the stone hearth and drinks his coffee as Scout lies adoringly at his feet.

Maggie sits in the rocking chair, her hot mug cradled in both hands as she savors every sip.

Owen's eyes are on her, and hers are on me. I honestly can't tell if she's utterly clueless as to his interest in her or simply in denial.

When Owen finishes his coffee, he carries his cup to the sink, washes it, and sets it in the dish rack to dry. "How 'bout I take the dog back outside for some exercise?" he asks me. "I'll have him run the agility course a few times to wear him out a bit."

"Thank you, Owen." As soon as he and Scout are out the front door, I turn to Maggie.

"Don't you even start," she says before I can get a word out. She gets up and takes her empty coffee cup to the kitchen.

Well, that answers my question. She's not clueless. She's avoiding the issue.

While Maggie putzes around in the kitchen, killing time, I haul myself up onto my crutches and make my way painstakingly to the bathroom to relieve my bladder and freshen up by brushing my hair and teeth. Killian should be home soon.

When I swing my way out of the bathroom—I think I'm starting to get the hang of using these crutches—I find the front door wide open and the cabin empty. My heart stops a minute, and then my pulse starts racing. "Maggie?"

Maggie pops her head in the open doorway. "Oh, sorry. I stepped outside to watch Scout run the agility course."

I shuffle toward her and step outside onto the front porch. I think it's the first time I've been outside since getting home from the hospital.

"Here, sit down before you fall down," Maggie says, directing me to the wooden swing hanging from the covered ceiling. She holds the swing steady while I lower myself onto the bench seat. Then she takes my crutches from me and leans them against the porch railing.

Across the yard, Owen is guiding Scout through the agility course, although it doesn't look like Scout needs any instructions. He's racing through the obstacle course with ease.

"I think you need to make the course harder for him," Maggie says to me.

When Scout finishes the course, Owen throws a tennis ball across the yard, and Scout tears after it.

When we hear tires crunching on the gravel lane, Scout freezes and turns to face the source of the sound.

Owen reaches into the back waistband of his jeans and takes hold of a black handgun, which he holds casually to his side. "Maybe you ladies should go inside."

"It's okay. It's just Killian," I say, staring at the front end of my Jeep as it pulls into view. It doesn't take me long to notice that the front corner bumper is dented badly.

Scout runs to the driver's door and waits for Killian to exit, his tail wagging eagerly.

Owen walks over to Killian, and the two of them have a rather lengthy conversation. Then Killian hands Owen two sacks of food to carry inside. Killian grabs a carton of beer.

"Food's ready," Killian says as he holds up the beer for me to inspect. "Ruth said this is your favorite." And then he steps up onto the porch and stops in front of me. "You doin' okay?"

"I'm fine, but what about you?" I nod to my Jeep. "Did you run into a bit of trouble? I don't remember my bumper being crushed like that."

Killian winces as he hands the carton of beer to Maggie, who carries it inside. Then he helps me stand and hands me the crutches. "Good thing it's reinforced," he says with a guilty grimace. "Somebody tried to run me off the road, so I returned the favor."

My eyes widen. "Were you successful?"

"I was. They went nose first into a shallow ditch." He leans in and kisses my forehead. "Sorry about the damage to your Jeep. The rear bumper is toast, too. I'll get it fixed. At least it still runs fine."

I shake my head in disbelief. Someone tried to run him off the road, and he talks like it's nothing but a big inconvenience. "I assume it was the poachers."

He shrugs. "Who else? I didn't get a good look at them or a license plate number."

"How'd it go with Ray?"

"I was right—he has a crush on you. But I agree Ray's on the level. I think the poachers were using him to find you."

"I knew he wasn't involved with criminals."

Killian's hands cup my face. "You can't be too careful, love." He gazes down intently into my eyes. "Would you be opposed to me kissing you? Just to make sure it was as amazing as I remember it?"

I love how he makes me laugh. "I'm okay with that."

He gives me a kiss—a hello kiss—like he's glad to be home. It's all very domestic. His lips are soft, yet firm, a little bossy as he nudges mine open so his tongue can slide in against mine.

"Mm," he says. "You taste like peppermint." He deepens the kiss, and all I can think about is his mouth on mine. One of his hands slips around to the back of my head, and the other slides down to cup my waist. Gently, he draws me against him, steadying me, until our bodies are pressed flush together. His erection nudges my belly, and the feel of his hardness makes my belly quiver.

"Ahem." Maggie clears her throat. "Are you guys coming to eat before the food gets cold?"

We break apart, and Killian catches me when I start to lose my balance. "We're coming," he says.

24

Killian Devereaux

Cameron Stewart, another one of the guys on Jake's team, arrives around four-thirty that afternoon in a rented SUV filled with surveillance equipment. He walks in the door and wipes his boots off on the welcome mat. "Hello, Hannah. I'm glad to hear you're doing all right."

"Hi, Cameron," she replies. "I'm doing well, thanks to this guy." She points my way. "Thanks for coming out on such short notice."

"No problem," he says.

I introduce him to Owen and Maggie, and then he and I

head outside to survey the property and make a plan.

"I hear you're staying a while," he says to me once we're outside. "Until this is resolved?"

I nod. "I'm staying indefinitely, if I have my way."

"Yeah?" He nods toward the cabin. His brows rise. "You and Hannah, huh?"

I nod. "Yep."

He claps me on the back. "I'm happy for you, man. Congratulations."

It takes us a whole ten minutes to figure out where we want to place the cameras so that we'll pick up any movement in the yard, as well as any vehicles coming up the lane. Owen comes outside to join us, and with the three of us working, we have the cameras installed in no time. They're wireless, and we connect them to Hannah's wireless router. It's a pretty easy setup.

Hannah and Maggie come out to sit on the front porch while we wrap up the installation. I download the monitoring app on her phone and show her how it works. If she needs to, she can summon the police from the app. Hopefully, it'll never come to that.

After all the work is done, we sit outside on the porch and celebrate with cold drinks. Scout's in heaven, having so many people to play with. Owen gets roped into throwing the ball until his arm aches.

Finally, just after dark, Cameron heads back to Denver to catch his return flight. Owen and Maggie say their goodbyes, too, and we're left alone.

Finally.

"I thought they'd never leave," I say with an exaggerated sigh.

Hannah's lying lengthwise on the sofa so she can stretch out her legs and get comfortable. Her cast is propped up on a pillow. She nods toward her cast. "Three days down. Only thirty-nine more to go."

I sit on the coffee table and face her. "Be patient, love. Your body needs time to heal." Then I check the dressing on her arm to make sure it's still healing nicely. "You'll be good as new in no time."

We sit for a minute, facing each other, as the tension and anticipation grow thick in the air.

"It's getting late," I say. "I should take Scout outside one last time before bed."

She nods. "Good idea."

When Scout and I return, I find the sofa empty. It's after ten now, and I know she's tired, so I lock up the cabin, check that the cameras are functioning correctly, and turn off the lights.

I see a light underneath the bathroom door. "Everything okay in there?"

"Yes."

"Need any help?"

She hesitates in answering, but I wait patiently. I have a feeling we're entering new territory tonight. I don't want to rush her or pressure her. We'll take this at her pace. She can have all the time she needs.

Finally, almost apologetically, she says, "Actually, I do need some help."

Trying not to feel jubilant, I turn the doorknob and find it unlocked. "Can I come in?"

"Yes, please. If you don't mind."

I stifle a laugh. *Do I mind? Is she kidding?* I slowly push open the door and step inside a warm, steamy room. The lights over the bathroom counter are off, but there's a small lamp on, casting just a little bit of light. Hannah's sitting in the bathtub, naked as the day she was born, her cast propped up on the side of the tub, resting on a folded towel. At least she's keeping it dry.

"I got myself into the tub," she says, "but I'm finding it impossible to get out on my own. If I try to lift myself up, I slip back in."

I can't hold back my smile. "I'd be happy to help you."

She shakes her head. "You're loving this, aren't you?"

"Of course I am," I say, grinning. "I got kisses today, I copped a feel, and now I'm getting an eyeful. At this rate, who knows what I'll accomplish before midnight. You've practically made all my dreams come true."

Raising her arms to me, she laughs. "I warn you, you're gonna get wet."

"Shouldn't that be my line?"

I'd swear she's blushing, but it's hard to tell because the bathroom is so warm and her cheeks are flushed.

She's already let the water out of the tub, and now she's sitting there shivering, her wet skin covered with goose pimples. I grab a dry towel off the rack, cover her with it, and slip one arm behind her back, the other beneath her knees, careful not to jar her ankle. I'm trying hard not to peek at her naked body, but that's a mighty tall order when I see miles and miles of smooth skin. There'll be time enough for that later. Right now, she just needs my help, not me gawking at her.

As I carry her out of the bathroom, she tries her best to arrange the towel over her naked body.

My chest rumbles with suppressed amusement. "Don't worry, love. I'm not looking."

She laughs. "You're a guy. Of course you're looking."

Busted. I did notice a few curves. "Well, I'm trying not to."

I carry her into the bedroom and set her on the floor beside the bed, holding her steady as she balances on one foot and quickly dries herself off. Somehow she manages to keep the towel strategically placed over her breasts and pussy. "Well done, Hannah. I hardly got a peek at anything."

She rolls her eyes at me but quickly redirects her attention when I pull my shirt up and over my head. Her eyes lock onto my bare chest, and I swear I can literally feel the heat of her gaze on my skin.

"I should grab a quick shower," I tell her as I back out of the room. "You stay put."

She nods but says nothing for a change. I think she's getting nervous. I guess that makes two of us. Whatever happens between us tonight, or any night, I want it to be good for her.

I take a quick shower, scrubbing myself briskly from head

to toe. I don't know what tonight will bring—maybe nothing—probably nothing—but I want to be prepared. After helping Cameron mount all those surveillance cameras, I'm a bit sweaty.

After my shower, I dry my body and hair with a towel and finger comb my hair into some degree of order. It's pretty short, so that's not too hard. I return to the bedroom wearing nothing but the towel wrapped around my waist because, like an idiot, I forgot to bring clean clothes with me into the bathroom.

I find Hannah sitting up in bed, supported by a pillow propped against the headboard. The sheet is pulled up to cover her breasts, and her arms are crossed over her chest. Her dark brown hair is loose on her shoulders, slightly damp and wavy from her bath.

I lean against the doorjamb. "You look beautiful."

She smiles. "So do you."

Pushing away from the door, I nod toward my duffle bag. "I forgot to grab clean clothes." I locate a pair of boxer-briefs, drop my towel, and pull them on. "Is this okay?"

She nods. "Sure. I sleep in my underwear, too."

Oh, fuck.

She would have to say that. I'm already hard, and I'm sure she can tell because the fabric of my briefs can only hide so much. "Look, I don't want to be presumptuous. You tell me what you want and don't want tonight, okay?"

She tosses the sheet aside, and to my surprise, she's wearing black bikini underwear and a black bra.

"How did you manage that?"

"I put them on while you were in the shower. I didn't want to be presumptuous either."

I flip the light switch off and stalk toward her, skirting around the foot of the bed to what has become my side. She follows me with her gaze as I climb onto the mattress, on my hands and knees, and prowl closer. "We're not having sex," I say. "I thought I'd throw that out there for the sake of clarity."

Honest to god, she looks disappointed. "We're not?"

I shake my head. "I can't risk hurting your ankle."

"What if we're really careful?"

"Nope. However, never fear, I promise I'll take care of you in other ways."

After propping her cast up on a pillow, I lie down next to her and lean over her, my mouth just inches from hers. "I'm going to kiss you."

She laughs. "I don't see anyone trying to stop you."

"Just wanted to be clear. You've told me no so many times before, and I don't want us to get our wires crossed."

She reaches up to thread her fingers through my damp hair, her short nails digging into my scalp and sending sparks of electricity down my spine. My balls tighten as my dick swells.

"I'm telling you yes now," she says. "Is that clear enough?"

Hell yes, it is. I kiss her forehead, then trail my lips down the bridge of her nose to settle on her soft lips. She sucks in a shaky breath and tightens her grip on my hair. She starts kissing me hungrily, like a woman who knows exactly what she wants, and her hunger only stokes mine.

I slip one hand behind her head and cover a breast with my other hand. Her lush nipple puckers when I brush my thumb over the fabric of her bra. Arching her back, she groans into my mouth.

I keep reminding myself to slow down—to be careful—but my ability to think clearly has gone out the window. This is *Hannah*, for god's sake. I'm in bed with Hannah—a place I never thought I'd be.

She takes matters into her own hands when she peels back the cup of her bra, exposing her bare breast and pressing it into my palm. Her nipple is a dusky pink bud, puckered up sweetly. I can't help drawing it into my mouth and flicking it with my tongue. When I suckle her gently, she tightens her fingers in my hair, pulling hard enough to make me grimace. Her hips start moving and she's making these incredible sounds that are driving me insane. My cock is aching now, hard as a fucking rock, and I'm desperate to sink inside her.

I release her nipple and take a deep breath. "Slow down, *couyon*," I mutter to myself.

Slow down, idiot.

"What?" she murmurs, still distracted.

"Nothing." And then I kiss her.

She skims a hand down my back, her nails digging into my muscles, and when she reaches my ass and grabs a handful, I know it's time to up my game before I lose all control of the situation.

As I pull away, our mouths separate, and she makes a plaintive sound.

"I got you, love," I tell her as I slip down the bed to the spot between her thighs. Her scent fills my nose, making me even harder.

Damn.

Careful of her cast, I nestle myself between her supple legs, shifting her good leg over to make room for my shoulders. When she realizes where I'm headed, she's only too happy to help me out. I brush her belly button with my nose, and she lets out a rushed breath. Then I skim down to her bikini line and tease the waistband with one finger.

"God, yes," she says breathily as she raises her hips off the mattress. "Take them off, Killian."

I'm starting to think she put them on just so I'd have to take them off. Her fingers are back in my hair, both hands gripping and tugging, full of demand. *God, I knew she'd be like this—direct. Not afraid to ask for what she needed from me.*

I press my nose against the warm gusset of her underwear, right between her lush lips, and breathe her in. Her scent makes my dick throb and my balls ache. When I lick her through the fabric, then blow hot air on her, she starts squirming in earnest.

"Lie still," I warn her. "You'll hurt your ankle."

"Forget about my ankle, Killian," she growls.

Double damn.

I like a girl who knows what she wants and isn't afraid to demand it.

After pulling the little strip of fabric aside, exposing her plump lips, I swipe a tongue through the silky wetness between them. She's already so perfectly fucking wet. I want to devour her.

"Take them off," she gasps as she rocks her hips.

Yes, ma'am. I kneel and work her underwear down her good leg. She bends her knee to make that easier. Then I gently pull them down her other leg and over the cast. When I settle back down, she opens herself to me. She's as hungry for this as I am. As I lick and tease her, she shows me where she wants my tongue. As I tease her clit, I slip a finger inside her slick opening. She cries out loudly, lifting her hips.

I lightly smack her ass. "I said lie still."

She lets out a frustrated groan. "For god's sake, Killian, I'm not going to break."

She tugs on my hair, urging me to rise up over her. I do as she wants, my thighs cradled between hers. When my erection presses against her opening, we both groan.

She reaches between us and wraps her fingers around my erection. "There are condoms in the top drawer of my nightstand."

I groan harshly. "Remember, we're not having sex tonight. It's too soon. Your ankle—"

She presses her wet heat against my trapped erection, rubbing herself against me. "In the nightstand, top drawer," she repeats.

"*Merde.*" *Shit.* "I only have so much willpower, you know,"

I say, laughing. How in the hell am I supposed to do the right thing when she's offering herself to me?

"I know. That's why you're going to get a condom."

"Fuck." I reach across her and open the top drawer, fishing around blindly until I find a box. I pull it out and hand it to her.

She promptly removes a packet, tears it open, and says, "Take off your briefs."

I do as she asks, whipping them off as quickly as I can. She rolls the condom onto my length.

I lean down and kiss her, my lips nudging hers open so I can slide my tongue against hers. She grips my head, panting against my mouth. We're both breathing hard.

"Inside me, please," she rasps. "Now."

Merde. "Yes, ma'am." I reach down to fist my cock and direct it to her opening.

She raises her hips as I slowly sink into her, working myself deeper and deeper. She's so soft and wet, her body ready and welcoming. We both groan in pleasure.

I start to move, slowly at first, giving her a chance to get used to my size. I'm a big guy, in all aspects, as she quickly realizes. She gasps when I sink inside her.

I brush her hair back from her forehead. "Okay?"

She nods. "It's fine," she breathes. "I'm fine."

I keep my thrusts slow and measured, gliding carefully inside her as her body adjusts to me.

When her nails scrape down my back to my ass, and she digs in, I take it she's ready for more. I pick up the pace, carefully at first, but she's encouraging me to move faster, harder, deeper.

"Killian, god, yes," she breathes. Her words are followed quickly by a keening whimper. "Harder! Please."

Damn, that's all the encouragement I need to let myself go. To let myself feel this incredible pleasure of being surrounded in her tight, wet heat. She's slick with desire, her hips raising to meet mine, and we're both straining together.

When she slips her fingers between us and strokes herself, I about lose my damn mind. Watching her tease her clit while I power into her is more than I can take.

"Fuck!" I growl, arching my back, throwing back my head as my orgasm rips through me.

"Killian," she gasps as her body tightens on me, her sex clamping down on my cock.

I feel the ripples of her climax all along my shaft, and it's perfect. *We're* perfect together. Our bodies are so in tune with each other. Her cries of pleasure are the sweetest sound I can imagine.

When my climax wanes, I slow my thrusts. Her muscles go limp, her arms falling to her sides. After pulling out, I leave the bed to dispose of the condom, wash my hands, and return quickly to rejoin her in bed.

"Come here, love," I say as I wrap her in my arms.

I pick up the empty condom wrapper, which I find lying discarded in the bed. "I hope there are plenty more where this came from."

She laughs. "An entire box of them."

25

Hannah McIntyre

Being with Killian is like nothing I've ever experienced before. He's all-consuming. He's all strength and power and stamina, and yet he's also a considerate lover. Everything about Killian is big—his arms, his chest, his legs. And, appropriately, so is his cock. I noticed that when I rolled the condom onto him.

After Killian disposes of the condom, he crawls back into bed and lies close to my side. He presses a kiss to my temple, then runs his fingers through my hair. "If your brothers knew what I just did to you, they'd have my head."

I laugh. "They'd probably give you a medal."

"I seriously doubt that."

"I mean it. They've been talking you up to me for months."

"You're kidding me."

"I'm serious. Especially Shane."

"I'll be damned."

"He thinks we have a lot in common."

"We do."

"My family doesn't like the idea of me living out here all alone. They think I need a man to protect me."

He chuckles. "I don't think you need any help at all, unless you're being chased by poachers."

"Touché. I guess we all need someone at some point in our lives."

He runs his finger lightly down the side of my face, tracing the curve of my cheek and following it down to my throat. "I admire you for following your own path in life," he says. "That takes guts, and you have it in spades."

I turn to face him and gaze up into his dark eyes. He has a handsome face, with strong cheekbones. When I cup his face and stroke his beard, which is surprisingly soft, he closes his eyes and leans into my hand.

Just looking at him makes me breathless. I let my fingers trace the outline of his biceps, then run my fingers down his forearm to his hand and link our fingers. His tatts are sexy as hell, full sleeves that end at his wrists. Just looking at him makes me hot and bothered.

I lie quietly, still feeling the residual pulses of desire coursing through my body. My sex is tingling still, and I feel a bit of a burn from being stretched.

"I should check your sutures," he says, getting up and grabbing the first-aid kit. He quickly redresses my injury, cleaning it and applying a fresh bandage. "Do you need to pee?"

I bite my bottom lip to keep from smiling. He sure has a way with words. But he's practical, and I appreciate that. "I probably should."

Without a word, he scoops me into his arms, carries me to the bathroom, and sits me on the toilet. "Holler when you're done," he says as he leaves the room and waits out in the hallway, giving me some much-appreciated privacy.

When I'm done, I pull myself up onto my good foot and wash my hands. I also take the opportunity to brush my teeth again. "Can you grab my crutches, please?"

"You don't need crutches when you have me." And then he walks into the bathroom, as naked as the day he was born, and scoops me up in his brawny arms. I catch a glimpse of our reflection in the mirror, and my belly flutters deliciously. All that bare skin, and all those muscles. It's intoxicating.

He carries me to bed and lays me down gently, then climbs over me to his side of the bed. After arranging my cast on the pillow, he draws the bedding up over us and leans in to kiss the side of my neck, just below my ear. I shiver in response and suck in a dizzying breath.

"I told Owen about us today. Cameron, too."

I smile. It's like we're in middle school. "I told Maggie."

Seeming satisfied with that announcement, he nods. "Good. They might as well know we're together—because we are, right?" His gaze locks onto me with the singular focus of a laser.

I can't believe I'm going to say this. I can't believe I'm doing this. Because even though I think this might be a bad idea—even though I'm afraid he'll regret it—I can't walk away from this chance to be with the most exciting man I've ever known. "Yeah, we are."

He nods, apparently satisfied with my response. "Just wanted to make sure we're on the same page. *Tu es ma petite amie, oui?*"

"I'm your *girlfriend?*" My French is rusty, but I think that's what he said.

He nods.

"Then, yes, I am."

He reaches past me to turn off the lamp and settles beside me in bed. "*Bonne nuit*, Hannah."

"Goodnight, Killian."

Scout jumps onto the bed and curls up at our feet, and we're one big happy family.

* * *

I wake with a panic, clawing at the hand that's covering my mouth.

"Shh," comes a low whisper in the darkness. He sucks in a breath—I think I drew blood. "Don't make a sound."

Killian slowly removes his hand from over my mouth. "The cameras are going apeshit." He holds up his phone and shows me the series of alert notifications taking up his phone screen. "Someone's outside."

As he quietly gets out of bed, I glance at the digital clock on my nightstand. It's three-thirty. No one should be outside my cabin at this god-awful hour. I sit up and turn so that my good foot is on the floor and I'm able to open the second drawer of my nightstand and grab my spare handgun.

Out of the corner of my eye, I notice Killian yanking on his black boxer-briefs. He grabs a tee and a pair of jeans off the floor and dons them quickly.

"Where's my underwear?" I mutter as I hunt around in the dark.

Killian tosses them to me. "Get dressed quietly and stay in the bedroom with Scout." When he comes to me, he's dressed, and his gun is holstered onto his chest. I watch in the dim lighting as he inserts an earpiece then clips a small black radio to his jeans. He tucks my hair behind one ear and inserts a similar device in mine, then hands me the radio.

He grabs my underwear out of my hands and works the left leg hole over my cast. I slip my right foot into the other leg hole and pull it up. He grabs my knit shorts and T-shirt lying on the seat of a chair and helps me dress. Then he clips a radio to my waistband, switches it on, and tucks earbuds into my ears.

"Can you hear me?" he whispers into his own mic.

I nod as I adjust the volume on the radio and click my mic button. "Yes. I mean copy."

He starts to move to the door, but I snag his hand. "I'm coming with you," I hiss.

He grasps my jaw firmly and stares hard into my eyes. "You stay right here, love." His voice is sharp. He cups my face and leans in to kiss my forehead. "I mean it, Hannah. You stay." And then he's gone, shutting the door quietly behind him.

"Fuck that," I mutter as I retrieve my crutches and push myself up onto my feet. I swing over to the only window in the bedroom and, standing to the side, crack the curtain just enough that I can peer out into the night. Thanks to heavy cloud cover tonight, there's not much moonlight to speak of. Scout paces in front of the bedroom door, huffing softly, and I listen for any sounds coming from outside. I hear nothing.

I'm not about to sit in here like a good little girl while Killian takes all the risk. If the poachers are here, there are at least two of them, possibly more. That's two-to-one, not in Killian's favor. If I help him, at least we can even the score.

"I count at least two at the tree line," he says quietly in my earpiece. "And I see the front bumper of the black SUV. I want you to call the sheriff's office."

"Roger," I say as I grab my phone and put it on silent. I've got Sheriff Nelson's office on speed dial. When a dispatcher answers, I fill her in. Then I tuck my phone into my pocket.

"Done," I tell him over the radio.

"Good. Now hunker down and stay out of sight. I'll hold them off until reinforcements arrive."

I never was one to follow instructions—just ask my parents. I crack open the bedroom door and listen. Nothing. Scout is eager to break out of the room, but I hold him back with one of my crutches. If anyone's going to get shot, it's a hotheaded puppy barking his head off at armed strangers.

Carefully, I slip through the door and close it behind me, shutting Scout in. Fortunately, he doesn't bark.

The cabin interior is dark, but I know my way around by heart. I shuffle down the hallway to the living area. There's barely any moonlight coming through the front windows, but it's enough that I can see that my shotgun is missing from the rack on the wall. And there's no sign of Killian in the cabin. He must be outside already. Damn it! He's out there alone, with no backup.

My heart practically stops when I hear two shots in rapid succession, then three more, followed by a muffled grunt of pain.

Shit!

I creep toward the living room window to peer outside. From where I'm standing, the porch is empty. There's no sign of Killian or the poachers. I'm working in the dark here, and I don't know how to help him.

Then I remember the app on my phone that shows the sur-veillance camera feeds. I open it and quickly flip through the live feeds—one just down the lane, showing the front end of a black SUV. There are feeds showing all four sides of the cabin, plus two encompassing the big front yard.

I don't see anyone, which makes it difficult for me to know what I should do. I don't see anyone behind the cabin, but I can't very well climb out a window with a broken ankle. My only way of getting out is through the front door, and that might make me a sitting duck—which would only endanger Killian in the process.

I spot movement along the side of my Jeep—it's Killian. He's facing the SUV. The intruders must be behind their vehicle.

When Killian raises his head just enough to see over the hood of the Jeep, two more shots are fired from the direction of the other vehicle. Killian drops back down after firing a shot of his own. It's a stand-off, two against one. He's keeping them from coming closer to the cabin.

If it weren't for my ankle, I could slip out a back window and make my way through the woods and come up behind the poachers. Then we'd have them cut off, trapped between us, and we'd just have to hold them there until the cops arrived.

The radio crackles quietly, and then I hear Killian's voice. "Stay in the bedroom." His voice is calm and quiet. "Owen's on his way. Please don't shoot him."

I suppress a laugh. "Copy."

Then we hear police sirens, multiple vehicles approaching, followed by the sound of an engine revving as the SUV makes a three-point turn and heads back down the lane to the main road, away from the cabin. Undoubtedly, they're hoping they can disappear before the cops pen them in.

When Killian stands, his posture relaxed, it's my signal that they're gone.

I open the front door and swing out onto the porch. "Chickenshits."

He comes up onto the porch, taking the steps two at a time, and walks me back into the cabin, shutting the door behind us and barring it. He leans down to get in my face. "What the hell happened to staying in the bedroom?" he growls at me.

"It was two against one. That's hardly fair."

He starts to retort but, instead, snaps his jaws shut and shakes his head. "I guess it's to be expected."

"What is?"

"That you don't listen. You're a McIntyre. It's in your DNA."

"Killian, I am not about to sit back and let—"

Lifting me, he sits me on the table and steps between my legs. "Of course not. You're a force of nature, and that's what I love about you." He steps closer, pressing himself against me and wrapping me in his strong arms. "Did you hurt yourself?"

"No. My ankle is fine." I'm ignoring the fact that he said the L-word. He doesn't seem one bit fazed by what he said. He doesn't even attempt to take it back or make a joke of it. Instead, his fingers thread through my hair, and he kisses me. Not a light kiss, but a deep, soulful kiss that does something to me. My chest tightens, and I can't catch my breath.

Headlights flood the front of the cabin as several cars pull into the yard. Killian abandons me momentarily to glance outside. "Two police cruisers and Owen. Looks like the chicken-shits got away."

That makes me chuckle.

He returns to the table and sets me on my good foot before he hands me my crutches. "Come on, McIntyre."

I like that. I think if he'd called me baby or sweetie, I might have punched him.

By the time I make my way outside onto the porch, Killian is deep in conversation with three uniformed deputies, Sheriff Nelson—who must have been roused from a sound sleep because he's out of uniform and his hair is sticking up in tufts—and Owen, who looks equally disheveled.

Owen glances my way and gives me a silent nod, which I return.

I guess if the poachers are here, they can't be harassing Maggie. Still, I worry about her. I motion Owen over, and he joins me on the porch. "If you're here, who's with Maggie?"

"Ruth is with Maggie and the boys. Between the four of them, they're armed to the teeth."

"Good. I just wanted to be sure. Thanks for watching out for my friend."

Look a bit bashful, he nods. "You don't need to thank me. I'm happy to do it." He glances out into the yard at Killian and the officers. "It looks like you're in good hands here, so I should get back." He turns to go.

As Owen walks to his vehicle, Killian joins me on the porch, slipping his arm around me and drawing me close. We wave as the sheriff and deputies leave, Owen, too.

Killian nudges the cabin open, then swings me up into his arms and carries me inside. I laugh as I grapple with the crutches.

"Back to bed with you," Killian says, carrying me to the bedroom.

26

Killian Devereaux

After everyone leaves, I call Jake with an update because this is definitely something he needs to know. It's five-thirty in the morning his time; hopefully it's not too early to call.

"Devereaux, what is it?" he answers in a deep, raspy voice. Yeah, I woke him up. A sleepy female voice in the background asks him what's wrong.

I give him a succinct rundown of the night's events. "The important thing is Hannah's fine, despite the fact she doesn't listen and doesn't follow instructions."

Jake laughs hoarsely. "You sound like every teacher she's ever had."

"Yeah, well, the bad news is that the chickenshits got away, and we're no closer to identifying them. The cops missed them by minutes."

Jake snorts. "Chickenshits?"

"That's Hannah's name for them."

"Figures. All right. Good work. Stay frosty. I know the sheriff's office is working hard on this. Hopefully they'll have a breakthrough soon. In the meantime, your number one priority is Hannah's safety. Leave the police work to the cops. You stick to Hannah like glue. Is that clear?"

"Crystal." *As if he needed to tell me that.*

"Good. Send her my love. We'll talk again soon."

After ending the call, I double-check that all the windows are locked and the front door is barred. I toss more wood into the stove before heading back to the bedroom. Hannah's already there, lying on top of the covers in just her panties and a T-shirt, her cast propped up on the designated pillow. Her long legs are bare, and seeing all that beautiful skin makes my pulse skyrocket. "Aren't you cold?"

"Are you kidding? I'm overheated from all the excitement."

"And your ankle?"

She huffs out a breath. "Fine, for the umpteenth time."

"Just checking." I make a quick pit stop in the bathroom, then return to bed and crawl in beside her. In his post-adrenaline state, Scout's anxiously pacing the room. "Come here, pal,"

I say, patting the mattress. "Settle down and go to sleep."

Scout jumps up onto the bed, circles a few times, then lies down at the foot of the bed. He lets out one tired *woof* before dropping his head onto the mattress.

Hannah sits up to scratch the dog behind his ears. "Good boy. Don't let cranky Killian bother you. He's sleep deprived."

"I am *not* cranky."

She lies back down and turns to me. "Then what are you?"

I realize I'm tense as hell and my voice is overly curt. I make an effort to soften it. "Sorry. I'm not used to this."

Her brow furrows. "How are you not used to this? You're in the security field. Surely your days are filled with all sorts of danger and excitement."

I reach over to trace the curve of her cheek, then one eyebrow and the other. "I'm used to danger and excitement, yeah. What I'm not used to is being afraid."

She scoffs. "You're not afraid of anything, Killian."

I roll up onto my elbow to get closer and drop a kiss on her cheek, then on the tip of her nose, then a peck on her lips, which are curving up into a smile. "You. I'm afraid of you."

She laughs. "Bullshit."

"You're fearless, which makes you prone to recklessness. I'm afraid of something happening to you."

She turns to me with a smile that makes my heart stutter and presses her lips to mine. "I'm not reckless, but I was afraid for you out there alone, facing off with at least two armed men and possibly more. I had to do what I could to help. I couldn't just sit idly by and let you take all the risk."

"You're such a McIntyre—ready to run into a burning building, no questions asked."

She smiles. "Hey, don't knock it. That's how my dad met my mom. She ran into a burning building—literally—and he, a firefighter, ran in after her to pull her out. So yeah, we protect the people we care about, no matter the risk."

I love the fervor in her voice. "So, does this mean you care about me?"

She sucks in a breath. "To be honest, I'm pretty enamored of you. Earlier, you said you loved that I was a force of nature. You said that was *one* of the things you love about me."

"There are quite a few things." I slip my hand under her shirt and skim my fingertips over smooth, warm skin. When my palm encounters a bare breast—soft and round—my dick begins to stir.

She grins. "You're not going to backtrack from that word?"

"What word?" I say, completely distracted by the sight of her breast.

"Love."

Oh, that one. Shit. "Nope. Not gonna backtrack. There are a lot of things I love about you. Your bravery, your passion, your loyalty to your family and friends. Not to mention your very fine ass." I slide my arm around her and pat her butt cheek.

She searches my gaze intently as if looking for something. "I've never met a man like you, Devereaux." Her hand comes up to cup my cheek, her thumb brushing lightly over my beard. "At least not one I wasn't related to."

"I don't beat around the bush. I know what I want, and I go after it."

She skims her hand down my chest, tracing the outline of my pecs, down to my abs, and presses her palms against my boxer-briefs, molding her fingers to the length of me. She smiles as I thicken more with each beat of my heart.

Every drop of blood in my body is heading south.

"We have plenty of condoms, you know," she says as she traces the head of my cock through the fabric. "We don't have to ration them."

Grinning, I lean in for another kiss. "Is that your oh, so subtle way of saying you want me again?"

She nods. "You're a fast learner, Devereaux. That's one of the things I love about you."

The L-word.

She said it, too.

Part of me wants to tell her I love her—flat out say it. No joking around, no kidding. Just fucking say it. But I know it's too soon. And the last thing I want to do is scare her off. Just because she's opened the door doesn't mean she'll let me stay.

And I want in.

I want to be a permanent fixture in her life.

I reach past her and open the nightstand drawer to grab another condom. The one thing I can do right now is teach her that I'll provide whatever it is she needs.

* * *

After long, leisurely sex, we clean up and doze off for a few hours, not waking up until sunlight is streaming through the open curtains. According to my watch, it's ten o'clock. I can't remember the last time I slept this late.

Hannah covers her eyes and groans. "I opened the curtains last night so I could see outside and forgot to close them. Sorry."

"It's okay." I hop out of bed and close the curtains. "That better?"

"Yes, thanks."

She moves as if to roll onto her side to face me but, apparently, she's forgotten about her cast. Lying on her side isn't really an option. "Damn it," she mutters.

The knowledge that she's naked beneath that sheet has my cock rising once more in all its glory. The movement catches her eye, and she skims my body with a sleepy gaze. She hardly got any sleep last night between the chickenshits showing up and then me ravishing her afterward.

"Dibs on the shower," I say as I skirt the foot of the bed and head for the door.

Her laughter follows me down the short hallway.

Once in the bathroom, I turn on the shower, and while it's heating up, I take a piss and brush my teeth. After I rinse and spit, I straighten to see her very naked reflection in the mirror in front of me. My gaze devours all that silky skin covering a supple, slightly muscular build. The woman has biceps and triceps, and they're sexy as hell. Her belly is softly rounded, yet I see a hint of abs. The girl's fit. I guess that shouldn't be a surprise with all the hiking and running she does.

It's the first time I've stopped gawking at her body long enough to get a good look. I attempt to redirect my thoughts. "Need something?"

She smiles guiltily. "Nope."

"You can't shower with me, love. We have no way of keeping your cast from getting wet. It's not waterproof, is it?"

"No, but I can watch you, can't I?"

Damn. Can this girl be any more perfect?

"You want to watch me? Sure, suit yourself."

"Let's go into town this evening," she says. "It's Saturday. Everyone gathers at Ruth's on Saturday night for drinks, pool, and darts. How about it?"

"You mean, like a date?"

Grinning, she nods. "Yeah. Like a date."

Jesus—our first date in public. "I'd love to, but are you sure you're up for that?"

"The only way to find out is to do it. It'll be fun. Ruth wants to meet you. Maggie will come, and she'll drag Owen with her."

"All right. If you think you can handle it."

She laughs. "Oh, I can handle it, big guy. I just hope you can, too." And then she pivots and swings herself back toward the bedroom.

"I can handle anything," I mutter as I step into the shower. The hot water feels good against my scalp as I duck beneath the spray.

*　*　*

After breakfast, we dress warmly and take Scout outside so he can run the agility course. He hardly misses a step as he maneuvers the obstacles with ease. It's definitely time to increase the difficulty for him.

Hannah fetches his tennis ball and throws it across the yard for him. "He's restless because I haven't taken him running."

"I'd take him, but I'm not leaving you here alone. Maybe later, when Owen and Maggie visit again, I'll take him on a run."

Hannah ups the game by throwing the ball far into the woods. Scout tears through the underbrush, crashing through leaves and twigs as he hunts for the ball. Each time he returns with the ball in his mouth, he looks pretty damn proud of himself as he drops it in Hannah's palm.

I reach over and pet the dog's head. "He's a good tracker."

"That's what I'm thinking. When folks get lost on the hiking trails, the sheriff puts out a call for volunteers to help in the search. I'm hoping to train Scout to track missing persons." She hands me the ball, which is soaking wet from the dog's saliva. "Throw it as far as you can."

I throw the ball and it disappears from sight, deep into the forest. Scout is off like a rocket.

On impulse, I pull off my hoodie and hand it to Hannah. I'm

just wearing a T-shirt underneath, and it's damn chilly outside. "When he brings back the ball, have him smell my sweatshirt and tell him to find me."

Her eyes light up. "Really? You think he can? He's tracked me before, but I've never asked him to track someone else."

"Try it." I run toward the woodshed and keep going into the trees, as far as I can go and still keep an eye on Hannah.

I can hear her praising Scout when he returns with the ball. She holds my sweatshirt out for him to sniff as she gives him instructions. "Where's Killian? Go find Killian. Go on. Go find Killian."

Scout crisscrosses the yard several times before he locks onto my scent. *Damn.* He's good. Then he comes running in my direction.

When he reaches me, Scout sits at my feet and barks.

"Good job, buddy," I tell him as I scratch the top of his head. "Come on, let's get back to your mama."

After we tire out the dog, Hannah sits on the porch swing reading on her tablet while I chop more wood for the stove. Despite the chill in the air, I'm sweating like a pig, so I whip off my T-shirt and work bare-chested. When I catch Hannah staring at me, she looks away, flustered, and goes back to reading her book.

I bury the ax in the chopping block and turn to face her, my hands on my hips.

When she realizes I'm looking at her, she glances my way. "What?" she asks.

Although I'm halfway across the yard, I'd swear she's blushing. "You likin' what you see?" I ask her. Hell, I'd like to walk over there, scoop her up in my arms, and carry her inside.

"Oh, yeah," she says, setting down her tablet. "What are you gonna do about it?"

I can't pass up an opportunity like that, so I march over there to her. As I climb the porch steps, she sits up in anticipation. I'm hot and sweaty, and when I lean close, my hands gripping the back of the swing, one on each side of her, she looks up at me with wide eyes.

Her gaze meanders down my chest to my abs, then flashes back up to meet mine. "You like what you see?" I repeat.

She nods.

"Good." And then I lean in and kiss her.

She starts to reach for me, but I snag her wrists and hold her hands to the side. "Hands off, darlin'. I'm a sweaty mess."

Her dark eyes glitter. "Maybe I like it when you're a sweaty mess."

I chuckle. "Oh, don't tempt me, love." Her stomach growls then, loud enough that we can both hear it. "Somebody's gettin' hungry. Let me get cleaned up, and then I'll fire up the grill and cook some burgers. Sound good?"

While I'm cooking outside, Hannah makes potato salad with the leftover spuds we cooked the other night. When I come in with a plate of perfectly seared burgers, she has the table set.

We do the dishes together after we finish eating, and then we end up on the sofa. Her ankle's aching from all the activity, so we decide to relax and watch a movie on her flatscreen TV.

Halfway through the film, she dozes off in my arms, and I don't have the heart to wake her. She didn't get enough sleep last night, and if we're going out tonight, she needs a nap.

I relish the feeling of her in my arms, warm and sleepy. I don't think I'll ever take this for granted. Gently, I brush her hair back, and she stirs sleepily. "Shh, sorry," I murmur. "Go back to sleep."

She turns into me, her face resting against my chest, and drifts away.

* * *

Early that evening, when Hannah comes out of the bathroom, I try not to stare. She's a beautiful woman under any condition, but all dolled up to go out, she's breathtaking. I suspect she's put on a bit of mascara and a hint of smokey eyeshadow, although it's subtle. Her lips look pinker than usual, with a hint of gloss. How in the hell does she make a pair of ripped jeans, boots, and a sleeveless top that shows more cleavage than I'm comfortable with look so damn good?

She's got a girl-next-door look, coupled with a fierce Indiana Jones vibe. She can either make your dreams come true or she can just as easily whack you in the balls.

Damn it.

This is a bar we're going to, so I know it'll be filled with guys looking to score. Now I think I know what she meant when she said she wondered if *I* could handle it.

I cross the room just to be near her and cup her face in my hands. "You look amazing." And then I kiss her, *because I can.* Because she's opened that door to me—or at least a good-sized window—and I'm walkin' right through it.

She smiles up at me. "So do you."

I look the same as I always do—jeans, boots, and a T-shirt. "Sorry, it's just the same ol' me."

"I know. You always look amazing."

"Sorry about your jeans," I tell her, nodding down at her cast. We had to cut off the bottom third of her left pant leg to accommodate her cast, and the rest of the pant leg is slit up to the thigh so we could get it over the cast.

She shrugs. "Sometimes we have to make sacrifices."

"Are you ready to go?"

She nods. "Let's do this."

Why do I have the feeling I'm in for trouble this evening?

I strap on my chest holster and slip on my jacket. Before we walk out the door, I grab my radio and earpiece and tuck them into my jacket pocket—just in case. It pays to be prepared for any contingency.

❧ 27

Killian Devereaux

It's nearly nine o'clock when we're on our way to her friend Ruth's tavern. Most of the businesses in the little downtown strip are closed for the night. Only the bar, the diner, and a laundromat down the street remain open for business. Still, the street is lined on both sides with parked cars. It looks like this is the place to be on a Saturday night in Bryce, Colorado.

Since street parking is full, I drive around to the back of the building where there's some available slots. I hold her crutches as Hannah lets herself drop carefully to the ground.

When she's steady on her crutches, I lean down to kiss her. Technically, I'm on duty, but I'm not here tonight as her bodyguard. I'm here as her boyfriend. That's a helluva big difference.

I take a second to slip my earpiece in and clip the attached radio to my belt. The wire is pretty well concealed by my jacket. I coordinated with Owen, who's going to be here with Maggie tonight. He's wearing his earpiece as well.

We enter through the back door and walk down a dimly-lit hallway to the front of the bar, passing the door to the kitchen on our left and two unisex restrooms on our right. The bar itself is packed. To our right are the tables and booths—most of which are occupied. Over to the left are pool tables and dart boards—all busy. There's a small dance floor in the center of the room where half a dozen couples are dancing to some honky-tonk song being played by a five-piece band on the stage. It kinda reminds me of home. You can't step foot in a Cajun bar without hearing live music, and of course folks are dancing.

Hannah waves at a corner booth. "There's Maggie."

As we make our way over there, sidestepping tables and servers rushing back and forth from the kitchen and bar, I survey the room, noting all the points of egress. Several people stop Hannah to say hello. A few of the women give her hugs. One guy—a blond cowboy—tries to give her a hug, but I stare him down, and he thinks better of it and goes on his way.

Hannah glances back at me and shakes her head with a laugh. "That was Steve Evans. He's harmless."

"Didn't look harmless to me. He looked grabby."

Maggie and Owen are seated on one side of the booth, the other side being empty. A woman with a long braid of straight black hair stands at their table, her hands on her hips. She's wearing blue jeans, well-worn cowboy boots, and a long-sleeved blue-and-white plaid shirt. I'm guessing she's Ruth, the owner.

When we reach the booth, I take the crutches from Hannah so she can slide into the seat. I lean her crutches against the wall near our table.

The woman with the braid eyes me blatantly as I approach, as if she's sizing me up. She has a stunningly beautiful oval face, high cheekbones, eyes dark as midnight, and dark lashes. Her skin is a warm brown. Clearly, she's Native American. "You must be Killian," she says.

"Yes, ma'am." I offer her my hand, and we shake. She's got a firm grip. Yeah, she's the boss around here. It's written all over her.

"Pleased to meet you," she says as I slide in beside Hannah. "I'm Ruth. I've heard a lot about you."

"Is that so?" I ask. "Seems I've hardly been in town long enough to be talked about." I know how small towns work.

Ruth winks at Maggie. "A little birdie gave me an earful."

"He got me out of that ravine in one piece," Hannah says as she hands me a menu.

Ruth pats me on the shoulder. "So I heard. Supper's on the house tonight, big guy. As a token of my appreciation for what you did for our Hannah. In case you weren't aware, we're pretty fond of her around here."

"I understand it's your brother we have to thank for flying Hannah out of that valley."

Ruth nods. "Micah flew choppers in the Army. He now runs an auto repair shop here in town, but in his spare time he runs a helicopter tourism business. His chopper comes in handy on occasion." She nods to the menus. "I'll send someone over to take your orders."

I look to the others—Maggie's sitting against the wall, Owen beside her. Owen hasn't said a word, but when we make eye contact, he nods in greeting. He's not one to talk a lot. I notice he's got his earpiece in, as I'd asked him to.

After we look over the menus, a young woman comes to the table to take our orders. She's young, blonde, bubbly, and all smiles.

Hannah orders a burger and fries, along with a bottle of Fat Tire. "I have a designated driver tonight, so I can drink."

I order the same, but without the beer. A soft drink instead.

Maggie orders a grilled chicken sandwich without the bun, and Owen orders a steak.

"How's your ankle?" Maggie asks Hannah.

"Good. I should be running again in no time."

I make a scoffing noise, and Hannah rolls her eyes at me.

Our server brings us our drinks.

Maggie takes a sip of her dark ale. "I guess dancing is off your itinerary tonight."

"I don't know," Hannah says as she sips her beer. "If I'm careful...." She looks my way.

"No dancing," I say, shaking my head emphatically.

"I don't know about that," Maggie says with a devilish grin. "Bella danced with Edward with a broken leg. I'm sure Killian can keep you from face-planting."

I look to Hannah. "Am I supposed to know what she's talking about?"

Laughing, Hannah bumps my shoulder with hers. "I can see we need to watch *Twilight* soon."

The whole time the girls are yammering, I continue to scan the room, getting a feel for the place and doing a bit of surveillance. I find Owen doing the same thing. I guess we can't help ourselves. It's second nature for both of us.

The blond guy who attempted to hug Hannah earlier stops by our table. "Hannah! How's your ankle? I heard you took a bad fall while hiking."

That's the official story. The local police recommended that we keep any details about the poachers out of the public news while the investigation is ongoing.

"Hi, Steve," she says, smiling up at the guy. Obviously, she knows him. "Steve and I work together," she says to me.

I reach for my Coke. "I see." But I don't like the way he's looking at her. Or the way he's eyeing me, like he's trying to size me up. *Don't even go there, pal.*

When our server returns with our food, I glare at Steve, and he gets the picture. "Well, I'll see ya later, Hannah, okay?"

She waves goodbye as she sticks a fry in her mouth. "Okay. See ya."

I glance down at Hannah. "So, how many men here have crushes on you? What's the total number?"

She laughs. "None of them. You're too sensitive."

"Hardly."

Owen catches my gaze and quietly says, "Check your nine o'clock."

I shove a fry in my mouth and casually glance to my left. There's a guy seated alone at a table for two. No food. Just a couple of beer bottles in front of him.

I continue to watch him out of my peripheral. Dark hair, dark eyes, about five-ten. He's too far away for me to see if he has a scar on his face, but he sure matches Hannah's general description of one of the poachers. The one she said was the boss.

I turn back to face Owen, who's sipping his soft drink. He's not drinking either tonight. I shrug. "Could be," I say quietly. "He meets the description. I need to get closer to see if he has a scar above his lip."

"He's watching her," Owen says quietly.

I grab Hannah's hand beneath the table to get her attention. When she's looking at me, I murmur, "The guy sitting alone, near the stage—do you recognize him? Could that be one of your attackers?"

She frowns. "Possibly. I can't see his face clearly enough to see if he has a scar."

It seems unlikely that we'd just happen to run into one of the chickenshits here in a public place, but I can't take any chances. It's entirely possible, especially if they're actively looking for

Hannah.

Owen nudges my boot under the table. "He's on the move."

Out of the corner of my eye, I notice that the dark-haired guy is walking toward the bar. "Be right back," I say abruptly, giving Owen a signal to keep an eye on Hannah.

I approach the bar, coming up alongside my target as he's ordering another beer, and I slip in on his right side so I can get a good look at his face.

Bingo! He's got a scar on his right cheek, exactly as Hannah described. When he notices me looking, I nod and do my best to sound friendly. "How's it goin'?"

He doesn't respond, though. Instead, he walks away from the bar and heads down the hall toward the rear door.

Well, shit.

Before I can follow, a woman behind the bar says, "So, *you're* the mysterious Cajun Hannah's been telling us about."

I turn to see Ruth standing across the counter from me. "I guess that's me. I'm pretty sure I'm the *only* Cajun Hannah knows."

She looks me directly in the eye, both her stance and her demeanor radiating confidence. "What are your intentions regarding Hannah? I warn you now, she's got a lot of friends here. Any one of us would be happy to run you out of town if you get out of line. Starting with me."

"I'm glad to hear it. Hey, did you happen to notice the guy who was just here beside me?" I draw my finger down my right cheek, tracing the path of the guy's scar. "Scar?"

She nods. "What about him?"

"Do you know who he is?"

"Sorry, no. I've never seen him before. Why?"

"He fits the description of one the men who assaulted Hannah. I just wondered if you knew him. The sheriff is trying to ID them."

Another bartender yells down the line at Ruth, asking for a draft beer. She grabs a tall glass from a rack overhead and pours it, then sends it sliding down the bar to a customer three seats away. "I'll ask around," she promises. "Can I get you a drink?"

"Thanks, but no. I'm not drinking tonight." I glance back at our table to check on Hannah. She and Maggie are laughing uproariously about something, probably something to do with Owen, as he has a rather dour look on his face.

I realize I'm right when Maggie bumps her shoulders into Owen's, grinning at him, but he doesn't even crack a smile. That makes the girls laugh even harder, and Maggie throws her arm around Owen and gives him an apologetic squeeze.

"I'll let you know if I see him in here again," Ruth says.

"Thanks." I return to our table and slide in beside Hannah. "He could be our guy. He has a scar just like the one you described."

Hannah shudders. "If his friend shows up, we'll know for sure."

The band starts playing a slow song, and couples take to the dance floor. We're done eating, so I hold my hand out to Hannah. "Would you like to dance?"

She grins at me. "Really?"

"Sure, why not?" The truth is, I love to dance. You can't grow up Cajun and not love dancing. It's in our blood. You get a group of Cajuns in one place, add a band and some live music, and everyone ends up dancing.

"Okay."

I slip out of the booth and grab the crutches, then I help Hannah to her feet. Once we're on the dance floor, I grasp her around the waist while she balances herself with the crutches.

"You really like to dance?" she asks me. "Most guys act like it's torture."

"I'm Cajun, love. It's practically a requirement."

One song turns into two, and we're swaying together to the beat of a slow song. My hands are on her waist, but I'm ready to catch her at a moment's notice.

"Do you really think that was him?" she asks. "The lead chickenshit?"

"Might have been. I guess we'll find out when we leave."

"You think they might follow us home?"

Home. I love the way that sounds. "Yes, if it's really him. He won't recognize me, but he'll recognize you."

She shivers. "Maybe coming out tonight wasn't such a good idea after all."

"I'll alert Nelson, just in case. We'll be prepared. Plus, we've got Owen for backup. Hey, the sooner these guys crawl out from under their rock, the sooner we can put an end to this cat-and-mouse game."

Hannah frowns. "What happens then, Killian?"

"What d'you mean?"

"Once they're caught and the danger is over, what's next?"

"You mean what's next for us?"

"Yeah."

I bring my hands up to cup her face. "I guess that depends on you. If it's up to me, I'm staying." Her lips tremble, and I suspect she's fighting a smile. "Do you want me to stay, Hannah?"

As she nods, her dark eyes fill with tears. "Yeah, I do."

"Okay. Then it's settled." And to seal the deal, I lean down and kiss her. "I'm staying. I'll call Shane in the morning and give him my resignation."

I laugh at the panicked look on her face. "Don't worry. It'll be fine. I've got some money saved up—and I'll figure out something else to do for work around here."

"This is what I was afraid of—you uprooting yourself because of me and walking away from everything you've built. Your friends, your job."

I slide my arms around her waist and draw her close. Her head fits perfectly just below my chin as I hold her to me. "I'm not losing anything, Hannah. I'm gaining something priceless."

That idiot Steve bumps into me. "Oh, sorry," he says, as if it was accidental. Yeah, right. "Hey, Hannah, how about letting me cut in?" He holds his hands out to her. "I promise I won't let you fall."

"Sorry, pal," I say. "She's spoken for."

"What?" Steve looks a bit dumbfounded as he stares at Hannah. "Who is this guy?" he asks her.

She grins. "He's my boyfriend."

"Your boyfriend?" Steve looks devastated. "What the fuck? Since when?"

"Since now," I reply. "So back off, buddy, or you and I are gonna have words." Then I make eye contact with Hannah. "I told you so."

Hannah shoves me playfully. "Oh, stop."

❧ 28

Hannah McIntyre

I feel giddy, like a high school girl out on a first date with the boy she's been crushing on forever. And here we are, arm in arm, dancing, and we just made it official.

Maggie comes up behind me, puts her hands on my shoulders, and whispers, "Having fun?"

Glancing back, I see Owen looming directly behind Maggie like a guard dog. I lean close to her and whisper, "We're going steady."

She laughs. "Good for you. I told you so!"

It turns out that two dances is my limit. My arms are shaking from trying to keep my balance, and my ankle is starting to throb.

I think Killian can tell, because he looks at me and frowns. "Let's sit down."

Owen claps Killian on the shoulder. "Hey, do you wanna play a game of Eight Ball?"

"Sure," Killian says. "As long as Hannah can sit down and rest."

Owen and Killian end up commandeering an available pool table, while Maggie and I take our seats to watch them play and cheer them on. Killian slides a spare chair over to me so I can prop my ankle up.

Ruth drops off fresh beers for me and Maggie, as well as soft drinks for the guys. Steve comes over to watch, and a small crowd of friends joins us. I think they're curious about Killian and Owen. I would be, too, if two über-hot guys showed up at my favorite watering hole.

While they're playing pool, Killian and Owen have some quiet conversations, and they don't seem to be keen to share with us.

Killian nods and types something into his phone while Owen takes his next shot.

"What's going on?" I ask Killian when he checks on me.

"Not much," he says. "We're just making some arrangements."

"For what?"

"You'll see."

Ruth comes to join us, standing beside the table where Maggie and I are sitting. She lays her hand on my shoulder and winks at me. "I like him." Then she looks to Maggie. "The other one's not bad either."

Trying not to grin, Maggie gives Ruth the evil eye. "Stop it."

The guys end up playing three rounds, Killian winning two out of the three. Owen offers him a raincheck on a bottle of beer.

Killian comes up behind my chair and leans down to brush his lips against my ear, giving me delicious goosebumps.

I shiver.

"You 'bout ready to call it a night?" he asks me. "This is a lot for your first time venturing out."

He's right. I am tired. Stretching out on my sofa at home, or better yet in my bed, sounds really good to me.

Killian goes to the bar to pay our tab, but Ruth brushes him off. "On the house tonight," she says, "as thanks for saving our girl."

We return to our booth to grab our coats and walk down the hall to the rear door. Just a few feet away from the door, Killian stops me. Owen moves on a few feet, closer to the rear door, and peers out the window.

"Be prepared, ladies," Killian says to me and Maggie. "We're not sure what to expect when we walk outside."

Maggie frowns. "What d'you mean?"

"I'm pretty sure the guy we saw earlier tonight is one of the poachers. He took off like a bat out of hell once he realized I was scrutinizing him. If it is him, he may have contacted his accomplice, and they might be out there waiting for us."

I glance down the hall to the back door and can see that it's dark out. Owen stands at the ready by the door, his hand on his firearm holstered at his hip.

"Stay inside with Maggie," Killian says to me. "I'll pull the Jeep up to the back door."

I grab his arm. "You can't go out there alone. What if you're right, and they're out there? At least take Owen with you."

"Owen stays inside with you two. I'll be fine."

Killian heads for the door, and before I can say another word, he's walking into a pitch-dark parking lot to get my Jeep.

A few moments later, he pulls up to the back door.

"Let's go," Owen says as he opens the door and ushers Maggie and me outside.

Killian's behind the wheel still. Owen walks me to the front passenger seat, opens my door, and helps me climb up while Maggie holds my crutches.

"False alarm, I guess," Maggie says as she hands me the crutches.

"Yeah, false alarm." I have to admit, I'm relieved no boogeymen have jumped out of the shadows. I'm not looking forward to confronting those guys again.

Killian makes eye contact with Owen, and the two look deep in conversation even though neither one says a word. Owen nods, then closes my door.

Killian reaches over me and locks my door. "Let's go home."

He's uncharacteristically quiet on the drive home. I expected him to tease me more about Steve, or maybe about our dances. Instead, he keeps checking the rearview mirror.

"Is something wrong?" I ask him.

His posture is tense. "We're being tailed."

I glance at my sideview mirror, but there's no one behind us. Still, the roads are dark and full of curves, so I can't see very far back. "You're sure we're being followed?"

"Yep. They followed us out of the parking lot."

"Who did?"

"Not entirely sure, but I can guess. It's a dark SUV with tinted windows."

My stomach sinks like a stone. "What do we do?"

"We act normal," he says as he reaches over to pat my knee. "We don't want to tip them off. Don't worry, everything's under control."

Under control? How can he remain so calm? I wish I could be as cool under pressure as Killian, but pardon me if I'm a bit concerned that we're being followed by two men who want me dead.

When we reach the turnoff to my place, Killian takes it and drives up the lane toward my cabin.

"Are you sure this is a good idea? We'll be sitting ducks up here if they cage us in. There's only the one way in and out."

Sure enough, as I'm watching my sideview mirror, another vehicle turns into my drive behind us. It's dark, so they're hard to make out. They turn off their headlights, but occasionally I see the glint of moonlight off their front grill. "They turned their lights off."

"It's all right. We're not the only ones with a tail tonight."

Before I can even ask what he means, we pull into the front yard of my cabin. The cabin's dark, except for the single bulb lighting up the porch. Killian parks the Jeep and kills the engine and lights, leaving us in a pool of darkness.

Sure enough, the SUV pulls in a few yards behind us. Two men jump out and take cover on each side of the vehicle, behind their open doors. They're aiming handguns at us.

One of them shouts, "Get out of the vehicle! Now!"

Killian reaches inside his jacket for his holstered gun. "Don't move, love. Stay in the Jeep and keep your head down." He disables the interior light and reaches for his door handle.

I grab his arm. "Please don't go out there. You're outnumbered."

"Not for long," he says with a hint of satisfaction in his voice.

I hear the crunch of tires on gravel before I see a familiar vehicle approaching. It's Maggie's red pickup truck pulling in directly behind the SUV, cutting the poachers off from behind. Then floodlights fill the yard from multiple angles, all trained on the dark SUV, and half-a-dozen uniformed deputies armed with shotguns come from all directions—from the woods, from behind the cabin—to surround the two intruders. Owen steps out of the pickup, his shotgun trained on the poachers.

"Sheriff's department!" Christopher Nelson yells. "Drop your weapons and put your hands up where we can see them! Now!"

Killian's standing outside the Jeep now, his hands clasping

his gun, which is pointed at one of the poachers.

I stare in awe at the sheer strength of force surrounding us. Not just Killian and Owen flanking the poachers, but also all the police officers.

When the poachers, who are greatly outnumbered, comply with the sheriff's orders, the officers swarm in, cuff them, and search them.

I pivot to face Killian, who has already holstered his gun. "You planned this. How in the world did you do it? When did you do it?"

Killian touches the mic on his radio. "Copy. I'm taking Hannah inside." He walks around the front of the Jeep to my door, opens it, and helps me down. He walks me up the porch steps and into the cabin. A moment later, I'm sitting on the sofa.

"Stay inside, love," Killian says. "I'm going outside to help." And then he's gone.

Scout paces restlessly in front of the door as the sound of heated voices comes through the wall. I hate being unable to see what's going on outside.

I'm tempted to move over to the window so I can see, when there's a knock at the door.

"Hannah? It's me, Owen. I'm comin' in." He steps inside, closes the door, and turns on the light that hangs over the kitchen table. "You doin' okay?"

"Where's Maggie? She's not out there with you, is she?"

"No. She's with Ruth back at the tavern. She's safe."

A few minutes later, Killian comes back inside. "All right,

they're gone. Nelson took the chickenshits to the county jail to await arraignment." He grins at me. "We got them, love. We got them."

Now that the excitement is over, Owen heads back to the tavern to pick up Maggie. Killian secures the cabin and comes to sit with me on the sofa. I realize I haven't stopped shaking since the poachers followed us up my lane.

Killian lays his arm across my shoulders and pulls me close, dropping a kiss on the top of my head. "It's okay. They're in custody. You're safe."

Then he pulls out his phone and makes a call. "I've got an update for you, Shane. The poachers have been apprehended by the sheriff's office. They've been taken into custody." He pauses to listen. "Yes, she's fine." Another pause. "I'm sure she wants to speak to you, too. But before I hand the phone over, there's something I need to tell you." He gives me a telling look and takes a deep breath. "I'm resigning, effective immediately. I'm staying here in Bryce, with Hannah." Another pause, this one longer. "I don't know, but I'll think of something."

He hands me the phone. "Your brother wants to talk to you."

"Hi, Shane," I say as I hold the phone to my ear.

"First things first, are you okay?"

"Yes, I'm fine."

"Are you sure?"

"Yes."

He sighs. "Well, that's what matters. So, you and Killian? He said he's staying in Bryce. With *you*."

"Yeah, he is."

"And you're okay with that?"

"I am. Really, Shane, I'm more than okay with it." I smile at Killian, who's listening to every word.

Killian snags my free hand and brings it to his mouth to kiss my knuckles.

"All right," my brother says. "Let me think this over. I'll get back with you both."

I say goodnight to my brother and end the call. "He said he'll think it over and get back with us, but I don't know what he has to think about. It's your decision, not his."

"It's *our* decision." Killian moves to sit on the coffee table so he can face me. He leans forward and cups my face. He kisses me, his lips warm and comforting. "It's late, and you should be in bed. Why don't you get ready while I take the dog out for a potty break? I won't be long."

"You have five minutes," I tell him. "And then I'm coming after you."

"I'll be back in four."

ꙮ 29

Killian Devereaux

Scout runs around the yard sniffing like a maniac. I'm sure he's bummed that he missed out on all the excitement this evening. He finally does his business and runs back up onto the porch. We come inside, and the dog gets a drink from his water bowl while I stoke the fire.

When I head down the hall, I find the bathroom empty, and I hear Hannah puttering around in the bedroom. By the time I'm done in the bathroom and make it to the bedroom, she's sitting up in bed, leaning on pillows propped against the headboard, her tablet in her lap.

"Whatcha doing?" I ask her.

"Reading." She lays the tablet down on top of the night-stand. "But honestly, my own life is more exciting than a novel at the moment."

"Scoot over," I tell her, and then I sit on the edge of the bed and reach for her arm. "Let me check your wound."

She glances down at the stitches. "They look good."

I apply fresh antiseptic ointment. The sutures do look good—no redness or swelling, no sign of infection. "Looks like you'll survive," I tell her. She has a doctor's appointment in about a week to get the stitches removed. "How does your ankle feel?"

"Not bad," she says. "I did just take a pain pill."

"Sutures out in a week, and your cast off in five weeks. You'll be good as new."

"What did Shane say to you?"

I was expecting this. "Not much, honestly. I think he was caught off guard. He said he'd think it over."

"I don't know what he needs to think about."

I shrug. "No matter. It's done." I brush her hair back and tuck it behind her ear. "I'll have to make one trip back to Chicago to get my personal belongings. I don't have much, as my apart-ment came already furnished. I live in his building, so I'm hop-ing he'll let me out of my lease early."

She laughs. "He'd better, or he'll have to deal with me."

I lean over and kiss her. "That's my wildcat. Don't worry. He's a good guy. It'll be fine."

I turn off the bedroom light and climb onto my side of the

bed. Scout jumps up to join us. After sniffing and rubbing on Hannah a bit, he settles down at the foot of the bed and curls up like a fox.

I lie on my back in the dark, my cock throbbing thanks to all the adrenaline still flowing through my veins. My body has a mind of its own, and that train has left the station without asking me. But she's been through a harrowing experience tonight, and sex is the last thing she needs. I don't want to push her, so I try to think about other things, such as what I'll need to pick up in Chicago, or what type of job I can find here in Bryce or perhaps in a neighboring town.

I reach for her hand and link our fingers. "Tell me about your job."

"Well, you know I work for a wildlife conservation organization. We rehab injured wild animals and provide education to schools and the public."

"Weren't you doing something with wolves? I remember something about wolves."

"When I was in graduate school, I wrote my thesis on wolf populations in the northern Rockies. When I finished school, I took the job here in Bryce. I don't get to work with wolves anymore, but I do get to work with other important species, like bald eagles, mountain lions, black bears, and coyotes."

"I'll need to find something I can do around here to support myself. I was thinking maybe I could find something in law enforcement. The sheriff seems like a good guy. I could work for him."

"We won't need much," she says. "I don't make a lot at the conservation center—it's more a labor of love. My Jeep's paid off, and so is my home. The land was a college graduation gift from Shane, and I actually helped build the cabin with a local co-op, so it was very affordable. I don't have a mortgage, and I keep my bills to a minimum so I can afford to do the work I love and not have to chase a paycheck."

"I like the sound of that. I guess I've always been a bit of a minimalist at heart. The personal stuff I have in my apartment in Chicago would maybe fill three medium-sized cardboard boxes. Speaking of my stuff, I'll need to return to Chicago to get it."

She squeezes my hand. "I'll come with you, if you want me to."

I roll to face her. "Of course I want you to come with me. We could fly to Chicago, and then we'll drive my Jeep back here. I guess I should have realized we were destined for each other. We drive the same vehicle."

Hannah grins.

"What's so funny?" I ask her.

"I'm imagining how my family will react when they see us together—I mean *really* together. They've been teasing me mercilessly about you since we met."

I lean in and kiss her. "Hopefully they'll be happy for us."

"They will be, trust me," she says.

She rolls on her side and pulls me close. Then she hikes her good leg up over my hips, pressing close to me. My cock, which of course is already hard simply because I'm this close to her, brushes against the sweet spot between her legs. The only thing separating her body from mine is a couple layers of fabric.

She kisses me hungrily and pulls me closer.

"Careful," I say against her lips.

"I'm fine." She pushes me on my back and rolls up on top of me so that she's sitting astride my waist, her weight on her knees.

"Watch your ankle," I warn her.

She braces her hands on either side of my head and leans down to kiss me. "We need to celebrate."

I grip her waist to hold her steady. "Celebrate what, exactly?"

"Everything. The poachers are in custody, you quit your job, you're moving here, we're together—"

I sit up and cover her mouth with mine. "All good reasons to celebrate."

When I press the tips of my fingers between her legs, she gasps. I can sense her heat and dampness even through her underwear.

I never thought this could happen. Hannah McIntyre—the girl of my dreams, who I've been chasing for what seems like forever—is sitting half-naked on my lap in a *bed*. "Are you for real?" I ask her, hoping this isn't just an elaborate dream cooked up by my subconscious.

She grins as she leans in and kisses me, her lips simultaneously coaxing and demanding. "I am. Are you?"

"Hell yes." Keeping her gaze locked onto mine, I slip my

hand down the front of her underwear, brushing against her soft, warm skin. My middle finger slides between the slick lips of her sex—my god, she's wet—and my thumb starts rubbing tight little circles on her clit.

Her gasp morphs into a throaty moan. "Oh, god, that feels good." Closing her eyes, she rocks against my fingertips, no shame, no hesitation. She knows what she wants, and she takes it.

When I increase the pressure on her clit, she gasps into my mouth, practically panting.

"Yes! Oh, my god, just like that. Don't stop."

She leans her forehead against mine, and I can feel the quivering in her taut thighs. She's close, I can tell, and I love knowing that I'm the one bringing her here.

"Killian," she breathes, and it's the most erotic sound I've ever heard.

I could spend the rest of my life pleasuring this woman. "Come for me, wildcat. I want to feel it. I want to watch you."

I think my words tip her over the edge because, almost immediately, she falls against me and shudders, a keening cry catching in her throat. I press my mouth to hers and drink in the sounds.

It takes me a minute to realize she's attempting to push her underwear down, but she'll never get them off with that damn cast in the way.

"Damn it," she growls in frustration as she tries to do the impossible.

"Here, let me." I grab hold of the soft fabric and tear the seam apart.

"Yes," she says, and then she reaches for the nightstand drawer. "We need a fucking condom."

There's no way she can extend her arm that far, so I steady her on my hips and do it for her. I hand her the packet, and while she tears it open, I lift my hips and shove my boxer briefs down past my thighs.

As she rolls the condom on my length, I lie back and relish this moment.

"Best day ever," I say through gritted teeth as she completes her task.

She pushes me onto my back and positions herself over my cock before sinking down onto me. The pleasure is incredible, so much heat and tightness. She raises herself, then drops down again, over and over, until gradually she's seated to the hilt. I have to grit my teeth to maintain control and not start shoving myself into her like a madman.

But I hardly need to move because she's doing all the work. She rocks on me, taking charge, her hands pressed to my chest, her fingers sifting through my hair. The look of utter bliss on her face matches the way I feel.

I'm afraid she's going to hurt her ankle, though, so I sit up, hold her carefully to me, and roll us so that I'm on top. Gripping her good leg, I hike her thigh up against my hips to open her up. She bucks into me, hard. Her face is damp with perspiration, her eyes glittering with arousal. I don't hold back, because

I don't think that's what she wants from me, and I want to give her exactly what she wants.

I'll prove to her, even if it kills me, that I'm exactly the man she needs.

ᘓ 30

Hannah McIntyre
Five weeks later

G od, it's good to have both boots on again," I say as I lace up my left boot for the first time in ages. I stand on both feet and test my ankle as I walk across the living room.

Killian looks poised to jump to my rescue at any second, should my ankle give out on me and I land on my butt. "Don't overdo it," he warns as he hovers.

He's sexy when he's being overprotective.

"I've got a great idea. We should go on a hike. Really put my ankle to the test."

He shakes his head adamantly. "No, we should not. Give it a few days, McIntyre. You don't want to end up back in the ER. Besides, your doctor said no running, no hiking... nothing strenuous for at least two weeks."

"How about grocery shopping, then? That's easy enough. We're getting low on supplies, and we're almost out of dog food."

He looks far from thrilled, but he doesn't argue. "Okay. I think we can manage a little shopping."

When I hold my palm out to him, he pulls the keys to my Jeep out of his front pocket and tosses them to me. Not only am I tired of using those damn crutches, but I haven't been able to drive in well over a month. I'm tired of being chauffeured around. I want my independence back.

"Come on, Scout," I say, whistling for my dog. He comes running from the bedroom. "I'll take him out for a potty break."

For the first time in a long time, I walk out my own front door on my own two feet. Scout bounds along beside me as we take the steps down to the ground. I spot a tennis ball, scoop it up, and throw it across the yard and into the woods as hard as I can. Scout takes off after it like a rocket.

Ah, it's good to be back.

Hopefully I'll be able to do a little running in a couple more weeks.

Scout comes racing back to me in no time with the bright green tennis ball in his mouth. He drops it at my feet, and I throw it again for him, this time harder and past the woodshed. And off he goes.

"Feels good, doesn't it?" Killian says from behind me.

I turn to see him standing in the open doorway. "It feels incredible. I hated having to use those crutches."

He smiles. "Now I'll get to see the real Hannah McIntyre, up close and personal, in her natural environment."

I walk back up the steps to stand in front of him, wrap my arms around his waist, and go up on my toes to kiss him. "Oh, buddy, you have no idea what I can do now that I have that damn cast off. I'm going to rock your world."

He nods back toward the cabin and grins. "Why don't we do some of that world rocking right now?"

At that moment, Scout returns with an excited bark and drops the ball at my feet. He's eager for another go. Killian snags the ball and throws it hard, sending Scout chasing madly after it.

I bite back a squeal when Killian picks me up and sits me on the porch railing. He insinuates himself between my thighs and pulls me close so that his hard-on presses against my sweet spot. The firm pressure against me is delicious, and I want more.

He takes hold of my ponytail with one hand while his other hand cups one of my breasts, holding me captive as he gazes down into my eyes. The hunger I see in his gaze steals my breath.

He kisses me, his lips hot and controlling, sending a shiver rippling through me. His tongue slides in to stroke mine, and his hand slides down to cup my ass and draw me even closer against him.

"You feel that?" he says. His voice is low and rough, edged with arousal.

"It's kind of hard to miss, big guy." And I mean *big* in every way imaginable.

His other hand releases my ponytail and grips the back of my neck, and damn! I'm surprised to find that as hot as I do. Normally, I don't like being manhandled, but for some reason when he does it, it turns me on.

"My mind is racing as I think of all the positions we haven't tried yet," he confesses. "I was so afraid of hurting you before, but now—" His hand slips down inside the back of my jeans, and he grabs a bare butt cheek. "Now there's nothing we can't do."

I slip my hands up beneath his shirt and drag my short nails slowly down his back. He groans loudly, and the sound makes my ache even worse.

Scout returns at that moment, dropping the ball at Killian's feet and sitting at attention as he hopes for another throw.

"Out of dog food," I remind Killian. "And beer. And steaks."

Killian growls as he removes his hands from inside my jeans. "Okay, grocery shopping first, then we come back here and get naked. We can try out some of those positions we've had to neglect. Deal?"

"Deal."

We put Scout inside and lock up the cabin.

"Do you want me to drive?" Killian asks, holding his hand out for the keys.

I give him a look. "Surely you're not serious."

He laughs as he opens the front passenger door and climbs in. "Just offering."

I settle behind the wheel and start the engine. It feels so good to be able to drive again. We take off down the lane and merge onto the road that heads to town. "How about we go to Chicago this weekend to get your stuff? I'm in the mood for a road trip."

"Sure," he says as he pulls out his phone. "I'll give Jake and Shane a heads-up to let them know we're coming."

It's a short trip down the mountain to town. I park in front of Maggie's store and hop out of the Jeep. Killian meets me on the sidewalk, and we walk inside holding hands.

Maggie's standing behind the sales counter, and she grins when she sees us holding hands. "You two are a sight for sore eyes," she says as she walks around the counter to greet us. She wraps me in her arms and gives me a big bear hug. "I'm glad to see the last of that cast."

"Me too," I tell her. "I told them at the hospital to burn it."

Killian grabs a shopping cart and heads straight for the beer cooler. "I'll get to work while you ladies catch up."

Maggie pulls me aside and says, "How are things going between you two?" She hands me a box of candy bars and points to an empty rack.

"Good." I try not to grin like a besotted idiot, but I can't help it. I start filling an empty rack with chocolate bars.

Maggie glances slyly at Killian, then back to me. "Is he as good in bed as I think he is?"

I can feel my cheeks burning. "Definitely."

"I figured." Maggie pretends to fan herself. "Some women have all the luck."

Killian joins us at the counter. There are two cases of beer in the cart. He holds out his hand. "Give me the shopping list. I'll grab what we need while you girls gossip."

I laugh. "We're not gossiping."

He gives me a look. "Yes, you are. I heard you two giggling like schoolgirls."

"Okay, fine." I hand him the list. "You get the stuff while we talk about you."

He wags a finger at me. "See, I told you."

"Just got some nice steaks in this morning from Lonnie, the butcher in town," Maggie calls after him. "Grab 'em while you can."

"Do you see what I have to put up with?" I ask Maggie, who's trying to keep a straight face.

"Oh, what a hardship," she says. "So, what's new?"

"We're heading to Chicago this weekend to get his personal belongings out of his apartment, and then we'll drive his Jeep back here. When we get back, he'll start looking for a job. He's considering law enforcement—can't you just picture him in a uniform?"

We hear the bell over the front door tinkling, and when I

turn, I see Sheriff Nelson walking inside.

"Speak of the devil," Maggie says.

"Mornin', Hannah," the sheriff says to me. "I saw your Jeep out front." He scans the store. "I'm looking for Killian." Nelson spots him in the bread aisle. It's not hard, as Killian towers over the store shelves. "There he is." He marches over to him.

Maggie hands me some packs of gum to shelve. "That's odd. I wonder what's going on."

A moment later, Killian pushes the cart over to me, Sheriff Nelson right behind him. "Chris has asked me to help out a local search team. One of the boys in a scouting troop got lost on Ridgeline trail this morning. There's added concern because a mountain lion was spotted on the same trail yesterday and again today. Will you be okay on your own?" he asks me.

I roll my eyes at him. *He did not just ask me that.*

"You've got your keys, right?" he asks. "Chris said he'd give me a ride back to the cabin so I can grab my gear. I'm sure someone can bring me home later."

"I can help search."

Killian frowns. "Hannah, no. It's too soon." He nods down at my left foot. "Your doctor said two weeks before any strenuous exercise. Give it some time, love."

I stomp my left boot on the floor. "See, it's fine. I'm coming, and I dare you to give me a hard time about it."

Killian practically glares at me. "You're not gonna be talked out of this, are you?"

"Nope."

Despite looking far from happy, Killian reluctantly nods. "All right, fine. But you stay on the trail, okay? No wandering off into rough terrain."

I shrug. "Fine."

His eyes narrow skeptically. "I'm serious. You have to promise me."

"I said fine."

Maggie's watching with amusement, her gaze bouncing back and forth between us. She shakes her head like an indulgent parent watching her two favorite kids arguing. "You two are adorable."

Killian motions to the cart, which is partly filled.

"Just leave it," Maggie says. "I'll hold onto your stuff until you get back."

Sheriff Nelson nods toward the door. "Why don't you guys grab your packs and meet us at the trailhead. I have someone there from the park service coordinating the search. Bring your climbing gear, Killian, just in case. There are some steep rock walls in that area."

"I'm a qualified climber," I say. "I'll get my—"

Killian points his finger in my face. "You are not climbing anything, love. That's nonnegotiable."

"Okay, fine." I know when not to push my luck.

✺ 31

Hannah McIntyre

Killian and I head back to the cabin and pack what we need—flashlights, gloves, hats, water bottles, protein bars, a first-aid kit, and thermal blankets.

Killian grabs his set of two-way radios, handing one of them to me. "We stay together. But just in case we get separated, I want to be able to reach you at all times. *N'est ce pas?*"

Right?

I love it when he slips into French. "Right."

While Killian assembles the climbing gear he brought from Chicago—ropes, ties, carabiners—I take the dog outside and let him run the agility course a few times to get some much-needed exercise before we leave.

"I wish I could take you with me, buddy," I tell Scout. "But you're not quite ready for that." Now that my ankle is healed, I can get serious about training him for search and rescue work. I think he'd be a natural.

As soon as the Jeep is packed, we take off for the Ridgeline Trail. When we arrive at the trailhead, we aren't surprised to find the parking lot filled with vehicles of all sorts. Members of local and state-wide search and rescue teams are here with their dogs, as well as local volunteers, law enforcement, and other emergency organizations. There's even a food truck handing out free food and drinks, and a medic crew and ambulance are here on standby in case they're needed.

I spot a couple huddled together, a man and a woman. The woman is in tears, while the man comforts her. I assume they're the missing boy's parents.

"Does this happen a lot around here?" Killian asks me as we haul our gear out of the back of the Jeep. He straps on his backpack and throws his climbing gear over his shoulder.

I nod as he helps me pull on my pack. "Tourists get lost out here. Even experienced backpackers can get into trouble."

We locate the resource coordinator and introduce ourselves.

"Mary Finch," says a tall, slender woman with short silver hair. She shakes my hand first, then Killian's. "Sheriff Nelson told me to expect you. We appreciate the help. We need to find this kid fast—there's a cougar prowling around the area."

The woman hands us a detailed terrain map of the trail. "Everyone works in pairs. You two are assigned to this area here." She circles a spot on the map with a fat red marker. "Chris said you're both experienced climbers, so I assigned you to a spot where there's a lot of rockface." Then she hands Killian a small black device attached to a carabiner. "Here's a satellite GPS communicator that will let you check your coordinates and send a text message back to camp. Good luck."

The trail is clearly marked, so we head out. There are lots of people coming and going, each carrying their own gear and maps. Our directions take us about a mile up the trail, where we stop.

Killian uses the device Mary gave him to check the map against our GPS coordinates. He nods to our right. "This is our section." He looks at me. "How about you stay here on the trail? We'll keep in touch via radio, and if I find anything, I'll let you know." He makes it sound as if he's doing me a favor.

I roll my eyes. "You're joking, right? You seriously think I'm going to stay here on the trail while you're out there doing all the work?" I point at some pretty dense forest. "Nice try, *pal*."

He scowls, clearly frustrated, and I imagine he's biting his tongue. Smart man. He exhales a heavy breath. "Hannah, please."

"No. And stop coddling me, Devereaux. I do *not* need to be coddled. I'm perfectly capable of hiking through the woods."

"Fine," he huffs as he motions toward the trees. "Ladies first."

I know he just wants to keep me in his sights in case I trip over a log, fall on my face, and rebreak my ankle. "Fine."

After walking about half an hour due north, Killian double-checks our location via GPS. "Let's spread out a little, but be sure to stay within sight. Remember, we may not be alone out here."

He means the cougar, of course.

As I resume walking, I adjust my backpack and tighten the straps. It feels good to be outside again. There's something so cathartic about being out in the wilderness—and at the same time, it's calming. This is my happy place. It's where I'm supposed to be.

I skim the reference sheet Mary Finch gave us. "The kid we're looking for is Scott Adams, age eleven, a Boy Scout." Killian's close enough that he can hear me. "Sounds like he's old enough to think he can take risks, but young enough to make mistakes."

As we search our assigned area, examining the ground and low brush for signs that someone passed this way, we yell the kid's name. Off in the distance, I can hear the faint voices of other searchers doing the same.

We walk for about twenty minutes, and I notice Killian keeps looking my way as if he's checking on me. He looks annoyed, probably because I'm off the marked trail. The terrain here is naturally uneven, as it's littered with downed branches, vegetation, and tree roots that stick up above the soil.

"Watch where you're walking, McIntyre. The last thing I want is for you to reinjure your ankle. I'd rather not have to explain to your family how in the hell I let that happen."

"How you *let* it happen?" Shaking my head, I laugh. "Let's get one thing clear, Devereaux. *I'm* responsible for the consequences of my own actions. Not you."

"Ha," he says. "That's where you're wrong. If anything happens to you, your brothers will have my balls."

"Well, if you don't lighten up and stop patronizing me, *I'll* have your balls."

Killian stomps in my direction until he's looming over me. "Baby, you already have them."

Unable to help myself, I crack a smile. I don't think I've ever enjoyed anything as much as I enjoy verbally sparring with him.

He pulls me close so we're face to face. "Are you always such a pain in the ass?"

"Yes."

He opens his mouth to retort but changes his mind and motions me forward. "Keep walking, McIntyre. We have a job to do. We'll continue this conversation later."

A few yards ahead, Killian throws out his arm and halts me mid-step. "Hold up." He crouches to examine the ground.

"What is it?" I peer down, trying to see what he sees.

"Fresh scat. A big cat's been through here recently. Cougar."

"Great. That's all we need—to come face to face with a mountain lion."

We keep forward moving, calling the kid's name and looking for signs of anything having passed through the area—a cougar or a child.

"Scott!" I yell. "Scott!"

Killian calls his name, too, his voice deep and booming.

We continue ahead, searching, calling, and listening. We cross fallen trees, the occasional creek, and lots and lots of ground. There's no sign of the kid, and no visual on the cat.

Eventually, the trees begin to thin out, and we enter a valley with increasingly large rock outcroppings. The terrain is dotted with fir trees and boulders.

Killian spots a big paw print and drops to his knees to examine it. "It's fresh," he says.

"Scott!" I yell. The more signs we see that a cat has been in this area very recently, the more worried I get for this kid's safety. An adult cougar would have no trouble bringing down an eleven-year-old child. It's not often that a cougar kills a human, but it's not unheard of in these mountains. There have been a handful of attacks just in the past few years. "Scott!"

I freeze in my tracks when I hear a high-pitched screech coming from somewhere ahead of us. I signal for Killian to stop. "Did you hear that?" I ask him. "Scott!"

A faint voice, barely audible, carries toward us on the wind. "I'm over here! Up on the rocks!"

Instantly, we pick up the pace, moving as quickly as the rocky ground will allow.

"Scott!" I yell. "Where are you? Keep talking."

"Here," he calls out. "Be careful! There's a cougar nearby."

"No shit," Killian mutters. And then he yells, "Hold tight, kid! We're coming."

Eventually, we reach a rockface that juts straight up about forty feet from the ground. A young boy wearing a navy blue winter coat and a matching knit hat is perched on an outcropping of stone about halfway up the rockface.

Killian stares up at him, hands on his hips. "How the hell did you get up there?"

"I climbed," the kid says. "The cougar was stalking me. Getting up here wasn't too hard, but getting down—that's not so easy." The kid peers nervously down at the ground far below him.

"Are you hurt?" I ask him.

He shakes his head. "No. Just cold and hungry. I've been sitting up here for hours. My butt's numb."

Trying not to laugh, Killian drops his supplies on the ground and begins organizing his climbing gear—harness, lines, carabiners. I radio the search headquarters and give Mary Finch the good news that we found Scott. I give her our coordinates so she can send a backup team to our location to assist.

Meanwhile, Killian already has his climbing harness strapped around his waist and hips and is prepping the rest of his equipment for an assent.

"How are you going to do this? Set anchors in the rockface as you ascend? I can belay for you."

He shakes his head. "I told you, you're not climbing."

"I didn't say I was climbing. I'll stay on the ground, but I can still hold your line."

"No. I don't want you putting that kind of pressure on your

ankle." He studies the rock formation. "I'll climb it freehand, get above the kid, set an anchor, and then rappel down with the kid."

"Killian—"

He shoots me a glare, as if daring me to argue with him. "I said no. It's too soon. You stand by on the radio."

I let out a frustrated huff. I feel ready, but he's right. It is too soon. Even belaying for him would put a lot of pressure on my ankle because I'd be potentially bracing myself against his weight if he slipped. "Okay, fine. Have it your way."

He raises an eyebrow at me, but wisely doesn't say anything. Instead, armed with a harness, climbing rope, half-a-dozen carabiners, and anchoring supplies, he approaches the wall and feels around for the obvious handholds and footholds.

I'm tempted to tell him to be careful, but I don't. It's a pretty straight forward climb—even I could do it, and I have a lot less experience climbing than he has.

I watch him methodically scale the rockface, one handhold and foothold at a time. It takes Killian about fifteen minutes to reach him.

After setting an anchor in the rock and clipping his line, Killian straps a harness around Scott's waist and uses locking carabiners to secure the kid's harness to his own. Then Killian coaxes the boy to wrap his legs around his waist and cling to him like a little monkey.

The kid holds on with a death grip as Killian carefully rappels down the rockface. As soon as his feet touch the ground, he unlatches Scott's harness and sets him down.

"That was awesome!" the kid says, gazing up at Killian with bright blue eyes.

"I'm glad you thought so," Killian says as he removes first the boy's harness and then his own.

"Can we do it again?" the boy asks.

Killian looks at me out of the corner of his eye before he says, "How about we work on getting you back to your parents? They're pretty worried."

I hand Scott a water bottle and a protein bar. "How about a snack?"

"Oh, man, yes!" He tears the wrapper open and takes a bite of the bar. "I'm starving."

We sit Scott down on a nearby fallen log so he can eat his snack. Killian and I subtly look him over to make sure he's not hurt. He has a few scrapes on his hands and one on his right cheek, but otherwise he seems to be in good shape.

"So, where's this cougar?" Killian asks him.

As he chews a mouthful of food, the kid looks around as if the cougar might be hiding in plain view, just waiting for a chance to pounce. "I saw him about an hour ago," Scott says with a mouthful of food. Then he swallows. "I think he was looking for a way to get up to me. When that didn't work, he climbed that big tree there. I could tell he wanted to jump, but I think it was too far. Eventually, he gave up and left. Scared me to death. I thought for sure he was gonna eat me."

After Scott finishes his food, we pack up our gear and start walking back toward the trail. We're halfway there when we meet up with Sheriff Nelson and one of his deputies—Officer Milly Sanders—and after assuring themselves that Scott's fine, they escort us back to the trail.

On our way to the parking lot, we meet up with Scott's frantic parents. His mother sobs as she holds him tightly in her arms. His dad stands beside them, his hands on his hips. He's trying to act nonchalant, but his eyes are rimmed in red, and it's obvious he's been crying.

After Mrs. Adams finally releases her son, the dad gets his turn. He actually picks the boy up in his arms and holds him tight, murmuring quiet words in his ear.

"Thank you both," the father tells us.

"We got lucky," Killian says. "We just happened to be in the right place at the right time."

The kid's more excited than scared. "It was so cool, Mom. I got to climb down the rocks using a harness. I want to be a rock climber."

The sheriff shakes Killian's hand and mine. "I can't thank you two enough for coming out today. This town appreciates it."

Once we get back to the parking lot, we join in the celebration with free hot dogs, burgers, chips, and cans of cold soft drinks provided by the food truck organizer. I recognize several of the people there, mostly local hikers and climbers who volunteer their time on search teams. Scott and his very relieved and grateful parents join in on the party.

The sheriff joins us at the rear of my Jeep. "We could use

another resource like you around here, Killian," he says. "God knows there's plenty of opportunities for rescue work like today."

"Maybe," Killian says. He nods my way. "She said I can stay, so I guess I'll be around for the foreseeable future."

Nelson smiles as he claps Killian on the back. "Glad to hear it." Then he winks at Killian. "Lucky man. Let me know if I can help you find work."

After wishing Scott and his parents good luck, Killian and I head back to town to finish our grocery shopping. It's evening now, and the shops will be closing soon.

As soon as we walk into the store, Maggie congratulates us on finding the lost Boy Scout.

Killian laughs. "Word sure gets around fast."

"You bet it does," Maggie said. "That's small-town life for you. Some of the search volunteers stopped in here a little while ago, and they told me that Hannah McIntyre and her sexy boyfriend found the kid."

I slip my arm around his waist and lean my head against his shoulder.

"Glad to be of service," Killian says to Maggie. He slides his arm across my shoulders and kisses the side of my head.

After we finish up our shopping and load our groceries into the Jeep, we head home. Killian fires up the grill and puts on some steaks while I give Scout a good workout in the yard. I focus on basic commands and heeling.

"Have you heard from Owen lately?" I ask Killian as he turns the steaks on the hot grill.

He shrugs. "He checks in with me every few days or so."

Owen left Bryce shortly after the poachers were apprehended and the danger to me and to Maggie was gone. The poachers are currently sitting in a county jail awaiting trial.

I was hoping that Owen might find a reason to stay, but apparently that didn't happen, and when I ask Maggie about him, she's very tight-lipped. "Does he ask about Maggie?"

Killian gives me a pointed look. "I know what you're thinking, but forget it."

"What? I thought he and Maggie hit it off really well. You're staying. He could have stayed, if he'd wanted to."

Killian sighs. "Owen's carrying around a lot of heavy baggage, love. I don't think he sees himself as fit company for a woman."

"That's a shame. I thought they were good for each other."

While Killian's monitoring the steaks, I head inside and disappear into the bedroom to change into a pair of soft knit shorts and a T-shirt. Then I head to the kitchen and prepare some side dishes and a salad to go with dinner.

Killian brings the steaks inside when they're done, and we set the table together and sit down to eat.

It's nice having him here with me. I could get used to this.

* * *

After dinner, Killian and I carry the dirty dishes to the kitchen sink.

He steps behind me and puts his hands on my hips and leans in to kiss the back of my head. "I'll bring in some more logs for the woodstove. Be right back." As he heads for the door, he whistles for Scout. "Come on, buddy. Outside."

He's going to be a great doggy dad.

After he stacks the logs by the stove, he joins me in the kitchen, grabs a towel, and starts drying the wet dishes, putting them away as he goes. I don't even need to ask.

I think I might be in love.

He bumps my hip with his. "That was a great meal, love. Thanks."

"You cooked the steaks," I remind him.

"Yeah, but you made the rest of it. Tomorrow I'll cook something for you."

While I'm finishing up at the sink, he casually slips behind me and presses his body against me. I feel his erection nudging my lower back. His hands slide to the front of me, and he urges me back against him. His lips are in my hair, gentle and teasing, sending tingles down my spine.

"I don't think I'll ever get used to this," he murmurs close to my ear. His warm breath ruffles my hair, sending more delightful sensations along my nerve endings.

With a groan, I lean my head back against his shoulder, and he trails nibbling kisses down the side of my neck.

"It's hard for me to be around you and not want you," he confesses as his fingers toy with the waistband of my shorts. "I feel like I'm dreaming, and yet this is real." He kisses the sensitive spot beneath my neck.

The feel of his lips on my neck is hypnotic, and with a soft moan, I close my eyes and lean back into him. He tightens his hold on me, supporting my weight so that I can just let go.

When his hand slips inside the front of my shorts, beneath my underwear, his fingers slowly descend to the warm, aching place between my legs. With a sound that's part whimper and part groan, I widen my stance to give him access to what he wants.

"Killian." My voice is little more than a breath, and I drop the kitchen cloth I'm holding to grip the edge of the counter. My head is spinning.

"Mm," he murmurs.

When his finger slips easily between the slick lips of my sex, I gasp, and he groans. I reach back and grasp the back of his head, my fingers clutching a fistful of his hair.

Chuckling, he presses his length harder into me, and my knees threaten to buckle.

Slowly, he slides my shorts and underwear down my legs, and they hit the floor. Then I hear him unfasten his jeans, followed by the tell-tale sound of a zipper going down.

My entire body shivers in anticipation, and I'm practically panting when he tosses his wallet on the countertop.

"Condom," he says in a rough voice. "In my wallet."

While I'm fumbling for protection, his warm hands slide down my butt cheeks and over my thighs, then back up. He grips my buttocks and squeezes them gently. As I try to rip open the packet, he bends down and playfully nips my ass, then soothes me with a kiss, followed by a light smack.

"Did you just spank me?" I ask incredulously.

"Yeah." He chuckles. "Did you like it?"

I growl in response, because there's no way I'll admit how much I did like it.

"I'll take that as a yes," he says, sounding pleased with himself.

I hear the rustle of soft cloth, and then his T-shirt flutters to the floor. He grasps the hem of my own tee and whips it up and over my head. Cool air soothes my heated flesh, making my nipples tighten.

I hand him the condom, and he rolls it on. Then he grips the back of my neck and bends me forward over the counter.

Good freaking dear god!

I don't think I've ever been so aroused.

And then he's there, pressing into my wet heat, and I lose my breath completely. Our labored breathing is all I can hear as he slides inside me, his hands gripping my hips hard. "Killian!"

He groans harshly when he's fully seated. "Don't move," he says. "Give me a minute." Then he raises one of my thighs to open me up even more.

We both gasp as he sinks even deeper.

"You okay?" he asks.

I moan. "Yes."

"Hold on to something," he warns me, and then he starts moving.

I swear, the ground shakes and shudders beneath me as pleasure swamps me. If he weren't holding me steady, supporting my weight, I'm sure I'd end up sitting bare-assed on the floor.

He maintains a steady, rocking rhythm, and somehow he's hitting my sweet spot just right. When his fingers slip in front of me to tease my clit, I see stars. My entire body shudders, and with an embarrassingly loud wail, I come in a wild rush, pleasure swamping me.

He keeps up a steady rhythm, his thrusts long and hard, matching his heavy breaths on my back. With a groan, he quickens his pace, and then he bucks into me with a shudder, his loud roar filling the cabin.

"You slay me, woman," he says.

After disposing of the condom, he scoops me up into his arms and carries me to the bedroom. "If you think once is enough, you have another think coming, love."

ꙮ 32

Killian Devereaux

The next morning, on a Saturday, we drop Scout off at Maggie's house, along with his toys and dog food, and head to the Denver International Airport to catch a midmorning flight to Chicago.

Hannah's brother Liam meets us at the airport and gives us a ride into the city—to the apartment building where I live. Liam lives in the same building, as do half of the McIntyre employees. I show Hannah to my apartment, and we drop our stuff off before heading up to the penthouse floor to say hi to Shane and his wife.

"I can't wait to see the kids again," Hannah says as we take the private elevator up to the top floor. "I'll bet Ava has changed a lot in two months."

"You like kids?" I ask her, trying to keep it casual. Kids are something we've never talked about before.

"Sure."

"Do you want kids?"

Grinning, she links her arm with mine and leans into me. "With the right man, yes."

Before I can reply, the elevator doors open to their private foyer. Cooper is waiting for us in the foyer, a tiny baby cradled in his arms and a burp rag tossed over his shoulder. "Perfect timing," he says by way of greeting. "Dinner's almost ready. I hope you're hungry."

"You better believe it. We're starving," Hannah says as she steps out of the elevator and takes Ava from Cooper. "Oh, my god, look how adorable you are," she coos to the baby. She sifts her fingers gently through the baby's soft patch of light-brown hair. "You look just like your daddy." She turns so I can see the baby's face. "She's got his eyes, too."

A pair of big blue eyes stare up at me.

Watching Hannah holding Ava does something to me. My pulse starts racing, and of course I can't resist picturing her holding *our* baby.

Cooper offers me his hand, and we shake. "Good to see you again," he says, a curious smile on his face. He tips his head toward Hannah, who has already disappeared into the apartment.

"It's about time you two quit dancing around each other."

Cooper is a force of nature. He's a silver-haired, blue-eyed former Marine shooting instructor, and Shane's business partner, right-hand man, and best friend. He and his partner, Sam, who's a helluva lot younger than Cooper, live here in the penthouse with Shane and Beth. One big happy family.

I hear a chorus of welcoming cheers coming from the penthouse. "Looks like we're expected," I say.

Cooper nods as he pats my back. "You can count on the McIntyres to throw a welcoming party for their daughter and her new beau. You didn't think they'd let that slip by, did you?"

Laughing, I shake my head. "Hey, you won't get any complaints out of me. I've wanted this for a long time and never thought it would happen."

Cooper's red-haired partner pops his head through the open door. "The kitchen timer's going off, babe—the wings are done. You want me to take them out?" Then Sam grins my way. "Hey, Killian, welcome to the family."

"I'm coming," Cooper says to Sam. He pushes me toward the penthouse door. "Come join the party, Killian."

It is indeed a party—that much is obvious when I walk into the penthouse. There are streamers and balloons everywhere. Blues music is playing softly over the sound system, and the dining room table is laid out with an incredible array of food. It looks like the whole McIntyre clan is here, plus Beth's family.

Bridget makes a beeline for me and throws her arms around my waist. She's a petite little thing, like her daughter Lia. As she holds me tight, I can feel her arms shaking. "Thank you, Killian."

"You don't need to thank me, Mrs. McIntyre."

She steps back and gazes up at me with tear-filled eyes. "Call me Bridget, please. And there's no way I can ever thank you enough."

Calum McIntyre comes up to shake my hand. He clasps my shoulder with a firm grip, and we stand eye to eye, man to man. "Welcome, son. We're glad to have you join us."

"Thank you, sir." This isn't just a welcome party. They're inducting me into their family.

I glance across the expansive space and spot Hannah with Beth and Shane. Shane's holding Luke, and Hannah's still mooning over the new baby.

When Hannah looks up from the baby and catches my eye, my chest tightens, and my breath catches in my throat. God, this could be us one day—we could be standing here with a baby of our own. And if we had a baby, that'd mean she was truly mine forever—my wife.

My wife.

Damn.

A stream of people come up to shake my hand—Jake, Jamie, Liam, Dominic, Sam, the big celebrity rockstar Jonah Locke, and Beth's brother, Tyler, and his partner, Ian. I get lots of hugs from the females of the family—Sophie, Molly, Annie, Beth, and Beth's mom, Ingrid.

Lia—Hannah's youngest sister—walks up to me and gives me

a fist bump. "So, you made the cut. Well done. I'm impressed."

Jake and Annie's son, Aiden—a brown-haired little boy with big brown eyes—walks up to me with a well-loved stuffed dinosaur tucked under his arm, and says, "Are you in love with my Aunt Hannah? Because that's what everyone's saying."

The entire room goes hush as all those pairs of eyes are directed at me. I catch Hannah's interested gaze from across the room—she's biting her lip as she tries not to smile. I answer Aiden with, "Yeah, I am. Is that okay with you?"

He shrugs. "Sure. I guess that means you'll be my uncle then, too, won't you?"

The kid might be jumping the gun a bit, but I nod anyway. I'll take what I can get. "I certainly hope so."

Jake comes up to me and throws a heavily muscled arm across my shoulders. "Let me buy you a drink," he says as he nods across the room to the bar.

I join the guys who are congregating around the bar. Liam hops up to offer me his barstool.

"So, what can I get you?" Cooper asks. He's standing behind the bar, acting in his usual capacity as bartender.

"Whatever you've got on tap is fine."

He pours me an ice-cold beer and sets it on the counter in front of me.

Lia walks behind the bar and levels her gaze on me. "Watch yourself, buster." She points to her eyes and then to me. "I'll be watching you. We'll *all* be watching you."

❧ 33

Hannah McIntyre

Watching Killian on the hot seat is one of the most entertaining moments of my life. He's trying to be cool and not let anyone ruffle his feathers even though Aiden's ready to marry us off. We're officially dating now, sure. And I'm really stoked about that. *But marriage?* Surely it's a little too soon to be talking about that.

But then I realize my parents got married only two months after they met, and after nearly forty years of marriage, seven kids, and five grandkids—with another on the way—they're just as much in love now as they were back then.

Killian meets my gaze, and I can feel the intensity all the way across the great room. We're like a pair of magnets being drawn together by an invisible force.

When I wave him over to join us, he weaves his way through the crowd, shaking hands and accepting hugs and pats on the back, until he's by my side.

Shane claps him on the back. "Welcome back. You sure I can't talk you into staying?" Of course he's just teasing Killian. Shane knows better.

I hand Ava to Killian, who fumbles for a split second as he settles the baby against his broad chest. He's got a death grip on the baby, one hand supporting her head and the other holding her to his body. That baby's not going anywhere.

"Sorry, man," Killian says to my brother. "No offense—because I've loved every minute I've worked for you—but I got a much better offer." He looks my way. "One I can't refuse."

Shane grins. "So I hear." His gaze travels to me. "My sister told me about the rescue you two performed yesterday."

Killian shrugs. "It was an easy climb. No big deal. We were in the right place at the right time when we found the kid."

"Let's talk later, in my office, when everyone's gone home." My brother's looking at both of us. "Hannah tells me you've been kicking around some ideas. I have a proposition for you that I think you'll like."

My sisters sneak up behind me and literally pull me away from my brother and Killian. They drag me across the room to the bar, where Cooper and Jake are pouring drinks.

"Drinks are on me," Lia says.

I laugh and ask for a bottle of my favorite local brew. Cooper pops the top off a bottle of Goose Island and hands it to me. Sophie's drinking a soft drink—she's pregnant. And Lia's drinking a bottle of her favorite beer—Zombie Dust.

"So," Sophie says, keeping her voice down. "Tell us everything."

I'm sitting between my sisters, sandwiched between the diva princess and the tomboy, just like I've been my whole life. I have far more in common with my youngest sister, but Sophie and I have always been close, too. We were sisters first, long before Mom and Dad had the twins.

"What do you want to know?" I ask them before taking a sip from my bottle.

"Everything!" Sophie says. "For starters, who made the first move?"

"I did," I say. "I grabbed him and kissed him. I think I shocked the shit out of him."

"I told you!" Lia says triumphantly, giving Sophie a smug look.

I try to turn the conversation away from me and my love life to Lia's. She and Jonah just got married only two months ago, at an impromptu ceremony at Shane's home in Kenilworth. I throw my arm over her shoulders and pull her close. We may be adults now, but I've never gotten tired of teasing her. "How's married life treating you?"

Lia actually blushes. She nods, as if seriously considering my question. "You know, I think the sex is better."

I practically choke on my drink, while Sophie, who's not the least bit surprised by anything that comes out of our sister's mouth, rolls her eyes.

"I'm serious," Lia says. "He's like the Energizer bunny all of a sudden. He can go for hours."

Sophie sighs. "Tell me about it." Of course she's thinking of *her* husband, Dominic.

Lia wags her bottle at us. "If you ask me, I think it's because he gets off on calling me *wife*."

"He probably does it just to get a rise out of you," Sophie says.

Lia nods. "I imagine you're right, because it pisses me off, we argue, and then we have make-up sex. I think he does it on purpose."

Speaking of the devil, Lia's husband walks up behind her and loops his arms around her neck. "What do I do on purpose?" he asks. Jonah Locke looks the part of a rock star—long hair up in a manbun, his arms covered in tatts. Lia tells us he has tatts in other places, too, but we've never seen *those*.

"You call me *wife* just to piss me off," Lia says.

Jonah leans in with a grin and kisses her cheek. "Works every time."

More siblings come to join us around the bar, and I sit back and listen to their banter with a sense of ease I haven't felt in years. I love my family, but every time I came back to Chicago to visit, I was fighting an itch to get back on the plane and return to the mountains. This time, it's different.

As I glance across the room at Killian, who's deep in conversation with my brother Jake and his wife, Annie, I feel a sense of contentment I haven't felt in years. Having him here with me somehow changes everything. I feel like the mountains came with me this time, and I'm not so anxious to return.

Killian catches me watching him and gives me a smile that says he's feeling what I'm feeling. As much as I'm enjoying this impromptu get-together with my family, I'm looking forward to heading down to Killian's apartment for the night. We'll get to christen his bed here tonight before we head home tomorrow.

Home.

We have a home together now.

He's coming back with me.

* * *

After everyone leaves, Shane invites me and Killian to join him in his home office. We follow him in and take seats across from him at his desk.

My brother takes a white business envelope out of his desk drawer and slides it across the table to Killian. Killian picks it up.

"Open it," Shane says.

Killian does as asked and withdraws a slip of paper.

"Shane, you can't be serious," Killian says as he glances at the printed words on the check. He shows it to me—it's a personal check, written out in my brother's own handwriting.

I nearly choke. "Two-hundred-and-fifty-thousand dollars? Are you kidding?"

"It's seed money," Shane says to Killian. "For you to start your own business. Whatever you want to do."

"I can't take this," Killian says. He returns the check to the envelope, which he slides back across the desk to Shane.

Shane pushes it right back to him. "Yes, you can." Shane's expression grows serious. "You saved my sister's life, Killian. There's no amount of money in the world that could repay that. If you don't take this check, I'll write another one for half-a-million. And if you don't take that check—"

"I get the picture," Killian says as he leans back in the black leather chair. He reaches for my hand and laces our fingers together. "You know how I feel about Hannah. It's not a secret."

Shane nods. "I know. That's why you'll take the money and use it to start your own business. I expect you to become financially secure enough to provide for my sister."

"Hey," I say, sitting up straight in my chair. "I don't need to be provided for. I make do just fine on my own, thank you."

Shane ignores my outburst and levels his gaze on Killian. "Do we understand each other?"

Killian nods. "Yes, but you'd better listen to your sister. If you don't, she can make your life miserable."

That makes me laugh, and I lean over to kiss Killian's arm. "Good answer, Devereaux."

Smiling, Shane leans back in his chair. "Then it's settled. So, any ideas?"

"Yeah," Killian says. He squeezes my hand. "McIntyre Search and Rescue. It'll be a nonprofit organization, so we'll need to do fundraising. But on the side, I'll teach climbing workshops, and I think Hannah and I are going to organize some overnight backpacking and climbing trips up in the mountains. It'll be fun. Something we can do together."

"Sounds good," Shane says. "But if anything happens to my sister on those climbing and backpacking escapades, you'll answer to me. Is that clear?"

Killian nods, a hint of a grin on his face. "I can try to keep her out of trouble, but no promises. Your sister has a mind of her own."

Shane's lips twist wryly. "So I've noticed."

* * *

After leaving the penthouse, we head down two floors to Killian's apartment. It came furnished, and it looks like something out of an interior decorating magazine.

"Fancy," I say as I stand just inside the door and observe the casual elegance of the coordinated living room furniture.

"Yeah, it's not me," he admits. "Too rich for my blood."

"Sophie must have decorated it." My sister is an interior decorator, and she often works on projects for our brother. "It's beautiful, but I'd be afraid to put my feet up on the coffee table. I prefer a home that feels lived in—something I'm not afraid to get messy."

Someone has already provided a stack of cardboard boxes, packing tape, and a big fat permanent marker, so we get to work packing up his personal belongings. He doesn't have much. Some books, CDs, and DVDs. In his bedroom closet we find several pairs of sneakers and boots, one pair of dressy black shoes, jeans, T-shirts and hoodies, a handful of white and blue button-downs, and two dark suits.

"For weddings and funerals," he says of the suits. "That's the only time I wear them."

He has some toiletries in the bathroom, and in the spare bedroom there's a set of weights.

We stay up late packing everything up and stacking the boxes by the apartment door. We'll carry everything down to his Jeep in the morning and head off on our long drive home. I'm looking forward to a road trip with my guy.

It's two a.m. when we stop and take showers, get ready for bed, and crawl beneath the covers. We're both exhausted.

Lying with him here, I feel surprisingly content. Usually, when I'm back in Chicago, I feel anxious and out of place, and I'm itching to get back to Colorado. But not this time. Yes, I'm looking forward to getting back home, but it's more about the excitement of starting our life together, making plans, and starting a new business venture.

I'm so ready to move forward with him. I turn to Killian and run my palm down his bare chest. "When we get home, I'll inform Ray that I'm quitting."

"Are you sure?" he asks. "I don't want you to feel like you have to quit. I don't want to interfere with your job."

"I love my job, but I want to work with you. Watching you rescue Scott Adams was a hell of a rush. I want to do that with you. I want to be your climbing partner next time. I want to spend time in the mountains with you. We can train Scout to be a search and rescue dog—together."

He rolls to face me, his finger gently tracing the curve of my forehead, then down the side of my face. "That sounds perfect."

He leans closer, and his deliciously male scent teases me, making my belly quiver.

I think about all the times he tried to connect with me since we first met. He's tried repeatedly, putting himself out there, setting himself up for rejection, and he never gave up. My throat tightens, and my chest constricts painfully. My heart hurts just thinking about it.

I reach up and touch his face, curving my palm to his cheek. I gently brush my thumb over his beard. He's done so much for me. He came all the way to Colorado to save me. He rappelled down into a ravine to find me in a blizzard, and he carried me to safety.

He's done nothing but give to me and risk himself in return. And what have I given him? Not nearly enough. "Killian?"

"Yeah?"

There's something I can give him. I made the first move—I

kissed him first, which opened the door between us. Now there's something more I can give him. "Killian, I love you."

There. I said it first. I gave him *that*.

He stares, looking a bit dumbstruck, as if he doesn't believe his own ears.

"Hannah." He cups my face and searches my eyes. "*Je t'aime, ma belle fille.*"

I smile. I know what that means.

I love you, my beautiful girl.

He leans in and kisses me, his lips warm and coaxing. "I love you, too." When he pulls back, his eyes are glittering like black diamonds.

* * *

We take our time getting back to Bryce. It's a long drive— just a little over a thousand miles. We do it in two days, taking turns behind the wheel, not rushing, taking time to stop and smell the flowers. We spend the first night at a roadside motel that looks like something out of the 1950s.

"Your brother is nuts," Killian says after we shower and climb into bed.

We lie there, both naked and damp from our showers, and brainstorm how we're going to use the money Shane gave Killian to start a business.

"You won't get any argument out of me," I say.

"You're absolutely sure you want to quit your job? Don't you want to take some time to think about it? There's no rush."

I roll on top of Killian, sitting astride him, and wrap my fingers around his length, which has been blatantly hard since our joint shower in the tiny bathroom. "Yes, I'm sure. Stop asking me."

He nods, and as I tighten my grip on his erection, he gives me his *full* attention.

I lick my lips. "I'm going to give you something else to think about."

His nostrils flare as he sucks in a breath. "Oh, yeah?"

I slip down his body until I'm kneeling between his muscular thighs, my mouth hovering over his cock. His erection lifts eagerly into the air, as if it knows what's coming. My warm breath washes over the head of him, and then I lick the crown, taking just a tentative taste.

He lets out a rough growl as he fists my hair. "Oh, fuck, baby. Yes! God, yes."

I work him with my mouth and fingers until he's shuddering, his limbs trembling.

"Where are the damn condoms?" he mutters.

Honestly, I forgot where I packed them. "We don't need them."

I grab his hands and pull him off the bed with me. Then I drop to my knees on a blanket on the floor and pull him to stand in front of me. I gaze up into his dark eyes and open my mouth.

His expression tightens as he reaches down and grabs hold of my hair. "God, you're beautiful."

I take his thick length deep and work him with my tongue and fingers until he can't hold on another minute. He comes in a heated rush, gripping my head hard in his hands as he cries my name.

34

Hannah McIntyre

Late the next night, we arrive home to a dark and empty cabin. Scout is staying with Maggie and her boys, so we won't get him until tomorrow. Killian starts a fire in the woodstove while I get ready for bed. Then he gets ready for bed, and by the time he crawls under the bedding with me, I'm half-asleep.

"Goodnight, McIntyre," he says as he presses a gentle kiss to my temple.

Snuggling into him, I sigh. "Goodnight, Devereaux."

Both of us exhausted, we crash immediately.

* * *

The next morning, I rise with the sun and dress for my first day back to work. Sadly, it's also going to be the day I give Ray my two-week notice. It's bittersweet to think about giving up my job. I love it, but I love Killian more. And the idea of working with him—hiking, climbing, backpacking in the mountains, spending every day with him—is too good to pass up.

When I come out of the bathroom, I'm dressed for work in black cargo pants, a tank top for an undershirt, and my long-sleeved uniform sweatshirt. I load my big pockets with a few necessities—bear spray, a small flashlight, and a pocket knife. I also carry a handgun and a hunting knife with me when I go out into the field, but I won't be needing those today as I'll be staying put in the center.

When I head to the kitchen, Killian has breakfast waiting for me on the table.

I glance down at an amazing spread. "You're going to spoil me."

He laughs. "This is nothing. You should see what my mama and grandmama serve for breakfast. It's practically a three-course meal." He smiles as he pours me a coffee, then hands me the sugar bowl and the caramel creamer. "Will you be okay today—turning in your notice? I can come with you if you want."

I can't help smiling because I think it's cute when he gets all protective. Totally unnecessary, but cute. "No, I'll be fine. But thanks for the offer."

"Do you want me to go get Scout this morning and bring him home?"

"Yes, please," I say, leaning in to kiss him. "That would be awesome."

He holds his hand out to me. "Your phone, please."

"Why?" Curious, I hand him my phone. "What are you doing?"

"I'm adding a little app the company created so that clients could signal their bodyguards in times of emergency." He makes a few adjustments before he turns my phone so I can see the screen. There's a bright red triangle on the screen with a giant exclamation mark on it. "If you activate the app and tap the red alert icon, I'll be notified immediately, and GPS will tell me your exact location. Got it? You try it."

I press the red alert icon, and immediately Killian's phone sounds a klaxon-type alarm, loud and shrill.

He reaches over to silence the alarm. "It's that easy. I want you to have it in case you get into trouble. You call me first, got it? Then call 911."

"Got it." I rise up off my chair and lean across the table to kiss him. "You get me the sweetest gifts."

While he's clearing the table, I run to the bathroom to brush my teeth and put my hair up in a ponytail. Then I kiss Killian goodbye and head out to my Jeep.

Killian's rugged and slightly battered black Jeep Wrangler is parked next to mine. The sight makes me smile—his and hers

Jeeps. His looks a little worse for wear, though, and could definitely use a wash. I thought I was hard on vehicles, but he has me beat.

On the drive to work, my pulse is definitely elevated. I'm glad to be returning to the conservation center, and it'll be great to see everyone again, but the knowledge that I'll be turning in my notice is weighing on me. I've thought it over, again and again, and the bottom line is, I want to spend my days working with Killian. I know I can learn a lot from him, especially when it comes to climbing.

As I pull into the parking lot at nine o'clock, I feel a bit overwhelmed. I've always loved my job, whether I'm giving a tour of the rehab center to schoolkids or going out in the field to check on animals we're monitoring. I love the people I work with; they're all dedicated to wildlife conservation and protection. It's not just a job to us; it's a calling. And Ray Calhoun has been an incredible mentor to me since I started here. I've learned so much from him, and he's given me so many opportunities.

When I walk inside, I'm greeted by the whole staff, who are congregating around the reception desk.

Ray is front and center, and he gives me a big bear hug. "Welcome back, Hannah. We missed you."

I start off my day by conducting a few class tours of the facility and working behind the scenes with some animals that recently came to us for rehab—mostly easy stuff. Ray says he doesn't want me going out into the field for a while, until I'm sure my ankle is fully healed. I discover that a few of the animals I was taking care of are now gone—successfully returned to their natural habitats while I was out on sick leave. I guess I missed a lot in the past six weeks.

I try to keep focused on the here and now—what needs to be done today. And I answer a lot of questions from my colleagues about what happened on Eagle Ridge, about my rescue, and about Killian. Apparently, word has gotten around about him, and my friends are curious.

By four o'clock, the center is quiet as most of the staff have left for the day. I wanted to wait until everyone was gone before I told Ray about my decision to leave. My stomach sinks at the thought of telling him. This is my first job after graduate school, and it's not easy for me to just walk away.

When I catch Ray in the classroom, labeling some new fossils he picked up on a recent field excursion, I take a deep breath to psych myself up. "Hey, Ray. Can we talk?"

He straightens and turns to face me, a warm smile on his handsome face. "Sure. Let me wrap up here, and we can talk in my office. I'll meet you there in a sec."

On my way to his office, I grab a cup of coffee, mostly to give myself something to do. I'm hoping that cradling a hot mug in my hands will soothe my jangled nerves. When I head to his office, I find the door open, which is typical. He's an open-door kind of guy, always available to anyone who needs him. I walk in and take a seat in front of his desk. But I'm too nervous to sit, so I end up standing and pacing as I rehearse my speech.

When I hear footsteps, my pulse rockets into overdrive.

Here we go.

Just breathe, Hannah.

You're not the first person to quit a job, and you won't be the last.

My heart thuds in my chest as Ray walks into his office, carrying a cup of coffee. "Hi, Hannah." He smiles widely. "God, it's good to have you back. I—we—really missed you."

That makes me feel even more guilty. "Thanks."

"So, how did your first day back go?"

"Great. It's good to be back here. I missed everyone, too."

He sets his cup down on his desk. "I'm so relieved you've recovered from that horrible incident." He glances down at my left ankle. "How's your leg? All healed?"

I nod as I wiggle my foot. "Good as new."

"Good. I'm glad to hear it. So, is your babysitter heading back to Chicago soon?"

"My babysitter—oh, you mean Killian. Actually, that's what I wanted to talk to you about."

He frowns. "What's wrong?"

I take a deep breath. "Nothing's wrong. It's just that Killian's not leaving. He'll be staying here in Bryce. With me. He's starting his own business here." Feeling guilty after receiving such a warm reception today, I wince. "So, I guess this is me, tendering my resignation."

Ray's expression transforms instantly into sheer shock.

"I'm really sorry," I say. "You've been such a great—"

His frown deepens into a scowl. "What the hell, Hannah? You can't be serious." His voice is uncharacteristically harsh.

The hairs on the back of my neck rise, and a shudder runs through me. "Yeah, Killian's forming a wilderness excursion company, and I'm going to help him run it. We're also going to train Scout to—"

Ray steps in front of me, really close—too close. He shakes his head. "Hannah, you can't." He lifts his hand, and for a moment I think he's going to touch my face, but at the last second he drops it.

Muttering, he turns away, then back to me. "I had no idea there was anything personal going on between you two. If I had—damn it, Hannah! You hardly know the man. You can't just quit your job for him."

"Actually, we've known each other for a while now, and there's always been something—some kind of connection—between us. It's only recently that we acted on it."

"You *acted* on it?" Ray's expression tightens, his complexion flushing darkly. "What does that mean? You let him *fuck* you? Jesus!" He begins pacing, clearly angry and agitated. "Hannah, I've been biding my time, waiting for you to come back to work before I—"

Biding his time for what? "Ray—"

"Hannah." He returns to face me and grabs my upper arms. Then he slides his hands down my arms to take my hands in his. "I have feelings for you, Hannah. I had thought—I'd hoped— that you felt something for me, too." He sighs in exasperation. "Please don't make any hasty decisions. Let me take you out for dinner tonight, just the two of us. We should have done this a long time ago. We'll drive to Loganville, and I'll take you to Valentino's. I know you love that place."

Oh, shit. Killian was right. And I told him he was crazy when he said Ray had feelings for me. I yank my hands out of his. "Ray, I'm sorry, but—"

"No! Don't say it." He presses his finger to my lips. "I'm not taking no for an answer."

"That's not up to you."

When I pull out of his reach, he frowns. "Listen to me, Hannah," he says, his voice softening as he tries to cajole me. "You and I are perfect for each other. We do the same work. We have the same passion for wildlife conservation and rehabilitation." He takes a step in my direction. "I always thought that, eventually, we'd end up together. It just makes sense."

"Ray, I'm sorry." I smile, hoping to soften the blow. "You've been a great boss and a fantastic mentor, and I respect you tremendously, but I don't feel that way about you."

"How can you tell if you haven't even given me a chance?" His voice has turned sharp again, resentful.

"Ray, you're my *boss*."

"So?"

"Aren't there rules against that?"

He gives me a tight smile. "I'm the boss, sweetheart. *I* make the rules."

Ray grabs my hand and pulls me flush against him. His other hand steals around to the small of my back and presses me even closer.

I can feel the ridge of his erection digging into me. "Ray, no!"

"You let Devereaux touch you, don't you? I bet you let him do all sorts of filthy things to you, so why not me?"

I can't believe this is happening. I try to pull away, but he's holding me fast. My heart jackhammers in my chest, knocking against my ribs and making it difficult to breathe. "Let go of me!"

His hand at my back slides up, and he grips the back of my neck, hard. His nostrils flare in anger—or perhaps it's arousal—and his lips are pressed into flat lines. "I've waited patiently for you, Hannah, but obviously that was a mistake. I was trying to be considerate—trying to give you time to realize how good we'd be together."

I laugh bitterly. "You call this perfect?" I ask as I struggle to free myself from his grasp. "This is sexual harassment, Ray. This is sexual *assault*. I could report you for this."

His expression turns cold. "You've been leading me on since you got here. All the pretty smiles and the chit-chatting, inviting me out to lunch—"

"Those were team lunches. Everyone was invited."

"All the times you sat next to me." His voice is pure accusation. "You've done nothing but lead me on."

The man has lost his mind, and I feel sick. "You're my *boss*, Ray. My mentor. I thought we were friends. I wasn't leading you on."

"Oh, we're more than friends, sweetheart."

He releases my hand to cup my breast, his thumb brushing

over my nipple. I shudder in revulsion, sickened by his touch. I trusted this man. I defended him to Killian when Killian said he thought Ray had ulterior motives.

"Enough! Let go of me, Ray." My voice drops an octave, and the words come out in sharp bites. "I'm not telling you again. Let go."

Then he kisses me—or at least he attempts to. Before his lips touch mine, I step back and drive my knee hard into his groin. It's not often I get to use the self-defense techniques my brother Liam ingrained in my head, but I'm damn well going to use them now.

Ray gasps, releases me, and steps back. "What the hell!" He bends over and wraps his arms around his waist, his teeth gritted firmly as he rocks on his feet.

At least I got my point across.

Suddenly he straightens, and with fury in his eyes, he charges me, knocking me into the wall behind me. He grabs my wrists and pins them to the wall. "You fucking bitch!" he growls. He presses his mouth to mine and tries to force my lips apart.

I see red. Twisting my wrists, I break free of his hold. Then I shove my elbow into his throat, slamming into the soft tissues around his trachea. He steps back and wretches, coughing and gagging as he wraps his hands around his throat. While he's distracted by the fact he can't breathe, I slip my boot behind his and knock him back. He falls to the floor. Before he can recover, I roll him onto his belly, yank his wrists behind him, and secure them tightly with one of the zip ties in my pocket.

"You don't fucking treat women like that, asshole." Furious, I grab my phone and open Killian's app to send him a red alert. Then I dial 911.

"You'd better hope the cops get here before Killian does," I tell Ray as I step back to catch my breath. "Because if they don't, I wouldn't want to be you."

ॐ 35

Killian Devereaux

When the red-alert goes off on my phone, my heart practically stops cold. There's only one person who has that app installed right now, and it's Hannah. She's in trouble. I grab my phone off the coffee table and check her location. She's still at the wildlife rehab center.

Immediately, I strap on my holster and gun, grab my keys and coat, and race out the door. I'm in my vehicle and heading her way within seconds.

I risk calling her, and she answers after the first ring.

"Killian?" She's out of breath but otherwise sounds in control.

"What's wrong?"

"You were right about Ray. He thinks—he attacked me, Killian."

My blood turns to ice. "Are you hurt? Did he *hurt* you?"

"No, not like that. I mean, I'm bruised, but I'm okay. Just a bit stunned."

"I swear to god, I'll kill him. Did you call 911?"

"Yeah. The police are on their way."

"Where's Calhoun? Are you safe?"

"He's lying on the floor of his office, his wrists secured with a zip tie. He's not going anywhere."

That's my wildcat.

For the first time in several minutes, I can finally take a breath. "Sit tight, love. I'll be there soon."

When I pull into the parking lot of the wildlife center, the building looks dark. Besides my Jeep, there are only two other vehicles in the parking lot—Hannah's Jeep and Ray's truck. Looks like I beat the police.

I park haphazardly, shut off my engine, and run up to the front door. Fortunately, it's unlocked.

"Hannah?" I yell once I'm inside.

"In here! I'm in the office behind the front desk."

I follow the sound of her voice and spot her immediately, standing in an open doorway, her arms wrapped loosely around her waist.

After performing a quick visual inspection, I pull her into my arms. "Are you okay?"

She nods. "You were right about him. I should have listened to you."

I step back so I can look her in the eyes. "Are you sure he didn't hurt you? Did he *touch* you?"

She pulls free. "He grabbed hold of me, and he kissed me." She shudders visibly. "But I'm okay, honest."

I glare at Calhoun, who's lying on the floor, practically hogtied. Feelings of rage nearly choke me. This motherfucker put his hands on Hannah. He *touched* her. I step forward and haul him to his feet, ignoring his cries of pain. I don't give a shit.

I shove him until his back hits a wall, then grab him by the throat.

His eyes are huge as he stares at me, wary of what I might do. It's just us here, as the cops haven't arrived yet. He's not sure what I'm capable of, and he has good reason to be concerned.

Gritting my teeth, I lean in close. "I should fucking kill you," I growl.

He flinches. "You can't hurt me. I'm incapacitated. It would be assault."

I pull him forward and then slam him back into the wall. "Like you just assaulted Hannah?"

"She deserved it! All this time, she's been leading me on, making me think we had a future."

"You lying piece of shit," Hannah cries from behind me. "I did not!"

Ray looks to me. "And we would have had a future if you hadn't shown up. You ruined everything."

Disgusted, I shake my head. "You know, she stood up for you," I tell him. "I told her you were up to no good, and she defended your sorry ass. And this is how you treat her?"

"You were trying to turn her against me so you could have her for yourself. Admit it."

"Turn her against you?" I laugh. "You never had her in the first place."

Police sirens get louder by the second.

I squeeze his throat just enough to make him wheeze. "Looks like it's your lucky day. I'm outta time." I nod toward the door. "Show them in," I tell Hannah.

As soon as she steps out of the room and I hear her talking to the cops, I slam my fist into Ray's abdomen. He keels over, bent in half. "Sorry, my fist slipped." I watch impassively as he struggles to catch his breath. Hell, he got off lucky. He deserves far worse.

Sheriff Nelson leads the way into the office, two deputies right behind him. "Why am I not surprised to see you here?" he asks me with a hint of a grin on his face.

I nod toward Calhoun, who's red in the face and still trying to catch his breath. "You can charge him with sexual harassment, assault and battery, false imprisonment—and I'm sure there are a few more charges that apply. Throw the damn book at him. He assaulted Hannah."

Nelson glares at Ray. "You have the right to remain silent," he begins.

I stand there, my arms crossed over my chest, and watch as

the sheriff reads Calhoun his rights and then hauls him through the building and out to a waiting squad car to be transported to the station.

I stick close to Hannah as she locks up the center.

"Are you all right?" I ask her as we watch two police cruisers leave the site. She's trying to hide the fact that she's shaking.

She walks straight into my arms, and I pull her close and hold her tightly to me. When I kiss the top of her head, she lets out a heavy sigh.

"I'm all right." She looks up, a frown marring her pretty face. "I'm just sad. I thought Ray was one of the good ones."

"I'm sorry, love."

"The good news is I don't feel so guilty now for quitting. I could never work there now, knowing what kind of man he is."

I laugh. "Honey, I don't think Ray will be coming back here— ever. Besides, he just bought himself a trip to the county jail, where I imagine he'll reside for the foreseeable future." I lean down and kiss her. "Come on, McIntyre. Let's go home."

I walk Hannah to her Jeep and make sure she's okay to drive. Then I follow her home in my vehicle. We park next to each other in the yard and walk hand in hand up to the porch together.

The first order of business is to let Scout outside for some much-needed exercise and playtime.

"Come here," I say to Hannah, leading her to the porch swing. We sit together and I lay my arm across her shoulders and pull her close. "I'm sorry about Ray." I lean over and kiss the top of her head.

She leans into me. "How could I have been so wrong about him? I feel like such an idiot."

"It's not your fault, love. Some people are good at hiding their real intentions."

Scout runs up onto the porch with a tennis ball in his mouth. He drops the ball in Hannah's lap and jumps back, ready to chase it.

"I think it's time to get serious about Scout's training," Hannah says as she throws the ball for him to retrieve.

"I worked with search and rescue dogs in the military. I can train him."

Hannah reaches up to run her fingers through my hair. "I don't know about you, but I'm starving, and I need comfort food. Let's go into town and eat at the diner. I could really use a turkey bacon melt and some big fat steak fries, along with a gigantic chocolate shake with whipped cream and sprinkles. How about it?"

Laughing, I kiss her soundly. "Yes, ma'am. Are you driving or am I?"

"I am." She grabs my hand and pulls me off the swing. "Come on, Devereaux. I'm buying."

Epilogue

Hannah McIntyre
Two weeks later

L ate November, Killian and I fly down to Lafayette, Louisiana, so I can meet his mom and grandparents.

No pressure, right?

Wrong!

I'm terrified.

As I sit buckled into my seat, I stare out my window at the lush green ground below. "What if they don't like me?"

"What?" Killian laughs. "Don't be silly. They're gonna love you."

"You can't know that for sure. What if they *hate* me? What if they resent the fact that you're not settling down with a nice

Cajun girl?"

He leans close, bumping his shoulder against mine. "I'm thirty-five years old, love. I think they've given up on me finding a local girl. They're gonna be thrilled to meet you. They won't care that you're not Cajun."

I don't believe that for one second. "But what if—"

"No *buts*, McIntyre. Relax. Mama and Grandmama want grandchildren, so trust me, they're going to love you." He links our fingers together and kisses the back of my hand.

Our flight lands midafternoon, and we rent an SUV to drive out to his family's farm, which is quite a ways out of the city in a remote rural area.

As we drive, I see lots of signs with French mottos: *C'est bon! C'est la vie!*

That's good! This is the life!

And billboards for Cajun restaurants, bars, and music halls. We pass small farms and rivers that snake through areas of lush green vegetation. As we pass a wide river, I spot a boat flying across the surface of the water. "What's that?" I point it out to Killian.

"An airboat. We use them all the time in the bayou. You want to take a ride? I'll take you out in the swamp, show you some gators."

"I'd like that. I want to see where you grew up, the kinds of things you did as a kid."

The closer we get to our destination, the more nervous I get.

Killian, who's driving, glances over at me. He lays his hand on my knee. "You're awfully quiet. What's wrong?"

"Nothing."

He reaches for my hand. "Come on. Tell me what's buggin' you."

"I'm just nervous. I know you think they won't care that I'm not Cajun—"

"Oh, trust me, they'll welcome you with open arms, even if you're *une Americaine*."

"What do you mean, even if I'm an American? We *are* Americans. *You're* an American."

"They see themselves as Acadians—direct descendants of the Acadians who were exiled from Nova Scotia by the British in the seventeen hundreds and sent down here to the bayou to live. You English speakers are *les Americaines*. Outsiders."

I groan. "Oh, they're definitely going to hate me. My family roots are in Scotland."

Killian lays my palm on his rock-hard thigh. "You're not afraid to go toe to toe with poachers, but you're afraid to meet your future in-laws."

In-laws? That's the first time he's even hinted at marriage.

As we pass farther into the countryside, we come across a few small businesses scattered along the main road. We see a couple of diners and bars, a small used car lot, a gas station, and a feed store. We cross over a number of streams.

Killian points out the window. "I loved fishing there when I was a kid." Then a few minutes later, he points out another one. "When I was a kid, my grandpapa and I would run our boat up and down this river huntin' gators."

He points out the elementary school he attended, the middle school, and the high school. "Half the current teachers in those schools were kids I grew up with. Not many of them moved far from home after getting their education. I'm one of the few who left home after high school."

"Why did you leave?"

He shrugs. "My dad was in the military, and I wanted to be like him. I didn't remember him, of course. He died when I was a baby. But I remember the stories my mom told about him and his exploits overseas. I joined the military hoping I'd see some of the same sights he saw and do some of the things he did. After I got out of the military, I didn't know what to do, and that's when a friend recommended me to your brother. The rest is history."

Killian turns onto an unmarked, gravel lane, and we drive quite a ways back, fenced-in pastures lining both sides of the road. We pass cattle and horses and a good-sized pond.

He points out the water. "My grandpapa taught me to swim in that pond. I fished in that pond every chance I could and hunted crawfish, which Mama used to make *Etouffee*. I'll make you some while you're here—crawfish tails, butter, flour, onions and peppers, garlic, chicken broth, and Cajun seasonings of course, served over rice. It's delicious."

When he follows a curve in the road, we come upon an old white two-story farmhouse with a wraparound porch. It's obviously at least a century old, if not older, and it hasn't been painted in a good long while. There's a large barn behind the house, several sheds, and a chicken coop. A tire swing hangs from the branch of a huge oak tree that casts shade on the front porch.

Killian pulls up beside a battered white pickup truck and shuts off the engine. "Here we are." He brings my hand to his mouth to kiss. "Ready?"

"I guess I'm as ready as I'll ever be."

He opens his door and hops down, then walks around the front of the vehicle to my side. I already have my door open and am in the process of jumping out. Just as he holds his hand out to me, I hear the front door open and the sound of footsteps on the wooden porch.

"Breathe, love," he says as he takes my hand and squeezes it.

We walk toward the porch, where a dark-haired woman stands with an elderly white-haired couple. She must be his mother.

The three of them stand there staring at me for a minute. Then his mother comes down the steps and walks right up to Killian and wraps her arms around her son. She says something to him in French I can't follow—it's too fast. And her French sounds very different from what I remember hearing in school.

Finally, Mrs. Devereaux releases Killian and turns to me, her gaze assessing.

I swallow hard. *Here we go.* "Hello, Mrs—"

Mrs. Devereaux hugs me to her like we're long-lost friends. Then she rattles something off in Cajun French so quickly, I don't have a chance of understanding any of it.

Killian smiles at me. "She said, 'Welcome home, my beautiful girl. You can call me Mama.'"

The tension instantly eases from my body, and I give her a grateful smile. "*Merci*," I tell her. "Mama."

Thank you.

After the grandparents come down the steps and take turns hugging us both, Killian puts his arm around me and pulls me to his side. "I told you there was nothin' to worry about."

When his mother says something, Killian translates. "She said she hopes you're hungry because dinner is ready, and we're havin' gumbo in your honor."

I do my best to answer her in French. "*Oui, Mama. Merci.*"

Yes, Mama. Thank you.

The hopeful light in her dark eyes when I answer her in French is everything, and for the first time since boarding the plane to Louisiana, I can finally relax.

* * *

Dinner is an experience. The food is delicious—it's a dish made with chicken and Andouille sausages, in addition to shellfish, and it's very filling. Killian's mom and grandparents never once stop talking in rapid-fire French, and he translates in real time for me.

After we're done eating and have had dessert—bread pudding with cinnamon and nutmeg, one of my all-time favorites—Killian and I clear the table and wash the dishes while his family retires to the living room to talk over coffee.

Killian bumps my shoulder with his arm. "I'd like to take you out this evening, if you're up for it. There's a place just down the road where I used to hang out with my friends. There'll be live music there, and dancing. I'd like you to meet my friends."

"Sure, I'd love to. But how do you know they'll be there tonight?"

He laughs. "It's Saturday night, love. They'll be there. They'll *all* be there."

After we carry in our bags, Killian's mom directs us to a small, yet comfortable bedroom on the second floor, with a full bed covered with a pretty blue-and-white floral quilt. The back window looks out over a stream that runs through a lush pasture. I unpack, then freshen up in the small hallway bathroom next to our room.

"Your mom put us in the same bedroom," I say to Killian when I return from brushing my hair and teeth. I honestly wasn't sure how the sleeping arrangements would work since we're not married.

He laughs. "Of course she did. I told you, she wants grandkids."

Killian picks me up and swings me in his arms. When he sets me down, he threads his fingers through my hair, which I left loose around my shoulders, and smiles down at me. "*Je t'aime, ma belle. Je t'aime beaucoup.*"

I love you, my beauty. I love you very much.

"*Moi, aussi,*" I say.

Me too.

He offers me his hand. "Ready for some great Zydeco music?"

"Killian, I don't know how to dance to that."

"Doesn't matter. Just follow my lead." He winks at me. "After a few glasses of moonshine, you won't even care."

"I really hope you're kidding about the moonshine," I tell him as we walk out to the SUV.

He takes me to an old barn down the road that's been converted into a bar. The gravel parking lot is filled with vehicles, some of which are overflowing onto the edge of an adjacent field. It's dark already in the early evening this time of year. Strings of fairy lights are draped throughout the parking area, lighting our way to the entrance. Even outside, we can hear the music inside as a live band plays a lively Cajun tune. A man is singing, but his accent is so thick I can't make out the words.

There's a chalkboard menu near the door that lists tonight's specials—gumbo, jambalaya, Boudin sausages, crawfish etouffee, shrimp and grits, wild duck, even alligator. For dessert tonight... pecan pie *a la mode.*

As we approach the door, it opens, letting out a gust of warm, fragrant air. Two women walk out, and they stop dead in their tracks when they spot Killian.

"I think I've lost my mind, Gen," one of the women says.

"Killian?" the other one asks. "I can't believe my eyes."

"Hello, Genevieve, Marguerite," he replies. "It's good to see you."

They both shift their curious attention to me.

"I went to school with these two ladies," Killian says to me. To them, he says, "This is Hannah McIntyre, my girlfriend."

"The prodigal son has returned," Marguerite says, shaking her head in disbelief. "Wait 'til the boys inside get a look at you."

We go inside. The interior is warm from the crush of bodies and smells of beer and spicy food. Across the room, on a wooden stage, a five-member band of middle-aged men plays Cajun music on fiddles, guitar, and an accordion.

The place is packed. The tables are full, as is the dance floor, and servers hustle back and forth from the bar to the tables, dodging dancers in the process.

"Here's a table," Killian says as he grabs my hand and leads me to a small round table for two.

We sit, and Killian hands me a paper menu.

"I'm still full from dinner," I say, "but I will try some of that pecan pie."

He nods. "And beer. You gotta try some good Cajun beer."

A woman comes to wait on us—Babette, who's clearly pregnant and probably close to delivering. Yes, she remembers Killian from school, although she was two years behind him.

With one hand on her burgeoning baby bump, Babette winks at me. "Oh, I think it's fair to say everyone who went to school within a couple years of Killian remembers him. He sure was a popular one. I remember my sister, Camille, and her friends goin' on and on about him."

We order a slice of pecan pie with vanilla ice cream to share. Then we wash that down with two bottles of a popular Louisiana brew, Abita's Turbodog. Then Killian orders something called Dixie Blackened Voodoo.

"This sounds like something Lia would like," I say as I take a sip.

The music is fast and lively. My gaze keeps going to the dance floor, which is packed with young and old, black and white. It seems nearly everyone's up on their feet, shuffling and scooting, twisting and turning, in their well-worn cowboy boots. I see everything from young couples to seniors, and a number of interracial couples. It looks like a friendly crowd.

"Wanna dance?" Killian asks as he holds out his hand to me.

I'm tired from a long day, but I can tell by the expression on his face that he's dying to dance, and I don't want to disappoint him. "I'd love to." I lay my hand in his, and he pulls me to my feet and out onto the dance floor.

"I have no idea what I'm doing," I say, laughing as he swings me.

"Doan worry, love. Just follow my lead."

Turns out Killian's a great dancer. He twirls me and swings me effortlessly. I glance down at his boots and mimic his movements, and I think I'm doing a decent job of it in no time.

One song blends into another, and then another. And when the tempo eventually slows for a ballad, he pulls me close and wraps his arms around me and leans down to whisper in my ear. "I remember being here when I was young, watching the couples dancing, and thinking that maybe I'd be here one day with the woman of my dreams in my arms. And here she is."

He kisses me then, like there's no one watching. We dance like no one's watching. Three dances turn into five, and yet we keep going, laughing and twirling as the night wears on.

Finally, when we sit back down to take a break, a stream of people, young and old, stop by our table to say hello. Killian introduces me to so many people I can't possibly remember them all.

When it's time to go, we drive back to his mom's house and sit on the front porch swing a while, enjoying the cooler weather after being inside that hot barn.

"Thanks for coming here with me," he says as he links our fingers together. "It means a lot to me, but it means even more to my mama and my grandparents."

I lean my head against his shoulder. "Thanks for asking me." I can't believe I'm sitting with Killian on his mother's front porch. If someone had predicted this just a few months ago, I would have said they were crazy. "You're a very patient man, Killian."

He lays his arm across my shoulders and tucks me in close. "I would have waited forever for you, Hannah. I knew the minute I heard you open your smart mouth that you were the one I'd been waiting for my whole life. I even told my mama about you. She said if it was meant to be, it would be. She said if I really wanted you, I should be patient and give you time."

"Your mom's a smart woman. I'm glad you waited for me. Really glad."

He releases me and stands, holding out his hand. "It's late, and I know you're tired. What do you say we go inside and christen that bed?"

I can feel my cheeks heating. "It's not a big house, Killian. What if someone hears us?"

He shrugs. "Don't matter. I told you, they want grandkids."

* * *

Thank you so much for reading *Search and Rescue!* I hope you enjoyed Killian and Hannah's story. The next release in the *McIntyre Security Search and Rescue* series is Maggie and Owen's book, *Lost and Found.*

* * *

Keep reading for two bonus chapters!
One about Beth and Shane McIntyre,
and one about Maggie and Owen.
I hope you enjoy them.

Bonus - Meanwhile Back in Chicago

Beth McIntyre

I t's late, and it's past bedtime for two sleepy kids. While I nurse Ava, Shane reads a bedtime story to our toddler, Luke. Luke is nestled against Shane's broad chest, sucking his thumb while his other tiny hand has a fist-hold on his daddy's T-shirt. I listen hypnotically to Shane's low, slightly raspy voice as he reads Luke his favorite story—one about Thomas the Train.

Ever since Shane's mom gave Luke a wooden Thomas the Train playset, the child's been fascinated by trains.

"Hannah seems really happy," I say as I think back to Hannah and Killian's recent visit.

"Who?" Shane asks distractedly as he turns the page and continues reading aloud.

"Hannah. She seems really happy. They both do."

This has become our nightly routine—the four of us lying in bed together, cuddling and enjoying some quality family time before we put the kids to bed. Ava still sleeps in the bassinette at the foot of our bed, and Luke sleeps in his crib in the nursery right next to our suite.

"Yeah. It was only a matter of time," my husband says as he turns a page.

"What was only a matter of time?"

"Before she realized they were perfect for each other. She hardly gave Killian the time of day since they met, but he never gave up. That kind of devotion is rare."

"I'm glad to see her happy with someone. I always worried about her being so far away from home and all alone."

"My parents are certainly relieved. They know Killian will take good care of her."

I chuckle as I elbow him lightly. "And she'll take good care of him. Never underestimate Hannah. We should go out and visit them sometime. I'd love to see the mountains."

"When the kids are a little older, sure."

Shane's gaze lights on our two-month-old daughter, who's currently latched onto my nipple and sucking eagerly. She's a noisy little eater, making loud smacking sounds. Fortunately, I haven't had any of the difficulties getting Ava to nurse that I did with Luke. Of course, the challenges with Luke were mostly the result of my inexperience and anxiety.

When Shane reaches the end of the book, Luke grabs another one from the little stack beside them and hands it to his father. "Dada more."

Shane laughs as he cracks open another book. "This kid would have me read all night long if he had his way."

Luke pats Shane's chest and says, "More."

Shane looks to me and rolls his eyes. "This could go on all night, you know."

As soon as Shane starts reading, Luke yawns widely and his blue eyes begin to drift shut.

I smile at the picture the two of them make. Father and son. Two peas in a pod. "Five minutes more," I whisper, "and he'll be out like a light."

While Shane reads the second book, I finish nursing Ava, who's falling asleep herself. I snap closed my nursing bra cup and carry her to the changing table for a diaper change. Then I lay her in her bassinet and head to our bathroom to get myself ready for bed. When I return, Shane has closed the book, and he's stroking Luke's back as the baby sleeps soundly against him.

I smile. "I told you. Five minutes."

"I don't think he made it that long."

Shane carefully rises from the bed, Luke secure in his arms. "I'll be back."

While Shane's putting our son to bed, I slip on a nightgown and walk out to the kitchen to get a drink of water. I love this time of night, when the penthouse is dark and quiet, and the view out the three exterior glass walls in the great room is magical. The lights from the surrounding buildings twinkle in the inky darkness, and the stars overhead seem close enough to touch.

The sound of bare feet padding along the wood floors catches my attention. I turn to see Cooper coming down the hall, from the direction of the suite he shares with Sam. He's wearing a pair of red flannel PJ bottoms and that's all. His short silver hair is mussed, and he has a sleepy, satisfied expression on his face. "Everything okay?" he asks when he notices me standing in the kitchen.

"Yes. I came out to get some water." Since I'm nursing, I try to make sure I stay hydrated. "How about you?"

He chuckles. "Sam's hungry. He needs a snack to tide him over 'til morning."

I laugh, too. "Sam's always hungry."

I pour a glass of cold, filtered water and sit at the breakfast bar to drink it while Cooper puts a tray together for Sam: cubes of various cheeses, crackers, and cuts of turkey, ham, and salami left over from the party. He rinses off some fresh strawberries and cuts them in half, then adds a few clusters of purple grapes and a handful of mixed nuts. Lastly, he cuts a slice of leftover cake.

I shake my head. "That's some snack. You spoil him rotten."

Cooper meets my gaze with a pleased grin. I don't think he minds in the least.

"Who's spoiled rotten?" Sam says sleepily as he joins us in the kitchen. He's dressed in a pair of silk boxers, and that's it. His red hair is sticking up in tufts as if someone's been tugging on it.

I smile, thinking somebody probably was.

I notice a few red patches on Sam's throat and chest. "Whisker burn?" I ask, grinning at him when his face flushes. With his red hair and fair complexion, he blushes a lot.

Sam winks at me as he walks up behind Cooper and slips his arms around Cooper's waist. Sam leans close and kisses his partner's bare back.

"Is this the after-party?" Shane asks as he rounds the corner and joins us. He switches on the baby monitor sitting on the counter so we can monitor the nursery.

"Looks that way," Cooper says in his deep, baritone voice. When he's tired, his southern accent is more pronounced.

"I worked up an appetite," Sam says as he lays his cheek on Cooper's back.

Shane and I both laugh. "I'm sure you did," I say.

The baby monitor crackles, and then we hear a shrieking cry from the nursery.

"That didn't last long," Shane says as he turns and heads back the way he came.

"He's got a pair of molars coming in," I explain.

Shane returns a moment later with a sobbing baby propped against his shoulder. Luke's chewing on his fist as fat tears stream down his cheeks.

Sam takes a teether out of the freezer and offers it to Luke. "Here, buddy, chew on this."

Luke pushes the teether away and locks eyes on me. "Mama," he wails, reaching for me.

Shane hands me Luke. I cradle him close and rock him in my arms.

"Looks like it's gonna be a long night," Cooper says, all sympathy. "Good luck."

Cooper and Sam head back to their suite with their charcuterie tray, and Shane and I retire to ours, with Luke. I sit in the rocking chair by the hearth and rock him back to sleep while Shane lies in bed watching me intently.

"What's so fascinating?" I ask him.

"You are."

I chuckle. "Me? Why?"

"I'm so in awe of the woman you've become, and the mom you are. Our kids are lucky to have you. Hell, *I'm* lucky."

Once Luke is back to sleep, I carry him to the nursery and lay him in his crib. When I return to our bedroom, Shane pulls me down on top of him, his hands going to my waist.

"No, *I'm* the lucky one," I tell him as I lean in to kiss him.

He laughs softly as he rolls us so that he's on top. "Keep telling yourself that, sweetheart," he says, as he slips a gentle finger between my legs.

I gasp as pleasure ripples through my sensitive flesh, a tingle coursing up my spine.

"I love you," Shane murmurs as he kisses me. "To the moon and back."

Bonus – Maggie's Houseguest

Maggie Emerson

I watch through my kitchen window at the man chopping wood in the backyard. He took off his long-sleeved flannel shirt, leaving himself in just a sleeveless tank top as he brings the ax down on log after log, splitting them in half as easily as if they were made of wet paper. His arm muscles bulge with each swing, his well-defined biceps and triceps standing out in clear relief.

I've never seen a man with so many muscles. And I can only imagine what the rest of him looks like—his abdomen, his thighs. His ass.

His hair, long and ash-blond, is tied up in a manbun to keep it out of his way. His focus on his work is laser-like. I wish he'd quit working so hard and come into the house for a while, maybe long enough to get a cold drink or find out what I'm making for dinner.

It's been years since I had a man sitting at my kitchen table, eating my food. The boys were only six and eight when I divorced their asshole of a father. I've been single ever since, going on nine years now. Sure, I dated on and off, but it never amounted to anything serious. I was too focused on my kids. They had to come first, since I was basically both mom and dad now. Their dad hasn't been a good role model since he was convicted of embezzling and went to prison.

I've been burned too many times by the very man who had vowed to honor and love me, in sickness and in health. Too bad he was lying through his teeth when he made those vows. And it's too bad I didn't find out the truth about him until after we'd had two kids.

Fortunately, my ex-disaster, Calvin, is still in prison in upstate Colorado, serving a ten-year sentence for embezzling money from the trucking company he was worked for at the time. The damn idiot.

I force thoughts of my ex out of my head and go back to making dinner—a big pot of chicken and dumplings, like my mama taught me to make. And I made a pineapple upside-down cake for dessert.

I hear the front door open and then slam shut. The boys are home from football practice.

"We're home mom," Riley yells as he runs upstairs to shower.

"Dinner will be ready soon," I call up to them. "Don't take too long."

I hope Owen will join us for dinner this evening. I've invited him before, but he always respectfully declines and takes a plate up to his room. I think he's afraid his presence here is an imposition, but I don't see it that way. He's been kind enough to stay with us while the investigation into the poachers who attacked Hannah McIntyre is underway.

I know I sleep better at night having him under the same roof as me. I saw him in action up in that ravine when we were searching for Hannah, and in the valley where we sheltered overnight during a blizzard. He insisted on staying out in the elements all night long, despite frigid temperatures, just to make sure no one snuck up on the shack where we holed up for the night. That man has serious skills.

I think the boys enjoy having him around, too. They never had much of a father figure to speak of. I want them to have a good role model around to show them what's what. The best way for boys to learn how to be a good man is to see one in action—and that definitely describes Owen Ramsey. Cal was a lousy role, and as far as I'm concerned, my boys are better off without his influence.

Once dinner's nearly ready, I wash my hands and dry them on a dishtowel. Then I walk out the back door and down the steps to the yard, where Owen's chopping logs for the wood-stove. He's only been here a few days, and already we have more wood cut and stacked than we've ever had. I can only manage so much chopping at a time before my shoulders give out on me. I'm not as young as I used to be.

When I allow myself to stare at Owen's shoulders, my belly quivers. It's been a long time for me. A very long time. And having Owen around gives me thoughts I have no business having.

Hell, I'm not sure how old he is, but I'd be surprised if he's over thirty-five. I turned forty this past summer.

"Dinner will be ready soon," I tell him as he's mid-swing.

I watch his arm muscles flex as he brings the ax down with a solid *thunk*, splitting a fat log cleanly in half.

His hazel eyes meet mine, and he nods. "Yes, ma'am. Thank you." He sinks the ax blade into the chopping block. "I'll go wash up now."

I nod. "I hope you're hungry. I made plenty."

He nods. "I am. Thank you."

Owen follows me in through the back kitchen door.

"Something smells mighty good," he says when he gets a whiff of dinner.

"Chicken and dumplings. Would you like to join us at the table this evening? The boys will be down shortly."

He glances at the kitchen table, which is covered with a floral tablecloth. "I'd like that, if it's okay."

"Of course it's okay. We'd love for you to eat with us."

He nods toward the front staircase. "I'll just run upstairs and wash up real quick, and put on a clean shirt."

As he walks away, I confess I enjoy the view of his tight ass in a pair of well-fitting faded jeans. His scuffed cowboy boots sound good as they strike the wood floorboards.

I busy myself getting everything ready. When Owen appears in the doorway ten minutes later, my mouth goes dry.

Good Lord, save me from temptation.

He's got a long-sleeved plaid shirt on, open at the collar, and I can see a peek at the ink on his chest, and the strong column of his neck. His hair is freshly brushed and put up in bun, neat and tidy.

"How can I help?" he asks as I'm carrying a heavy serving bowl to the table. "Here, let me." He takes the bowl from me and sets it on a trivet on the table.

"Thank you," I say. "Please have a seat."

But instead of sitting, he follows me into the kitchen. "Is there anything I can do to help?"

"Well, you could grab four glasses from that cupboard there."

Riley and Brendan come tearing down the back staircase into the kitchen, both of them talking at once as they claim their seats at the table.

"What's for dinner?" Riley asks.

"What smells so good?" Brendan asks. "I sure hope you made a lot of it. I'm starving."

I laugh. "You're always starving. And yes, there's plenty," I tell him. "Don't worry."

As Owen sets four glasses on the table, one at each place setting, he eyes the boys, who are seated and anxiously waiting for the food. "Why don't you boys help set the table? Riley, why don't you get the plates? And Brendan, you can grab flatware for everyone. I'll grab us some napkins."

The boys both look to me, confusion on their faces. It's quite comical. "You heard the man," I say. I guess I'm guilty of letting the boys off the hook when it comes to dinner chores. I've just found it quicker to do everything myself.

My sons jump to their feet and carry out Owen's instructions. If I'd asked them to help out, they'd have lollygagged so long that I'd have ended up doing it all myself just to save time.

Owen has a way with the boys. When he speaks, they listen. When he tells them to do something, they do it. I guess that's what teenage boys need. Someone to make them listen and take notice.

Pretty soon the table is set, and the boys are seated. Owen carries over a basket of warm dinner rolls, and I bring the green beans and the salad. It's a simple meal, but filling. There should be enough food here to satisfy these three big appetites.

As the guys dig in, I bring a pitcher of homemade lemonade to the table.

"How was football practice?" I ask the boys.

Riley is a senior this year, and he's a quarterback. Brendan is a sophomore and plays wide receiver.

Riley swallows a mouthful of food. "Good. Coach said I can start at our first game."

"That's fantastic," I say.

Owen listens but doesn't say anything. He eats quietly, his sharp gaze taking in every nuance of the conversation.

When everyone's done eating, I stand to clear the table. "I'll get dessert."

Owen quietly says, "Riley, Brendan, your mama worked hard to cook this meal. Why don't you help out by cleaning the table?"

The boys jump to their feet to do as Owen asked. He's like a teenage boy whisperer.

While I'm bringing the pineapple upside-down cake to the table, Owen brings four dessert plates and clean forks.

"Thank you for a delicious dinner," he tells me as I cut into the cake.

After dinner, the boys head upstairs to play video games for a while before they hit the hay. Owen helps me clean up in the kitchen. He washes the dishes, while I dry and put them away. This old farmhouse doesn't have an automatic dishwasher.

It's nice having someone to share the work with. It reminds me of what I'm missing. What I've been missing for nearly a decade.

I can't tell if it's my imagination or not, but sometimes I get the feeling Owen likes it too. When I catch him watching me with a quiet yearning, he looks away. I don't know if the hunger I see in his eyes is real or just wishful thinking on my part.

Probably wishful thinking.

He sure never acts on it.

Even though I wish he would.

I know I'm too old for him, but just once wouldn't be too bad, would it? It would be like a friend-with-benefits thing, like you see in rom-coms.

The funny thing is, I know absolutely nothing about him, other than he's a former Army Ranger and that he lives alone, off the grid, on a mountain in Tennessee. That's it. That's all I know.

"Anything else I can help out with before I turn in?" he asks me when the kitchen is spotless, and the trash has been carried out.

He has a nice baritone voice—low, a bit rough, the kind of voice a woman wants to hear whispering in her ear at night. The kind of voice that will give her the most amazing shivers.

"Maggie?"

I shake myself. *Jesus, pay attention, Maggie.* "Um, no. That's everything. Thanks for helping me clean up the kitchen. And thanks for chopping more wood. I appreciate it."

"My pleasure." He dries his hands on a dishtowel. "I'll check on the horses before I bed down."

"Thank you."

He knows horses. He knows how to wield an ax. And he knows how to use a gun. He's prepared for anything.

"Night then, ma'am," he says, standing there in the kitchen in no apparent hurry to leave.

"Why don't you call me Maggie?" I ask him. "There's no need to stand on formalities."

He looks away. "I wouldn't want to be presumptuous."

I fight not to smile. Maybe I want him to be presumptuous. "I don't think there's any danger of that."

He grins. "All right, then. Goodnight, Maggie."

My pulse races as I imagine walking up to him, threading my fingers in his hair, and kissing him like there's no tomorrow. Would it be so bad for me to make a move on him? Would he be repulsed? Would he think I'm too old for him, the mother of two nearly grown boys?

My courage disintegrates and a sigh slips out. "Goodnight, Owen."

Two days later, the poachers who were after Maggie are apprehended and arrested. They're subsequently locked up in the county jail awaiting arraignment. The judge denied them bail on the grounds they were flight risks.

The next morning, without warning, Owen packed up his duffle bag, shook my hand, and said his goodbyes.

"Job's over," he says. "I guess I'd better head home."

"I guess so," I say in a quiet voice. *Please don't go.* "It was nice having you here."

We stood there staring at each other for the longest time before Owen looked away.

"Thanks for your hospitality, Maggie. I—" And then he shook his head and headed for his rented SUV and left for Denver to catch his flight home.

Owen could have stayed if he'd wanted to. He's a grown man, capable of making his own decisions.

I spent the rest of the day berating myself for coming right out and asking him to stay a while longer. For not taking a chance. I should have taken a chance. What's the worst that could have happened? My feelings could have gotten hurt? My self-esteem, which isn't great to begin with, might have gotten a bit more bruised?

I'll never know, because I chickened out and didn't say a word. I let him walk away, climb into the rented SUV, and disappear from my life.

* * *

Thank you so much for reading *Search and Rescue!* I hope you enjoyed this first book in my McIntyre Security Search and

Rescue series. My next release is Maggie and Owen's book, *Lost and Found.*

* * *

If you'd like to sign up for my newsletter, download my free short stories, or locate my contact information, visit my website: www.aprilwilsonauthor.com

* * *

For links to my growing list of audiobooks and upcoming releases, visit my website: www.aprilwilsonauthor.com

* * *

I interact daily with readers in my Facebook reader group (Author April Wilson's Reader Group) where I post frequent updates and share weekly teasers for upcoming releases. Come join me!

Books by April Wilson

**McIntyre Security
Bodyguard Series:**

Vulnerable

Fearless

Shane (a novella)

Broken

Shattered

Imperfect

Ruined

Hostage

Redeemed

Marry Me (a novella)

Snowbound (a novella)

Regret

With This Ring (a novella)

Collateral Damage

Special Delivery

Finding Layla

**McIntyre Security
Search and Rescue Series:**

Search and Rescue

Lost and Found

A Tyler Jamison Novel:

Somebody to Love

Somebody to Hold

Somebody to Cherish

**A British Billionaire
Romance:**

Charmed (co-written with
Laura Riley)

**Audiobooks and Upcoming
Releases:**

For links to my audiobooks
and upcoming releases,
visit my website:
www.aprilwilsonauthor.com

Printed in Great Britain
by Amazon